THE SINNERS OF ST BENEDICTS DUET

GODS & ANGELS

GODS & ANGELS

ELIZABETH STEVENS WRITING AS

E.J. KNOX

Kinky Siren
an imprint of Sleeping Dragon Books

Gods & Angels
by E.J. Knox

Paperback ISBN: **978-1925928488**
Digital ISBN: 978-1925928334
Hardcover ISBN: 978-1925928495

Cover art by: Izzie Duffield

Worldwide Electronic & Digital Rights
Worldwide English Language Print Rights

This one's for my spark.
Nice to have you back.

Contents

Author's Note

This is a dark, angsty, contemporary high school enemies-to-lovers romance with enough steam to melt your screen. Do not engage in public consumption unless your poker face is impenetrable.

Do not read if you don't like broken alpha males claiming what's theirs, a feisty heroine determined to break the bonds of an unwanted future, complicated love triangles full of passion and dirty words, or books with a choose your own ending (I know, I don't like them either, but I just couldn't help myself with this one).

This story features the heroine in sexual situations with both love interests. While not considered cheating by the characters, you may have different feelings (and that's okay). Proceed with caution.

This book is written using Australian English. This will affect the spelling, grammar and syntax you may be used to. It might come across as typos, awkward sentences, poor grammar, or missed/wrong words. In the majority of cases (I won't claim it's infallible, despite all best efforts), this is intentional and just an Aussie way of speaking (it took my US beta readers a bit to get used to). I can't say 'the' Aussie way, since we seem to differ even within the same state. Just think of us as a weird mix of British and US vernacular and colloquialisms, but with our own randomness thrown in. I still hope you enjoy it, though!

CHAPTER ONE

My heart beat quickly in my chest and my stomach did a happy little flutter, as the car slid between the great stone pillars of the Callahan Estate. With a nod from the gatekeeper, we started up the gravel drive.

I craned forward in my seat as though that was going to get us to the front door faster.

"Harlow," Dad chastised. "Some decorum, please."

"She's excited," Mum said fondly.

"She needs to learn what behaviour is appropriate and what is not. She can be excited, but she need not show it so...enthusiastically."

"She's twelve, Rex."

"Exactly," Dad said. "Not that long ago, she'd have been considered a woman already."

"Not anymore," Mum said pointedly, and I wasn't sure what the look they gave each other meant.

Dad nodded. "I'm aware."

"We agreed," Mum said quietly, as though I wasn't sitting right there and could hear every word, "that we'd just let it happen."

"Let what happen?" I asked.

Dad looked at me from the corner of his eye. "Is Apollo ready for school?"

I felt like there was more to the question. Like there was a question under the question that I didn't understand. The expectant look Dad gave me just made me more sure, so I just shrugged, mumbled something incoherent, and went back to staring at Callahan Hall as it grew larger in the window.

When the car pulled up at the front door, the butler was waiting for us with Mrs Mack the housekeeper, a few of the maids, and Apollo's mum, Frenella.

"Frenella, it's been an age," Mum said to her.

"Far too long, Sissy. You made good time," she said as she and Mum embraced.

The staff went about unpacking our bags for us and Frenella led us inside.

"Have you got everything ready for school, Harlow?" Frenella asked me.

I nodded. "I think so. Mrs Thomas checked the list five times! And she said that someone would have to iron everything again when we got there."

"We sent it all straight on," Mum said. "Make sure everything's all ready for her first day."

"We did the same. We're paying enough for his room, it may as well be ready."

"Archer in his office?" Dad asked.

"He was," came the deeper tones of Archer Callahan as he

glided across the parquetry towards us. "Good timing, Vanguard. Kieran's still here."

"Excellent. He and I have business," Dad answered, and he disappeared with Archer into his office.

Whenever Dad was at the Callahan Estate, they were always in Archer's office. I never knew what they did in there but, the one time Apollo and I had tried to find out, we'd been kicked out with some very stern words. It felt like, the older I got, the less time I got to spend with my parents. I was either at the Callahan Estate without them, or we were all there and I still didn't get to see much of them.

"Harlow!" Apollo called from the top of the stairs and my bad mood was instantly forgotten.

I looked up and saw him racing down.

"It's only been a month," I told him.

He pulled up to stop in front of me. "It's been forever!"

Mum put a hand on my head. "Why don't you two go and play?" she said.

"Mu-um," I complained

I saw her and Frenella exchange a look.

"Sorry," Mum said, failing to hide a smile. "You're far too old for playing."

"What are you going to do?" Frenella asked.

"Ice cream eating competition!" Apollo cried excitedly.

I looked at him and we shared a grin. "Do you have rainbow?" I asked as we ran towards the kitchen.

"Won't it be cute when they're welcoming us into their home?" we heard Mum say to Frenella.

"Aw, their first dinner party," Frenella cooed.

Apollo and I grimaced at each other and stuck our tongues out. It was no secret that our parents thought we were going to get married. It was also no secret that Apollo and I disagreed.

"You better have rainbow," I told Apollo.

Apollo rolled his eyes. "Rainbow's just vanilla with colours."

"Don't ice cream shame me, Apollo Callahan," I told him. "The colours are the best bit!"

His side eye as he pulled the freezer open told me what he thought about that. "Yeah, we have rainbow. I made sure Mrs Mack got you lots."

"The colours–" I started.

He finished for me, "...make you happy. I know," he said with a big smile. "That's why I got it."

Apollo Callahan had the unfailing ability to make me smile, big and warm. The kind that gives you a happy bubble in your chest and makes your cheeks ache.

He was my best friend. The person who knew me best in all the world, and I knew him the best. We spent almost every school holidays together and talked almost every day but, in just under a week, we were going to the same boarding school. Everything was going to change, and it was going to be the best day ever, every day.

An hour later, once two litres of ice cream had been butchered and the both of us were feeling very ill, we had to finally concede a draw.

"On the face of it," Apollo said as we kicked off our shoes in preparation for stage two of the competition, "starting with the ice cream might have been a poor choice."

"But it goes ice cream, sock skating, then mattress surfing." I stopped to consider it. "Actually, yes. Starting with the ice cream seems like the worst choice."

"Okay, tomorrow," Apollo said, "let's do it backwards."

I nodded. "Okay." Then as fast as I could, so he had the least amount of time to react, I said, "Readysetgo!" and took off down the passage.

"No fair," he laughed, and no doubt hurried to catch up.

As Apollo and I skidded into the front hall, I saw Archer at the door to his study. Frenella was coming down the stairs. There was something about the atmosphere between them that I didn't like. Especially since neither of my parents were in sight.

"Apollo," Archer said smoothly. His tone told us he wasn't well pleased about us skidding around the house in our socks.

Imagine if he'd witnessed stage three.

Apollo pulled up short. "Sorry, Dad."

Archer shot a look to Frenella, who came to stand by me, but his words were directed at Apollo. "There's someone you need to meet."

"Who is it?" I asked.

"Not you," Archer snapped, and I recoiled.

Archer wasn't the warmest of men, but he'd never quite looked at me with such dismissive repulsion.

"Best you come with me, dear," Frenella said, starting to pull me away. "We'll go find Sissy."

But I didn't want to find my mum.

Apollo and I reached for each other, but Frenella placed a

restraining hand on my arm, and Apollo seemed scared to take a step forward.

"Why can't Harlow come?" Apollo asked his father.

"A girl has no place in men's business," Archer replied sternly.

"That's not fair," Apollo argued. "Where I go, Harlow goes."

Archer may as well have had smoke billowing out his ears. "Grow up, Apollo. Taking your place at the head of Saint Benedict's hierarchy will not be achieved with *fairness*." He spat the word like it was something disgusting and glared at Frenella and me. "This is your doing. You've made him soft."

Frenella held my shoulders tightly, like she was protecting me. "I gave him a childhood," she told her husband.

Archer stormed over to Apollo and grabbed his arm roughly. "My son will not be the first of his line to serve another God. This ends now."

"I'm not going without Harlow!" Apollo insisted.

Archer's arm flew back across his body. Apollo and I both flinched.

Once.

Archer had hit him once.

But it had been enough to cement the obedience into him. Archer's word was law. The consequences would not be pleasant.

Apollo ducked his head in submission and Archer dropped his arm.

"Good boy," he said, pride and perhaps even love in his tone. He looked at his wife, who was glaring at him. "It's for his own good. We send him there this soft and he won't come home alive."

Dread settled in the pit of my stomach as Apollo, and I looked at each other wide-eyed.

I wouldn't pretend I hadn't seen the hulking figures who graced our fathers' doors in the dark of night. Sometimes they had what I hoped was red paint on them. Sometimes I saw a gun or a knife. They were mean men with hard eyes and scars, always scowling and always uncomfortable.

"Come on, dear," Frenella said to me. "Your mum's in the conservatory."

Apollo and I gave each other one more longing glance before his parents separated us.

"Who's Apollo meeting?" I asked Frenella as we walked away.

She fiddled with the pearls at her wrist absently. "Every God needs his Angels," was her reply.

"What does that mean?"

"It means," she sighed, "that as much as you and I have our places set for us by the circumstances of our birth, Harlow... The men have expectations put on them as well."

I nodded, but I didn't really know what she meant. I think she could tell. She stopped to lean down closer to my level and smiled at me. It was one of those smiles that didn't quite reach her eyes.

"You know how Archer and your father... Well, they keep their business to themselves?"

I nodded. "Yes. They don't like talking about it."

"No, they don't. Not with us anyway."

I felt like I had half the pieces in the jigsaw in place and I could almost see the others, but they were just out of reach. Like deep down I knew what she meant, but the full reality was just beyond my twelve-year-old understanding.

"Is this like the way you and Mummy have to look nice and smile even when you don't mean it, and have all those fancy parties?" I asked carefully.

A sliver of relief passed over Frenella's face. "Yes, Harlow. Just like that. The men have their business, the women...well, we have our roles to play as much as they do. Part of Apollo's role is power. He is the heir to the Callahan name and as such he's expected to achieve certain...status."

I still didn't really understand.

"Everything's going to change now," she said, but she said it like it was a bad thing. "Apollo has...duties. Duties his father will not let him back down from. Our world..." She sighed and I saw the love for her only child deep in her eyes. "Our world doesn't look kindly on what it deems soft. So, you, me and your mum? We walk the walk, and we talk the talk, and we look the other way when we see too much." She brushed my hair from my face. "We leave the men to maintain the fragile status quo because one wrong move... One wrong move and the people we love could die."

I searched her eyes, hoping this was all some kind of sick joke. People's lives weren't like this. But then, it explained so much. So many half-seen or half-heard truths, feelings that the world I'd been born into wasn't like everyone else's.

"Apollo could die?" I breathed, my heart thudding painfully.

"This is why God has his Angels," Frenella said, almost like it was a mantra.

I shook my head. "I don't know what that means."

She hugged me tight. "You will. Sooner than you want."

I pulled away from her. "Why did no one ever tell me this before? Why did they keep me so...so...?" I didn't yet have a word for what I was. Later in life, I knew that one conversation made only a very small dent in my naive ignorance.

"Because I shouldn't have. It's not a woman's place to worry about the business of men. We look the other way, we pretend all is well, and we suffer in silence, knowing each of us is doing the same. But I see you love Apollo and I fear for him. He's my only child. I fear he will lose himself without you."

That felt like an awful lot to put on the shoulders of one so young. What did Archer expect of Apollo to put that much fear in Frenella?

My heart pounded hard. I needed to see him. To make sure he was okay. I pulled from her grasp and ran back to the hall. Archer's door was firmly shut, and I knew what sort of reception I'd get if I barged in there. Archer had never even threatened to raise a hand to me, but I was scared he would if I dared enter his office now.

All I could do was sit on the stairs, leaning on the banister rails and stare at the office door, willing it to open and Apollo to walk out unharmed. I sat on those stairs for what felt like hours, thinking myself well hidden behind the banister railings. Just as my eyes were closing from sheer boredom, I heard the tell-tale sound of Archer's office door open.

Archer walked out with a big man, and two boys probably in their late teens. One was dark haired, and one was lighter haired, but they were obviously brothers.

"Pleasure doing business with you, Mr Callahan," said the big man with the scar down his face. He had a thick Scottish accent.

Archer shook his hand. "The pleasure is mine, Cillian. Binding our boys is just good business. Valen will make an excellent Angel."

As they moved towards the door, Apollo and another dark-haired boy about our age came into view, eyeing each other carefully. It was a side of Apollo I'd never seen. He looked starkly like his father, superior and disdainful. It made something in me shrivel uncomfortably.

I stood up quickly and all eyes were on me.

I finally pulled my focus from Apollo and my heart fluttered in my chest.

The dark-haired boy was...

At twelve, I didn't really have a word for it. Five years later, I still wouldn't really have a word for it, but he still managed to make my heart flutter uncontrollably.

His eyes bored into me, and I couldn't tell what he was thinking. Unlike the boy beside him, he looked rougher. There was a cut on his cheek, and he had... He had a tattoo on his arm, peeking out from his pushed-up sleeve. At the time, I naively thought it was one of those temporary ones. I'd soon learn that lesson.

"Harlow," Archer barked, and my eyes flew to him. "What are you doing?"

I swallowed hard, but my reply was distracted by the light-haired teen. The way he was looking at me. It didn't give me butterflies. It gave me chills. Fear crawled along my arms and made me wrap my arms around myself.

"Harlow!" Archer barked again.

I licked my lip and forced my eyes back to him, but I felt the other teen's eyes still on me.

"I… I'm sorry, Archer. I…" I didn't know what to say.

"Why don't you go and have tea with the other women?" Apollo said and I recoiled at the tone of his voice.

He'd never spoken to me like that. The way his father had just spoken to me.

What had happened in that office? Where was my Apollo?

Feeling tears pricking hot at my eyes, I turned and ran for my room.

Later that night, Apollo crawled onto my window seat with me and tried to apologise. He gave no explanation as to why he'd spoken to me like that, but it wouldn't be the last time. In fact, it was the first in a new normal of the public Apollo versus the private Apollo, the arrogant Apollo versus the sweet Apollo. And I was just desperate enough to keep a piece of my best friend with me that I didn't tell him off for it.

Many times over the next few years, I remembered my conversation with Frenella and I wondered, if I'd had the confidence to stand up to him back then, maybe I could have stopped him from fulfilling his destiny quite so spectacularly.

Chapter Two

A year later and life had certainly changed, but I wasn't sure it was the best day ever, every day.

I was less naïve. If only slightly.

I knew what God and his Angels meant, and I didn't like it.

There was a hierarchy at Saint Benedict's College. Every family had blood on their hands, of that I had no doubt but, those that had the most, ruled the school. And at the top was God and his Angels. Collectively known as the Saints. They were all entitled and cocky. But no more so than God.

Being God may as well have been exactly what it sounded like.

It meant privilege and arrogance beyond comprehension. It meant belittling and bullying and a lot more that I knew Apollo kept from me. Things like sex and violence. I saw the hints of weapons that the boys thought they hid from the nuns. I knew enough to be pretty sure that God had sent girls to make Apollo 'a real man'. There was just something different about him now.

By the time we were preparing for our second year at Saint Benedicts, Apollo was already a changed man. And I could only do so much when my time with Apollo was hampered by Valen

Kincaid, the dark-haired boy with tattoos down his arm and Apollo's first Angel. By the end of the year, the future God of Saint Benedicts had filled two of his Angel positions with the introduction of Marco O'Malley. Between Valen and Marco, any time I spent with Apollo was filtered, was public. Valen even invaded our holidays, occupying the room next to mine at Callahan Hall.

I didn't know what Apollo had said to Valen, but he'd made it his mission to make sure the whole school knew I was Apollo's, and Apollo did nothing to stop him. It hadn't taken long before none of the boys even looked at me. The one boy, who had the misfortune of getting the memo late and kissed me, had ended up with a broken jaw to match Valen's bloodied knuckles. The rest feel into line pretty quickly after that.

I hated Valen Kincaid.

I hated who Apollo was becoming.

Everything had definitely changed, and I wished I'd paid more attention to Frenella when she'd tried to tell me that it was coming. Maybe if I'd been more prepared, I wouldn't have looked the other way. But by the time I knew I shouldn't be silent any longer, I'd been silent too long.

But nothing changed quite so much until the week before our second year.

An icy reception greeted us when Mum, Dad and I arrived at Callahan Hall.

Frenella and Mum still embraced, with forced smiles and warm words. But they hurried me away as quickly as they could. It didn't stop me from feeling Valen's contemptuous glare from up on the stairs. I looked up and saw Apollo standing there with him. Apollo gave me a terse nod and I felt that small part of me shrivelling again.

"Vanguard," Archer said as he nodded at Dad.

"Archer."

"Let's get this over with."

I felt panic well up in me. I may have been kept in the dark about a lot of what they did and why, but I knew something was going on. Something between our dads, and Apollo was just standing there like he didn't care.

"Apollo," Archer barked. "Dismiss your wolf and get down here."

Apollo gave Valen a nod, then jogged effortlessly down the stairs.

That one action told me how much he'd changed. No longer was he just running down the stairs, just existing so he could get to me quickly. He was restrained, practiced, like he knew all eyes were on him. He moved with the beginnings of the smooth confidence of a man who knows he's…well, God.

As he passed me, there was a moment where I saw the old Apollo in his eyes. He didn't know what was happening either.

"Mum?" I asked her.

She just shook her head, took my hand and tugged for me to follow her. Follow her, I did. She led me up the stairs. I didn't miss the small touch between her and Frenella as we went.

"Valen," Mum said as we passed him, still standing as though sentry.

He inclined his head. "Mrs Vanguard. Miss Vanguard."

It was always Miss Vanguard. Like he was more servant than friend. It would take me years to see that, for Apollo and Valen, they were one and the same; there was no friendship without service, and no service without a friendship more like brotherhood.

Mum took me into my room and shut the door.

"What's happening?" I asked her.

As she turned, I saw her hand was shaking a little, but she was putting on a brave face. "You know how Frenella and I have always joked about you and Apollo getting married one day?" she said.

I nodded slowly. "Yeah…"

She nodded as she started moving around the room, like she was getting an outfit ready for me. "Well," she said, forcing the joviality. "Well, that's going to happen."

I frowned. "No, it's not."

She gave me a look and I didn't know what it meant.

"No," I repeated. "The school just thinks we're together because Valen—"

"This has nothing to do with what the children at Saint Benedicts do or do not think, Harlow," Mum said harshly, then let out a deep breath. "I'm sorry."

"Mum, I don't understand."

She nodded again. "I know. I…" She sighed, sat down on the bed and patted the spot next to her.

I dropped into it, and she looked at the wall like she was praying for courage.

"You are to marry Apollo, sweetheart. There's nothing we can do. The two of you get along so well, that it was probably going to happen anyway. Now, it's just…a certainty."

I didn't know what to say. "But I don't want to marry Apollo."

Mum sighed again and I thought she was holding back tears. "You don't now. Who knows what the future will bring?"

"If Apollo keeps up this future God charade, then I can tell you what the future will bring," I muttered.

"I know, sweetheart. I know it's hard."

"It's not hard. I just say no."

Mum took my hands. "You can't say no, Harlow."

"Why not?"

"You need to do this, sweetheart," Mum told me, and I saw fear in her eyes. "It's how it works."

How it works. This world I was only permitted to understand half of. This world where I was deemed too soft to make my own choices or be my own person. This world that took sweet boys and turned them into hardened men.

I could see it in her eyes. I was going to have to do it. At least, I was going to have to agree now. Surely, I'd have at least five years before we could be expected to marry. That was plenty of time to make an escape plan.

I nodded in an effort to reassure her. "Your marriage to Dad was arranged."

Her nod wasn't quite so reassuring. "Yes, but... This is a little different." Her eyes beseeched me to understand as she ran her hands over my hair. "We owe the Callahans, sweetheart." Her voice shook. "We...had no choice. Your father was backed into a corner. A life for a life. The life they demanded was...yours."

I felt my eyes widen. I thought this was a marriage deal. "They're going to kill me?"

She smiled, but it didn't reach the sadness in her eyes. "No. No, they want your hand. Apollo as your father's heir."

I might have been kept from the full nuances of the men's business, but I knew enough to make an educated guess.

"Archer wants Daddy's money..." I said.

Mum nodded. "Archer would kill for your father's money."

When most people said that, it was rhetorical, hyperbole. Something about the way Mum said it made me think she was serious.

My mind ran miles a minute.

Dad owed the Callahans. My hand – my inheritance – was payment. And someone would die if I didn't go through with it. Well, there went any thoughts of an escape plan.

"Archer hoped you and Apollo would happen naturally," Mum continued. "Over time. Then..." She cleared her throat. "Now, he doesn't have to wait."

This – Apollo and I – was more than just the wishful thinking of two doting mothers, then.

"When... When do I have to marry him?" I asked, assuming it was something as stupid as next week.

Mum shrugged. "There's no date in the contract. It was agreed to wait until you finish school to draw up the...particulars. At present, it merely stands as a contract owing and the...consequences if it is broken..."

I didn't need to ask what the consequences were. Even if I hadn't already guessed, I would have by the way her voice trembled, the look of fear in her eyes, the way her hand reached for mine. I could see she was trying to hide it, the way the women were always supposed to hide it, but she couldn't. She was that worried.

I nodded. "Okay," I told her, sounding braver than I felt. "Okay, I'll marry Apollo. One day," I added as though I had any power in the situation at all.

Mum hugged me tightly. "Thank you, sweetheart. Thank you."

As we sat around for pre-dinner drinks that night, our fathers made the announcement.

"Harlow and Apollo will marry," Archer said.

"And Apollo will be the heir to the Vanguard fortune," my dad finished, his voice tight, and everything in me fell.

I watched Archer and my father shake hands. My fate sealed. At least, if I was being made to marry someone, it got to be my best friend. If that counted for anything anymore. Everyone at Saint Benedicts had already been told I was Apollo's. Valen had made sure of that. Why not make it reality?

There was still obvious friction between our fathers, though Archer seemed very pleased with himself as our mothers lavished praise and excitement on the men. There was an undercurrent of tension in the room, like we were all walking on eggshells. We all had our part to play. If we didn't, people died. Well, I could play a part. How hard could it be?

In our corner of the room, Apollo took my hand. "I'm sorry, Harlow."

"What for?" I winced at the venom in my voice.

"We'll get through this. Together."

I was feeling slightly less optimistic about that. "Really?"

His hand squeezed mine. "I'll always protect you, Harlow. Our world will never hurt you."

Clearly, he knew more than me. Equally clear was that he wasn't about to enlighten me. I didn't know how he expected to protect me. My place was clearly fixed as far as our parents were concerned, and now Apollo had firmly placed me there as well, even if it was from some misguided belief that he was doing what was best for me.

As a woman in this world, I'd begun to understand I held little power, but at least I'd had my father's inheritance to give me some influence and authority. Now it – and I – was promised to Apollo, I had none. I was the same as the rest of them.

Trophy.

Enabler.

Prisoner.

Chapter Three

It was the entrance that every girl dreams of at least once in her life. Even if the fantasy is immediately discarded as ridiculous. Frivolous. Impossible. The thought crosses her mind. Just once. At least once.

For me, once was now my reality.

I should have been happy. I should have that bubble of warm joy steadily expanding in my chest, a matching smile spreading on my face, as I walked towards him. Him with his hand outstretched towards me, nothing but love and devotion on his face.

I wasn't unhappy, but I was bored. This wasn't for us. It was for them. It was, for lack of a better word, protocol. But four years of following it had made us experts. With practise, we'd become perfect. A routine – a relationship – born of necessity and the lingering love between childhood friends.

As I descended the stairs slowly, my hand on the railing, my skirts flouncing lightly around my legs, it was a scene quite literally out of a movie. The chandelier hung high above us. People milled about in their finery, drinks in hand, watching me descend. Waiting staff bobbed about with silver trays of tiny delicacies. And waiting for me at the bottom of the stairs…

Waiting for me was a prince.

A king.

A god.

Apollo Callahan was all that and more.

As I looked up at him, he winked at me and my smile felt more real, more natural.

His tall frame was wrapped in the most expensive, perfectly tailored tuxedo. A Jacquard jacket with silk lapels. Slim black pants. White pleated shirt. Black silk bow tie. He had become the dream of most every girl at Saint Benedict's College. With his dark blond hair swept up from his face. It wasn't the charming smile nestled in his dashing features that got me. It was the cheeky twinkle in his deep sapphire eyes.

I reached the bottom of the grand sweeping staircase and took Apollo's hand. He drew me the last few steps. It wasn't so hurried that it was unseemly, but enough that it was obvious he needed me in his arms.

When my foot hit the floor, his hand went to the small of my back and he leant in to kiss my cheek. The people gathered clapped politely and there was a general murmur of approval making its way around the room.

"Phase one complete," he whispered in my ear. "How many more hours to go?"

"Too many," I answered as I looked around at the pearl-draped women with their dainty wine glasses. "Can't we just go and eat ice cream until we bust?"

I felt him smiling. "I suppose you want rainbow?" he teased.

"Don't ice cream shame me, Apollo Callahan."

"I wouldn't dare, Harlow Vanguard," he chuckled. "You ready?"

I nodded. "As ready as I'll ever be."

"You look stunning, by the way."

I smiled at him as I looked into his eyes. "Thank you. You don't look so bad yourself."

He chuckled, his body leaning into mine instinctively. "I'm overheating. You're lucky you get naked shoulders and a breeze around your legs."

I laughed, my hand going to his chest. "We could swap, if you like?"

His nose nudged my jaw just under my ear. "I wouldn't want to miss seeing you in it."

"Apollo. Harlow," came the deep, warm tones of a familiar voice.

Apollo took his nose out of my hair and smiled at his father. A smile that didn't reach his eyes. "I thought you'd be later."

Archer Callahan looked around as though surveying his kingdom and my eyes followed his. His guests were refined and polished but, in the shadows and halls, lurked the truth; all of them carrying at least one holster or knife somewhere it was as easily hidden as it was 'accidentally' flashed.

"It took less time than expected," Archer admitted. "Neo Kincaid leant his not inconsiderable help to the cause." He finished up quickly – as though the faster he talked, the less I'd understand – and turned his smile on me. A smile that *did* reach his eyes. "Harlow, you look wonderful, as always."

He took my hand and I let him kiss it.

"Thank you, Archer. You and Frenella have outdone yourselves"

I felt Apollo's hand grip my back tighter at the shared in-joke.

Archer and Frenella Callahan threw the best parties in our society. It was a given. They upped the ante with every single one. Not that they needed to because no one was stupid enough to try to best them, and no one ever would. Not until they all expected me to take the reigns.

Something that Archer liked to remind me of as often as possible. "This will all be you soon enough."

I forced my smile wider. "I'm certain I could never do better than you." It couldn't be that hard, but it was the right thing to say.

"It's all my amazing wife, my dear. I just sign the cheques."

I gave him the agreeable laugh he expected. "The pen is mightier than the sword."

Archer's name was called from elsewhere. He gave me a wide grin as he started heading that way. "So it is, Harlow. So, it is." He looked pointedly at his son. "If you see Valk, tell him his father's looking for him."

My stomach fluttered and my breath skipped, but I hid it behind a breath supposed to make the men think I had no idea why Valen's father would want him or what on earth they might get up to when he did find him. I followed it up with a sweetly innocent smile, which was returned.

"Drink?" Apollo asked when his father was gone, visibly

relaxing. "Shall we get drinks?"

I inwardly groaned but nodded my head. "Yes."

Apollo steered me through the milling people into the ballroom, where there were even more people, towards the bar at the end. Much like the rest of Callahan Hall, it was a huge, ornate thing designed purely to show off how much money they had. The bar stretched across the whole back of the ballroom, except for a door that led through to the cellar stairs and kitchen. It was wood inlaid with gold, and brightly lit. Behind it, at every soiree the Callahan's threw, were at least six bar staff.

"Same as usual, Mr Callahan?" the waiter who saw us called.

He gave her a single nod in reply.

In moments, a tumbler of deep amber liquid and clinking ice was placed in front of Apollo, and a glass of frosted white wine was placed in front of me. Pinot Gris. The drink I was expected to down at all these things until my palette was 'sophisticated' enough to appreciate a fine red. In Pinot Gris' defence, I didn't dislike it. I just didn't like having my drinks – like so much in my life – chosen for me.

Apollo picked up my glass and passed it to me.

"Thanks," I said, to both him and the waiter.

He put his hand at the small of my back again and picked up his own.

Such a small thing, but it screamed volumes. Whenever we stood next to each other, Apollo was touching me. A hand on my back, like now. His hand in mine. Caressing my cheek as he smiled at something I said. His arm around my shoulder. The action had long since stopped being conscious, of that I was sure.

Now and then, he'd go to do something and realise he couldn't because my hand was in his.

Whenever we were in the same room, he constantly found me. He'd make sure I felt remembered and wanted and like I belonged there. His winks or cheeky smiles always made me feel like we alone shared the joke – whatever it may have been. I didn't just belong in this world, I belonged with him.

He looked out over the crowd as he sipped. There was so much of his father in him these days. As Apollo had got older, I'd seen him pick up more and more of Archer's mannerisms, his quirks, the way he held himself. At school, he surrounded himself with people who just reinforced this as the correct behaviour. Gone was the little boy who hid in the storeroom under the stairs as his father yelled at him and, in his place, was a man who emulated him in every way.

Apollo may have only just turned eighteen, but he'd left boyhood behind long ago, no matter how much I teased him otherwise. The way he moved through life. Confident. Powerful. Authoritative. Bowing to no one. To call him anything but a man would be disingenuous, and a lie.

I heard Apollo sigh, then he threw back the remainder of the tumbler, put it down with a shake of his head to the waiter ready to refill it, and looked at me.

"I guess we should get schmoozing?" he asked, clearly as thrilled by the prospect as me.

The only difference was, the world would probably come to an end if I tried to down my wine as quickly as he'd downed his Scotch. He could have all the liquid courage – or anaesthetic – he wanted, while I was supposed to maintain a demure and sensible composure.

Much like the sweet little boy was gone, so was the naïve girl who thought the world was full of hope and opportunity. I was kept ignorant, but I liked to think I wasn't naïve anymore.

I gave him a supportive smile. "Together."

He kissed my cheek with a smile. "Together," he said as he took my hand and we started off.

We did what we were expected to do. We mingled. We danced. We made sure every single person saw us being cute and adorable and loved up. It wasn't hard, not with Apollo by my side. I did love him. Having a good time with him was simple and easy. I just hated the parade. I hated the expectation. I hated knowing that all eyes were on us, looking for a flash of diamond on my finger at every opportunity. We had been contracted to marry for four years now, what were we waiting for already?

The younger portion of the crowd had retired to the Billiards Room some hours later. All people we went to school with and who were at the party with their parents or in their stead.

Those in the room constituted the elites of Saint Benedicts. They ruled the school under the watchful eye of Apollo, their God. They weren't all here, but the most noticeably missing were the four Angels. Apollo's Lieutenants. His muscle. His brawn. They weren't appropriate for this sort of thing. Better kept for school where the pretence maintained was completely different.

I stood in a corner with Triss, Alanis, Coral, Exie, Lula and Yola. We made small talk, but it would have been ridiculously naïve to pretend that we weren't all keeping one eye on the boys playing pool. Their brothers. The first sons, set to inherit everything. Keep your enemies close.

Apollo had taken off his jacket and bow tie and rolled up his sleeves. There was a half-empty bottle of Cognac at his side. He passed the vape pen off to Smith as he took a cue from Wyatt. He smiled as Bronn ruffled Kobe's hair and the younger boy cried out in protest.

We may have all been the children of peers, but we had our own pecking order. Our ages ranged from fourteen to eighteen, with Kobe and Dean the youngest boys by a couple of years. Most of them were in my year. The girls on the other hand, they were all sixteen or over as it wasn't seemly for the younger girls to come to these things. The boys, yes. The girls, no.

I caught Apollo's eye and he gave me another of his cheeky winks. It pulled a smile from my lips unbidden. He was a great many things was Apollo, but he knew how to make me feel special.

"Where are those fuckers?" Tyson asked.

Apollo frowned in perfect imitation of Archer intimidation. "Language in front of the ladies," he snapped.

Tyson came to heel quick smart. "My apologies, ladies," he said with a small bow in our direction.

His little sister, Triss rolled her eyes at me with a wry smile.

Of all the elites' girls, Triss and her best friend Exie were the only ones I actually liked hanging out with. They were the year below me – Triss being a mere nine months younger that Tyson, putting her in the same year – and felt by-and-large the same way about the world as I did. Suffer in silence, knowing we were all doing the same. Silence didn't mean we didn't communicate in other ways.

Apollo looked around, then at the watch on his wrist. "He said he was on his way."

"And I was," came the gravelly answer from the door.

Everyone turned to face him. Because who wouldn't?

My eyes were drawn to him whenever we were in even remotely the same vicinity. My eyes drank him in while my stomach fluttered angrily, my heart thudded uncomfortably, and a pool of warmth flooded me entirely inappropriately.

He'd at least dressed semi-appropriately for making an appearance at a lavish Callahan soiree where he might have been seen by someone who mattered. Dressed in a dappled grey suit, with black shirt and tie, the colours suited him. His hair was so dark, it was almost black, cut short at the sides and long on top. And though the top almost always dropped down over his face, seared into my memory were the piercing grey eyes that had a constant glare of contempt for me. His face was chiselled, always drawn in a look of annoyed disinterest or superior boredom. When he moved, his body glided like a panther, as though he had absolute control of every single muscle.

At Saint Benedicts, he was one of Apollo's Angels. I didn't need rumours to know there was nothing saintly about him. You only needed to take one look at him to know the man was born to sin. The fact I'd once walked in on him proving exactly that had been an unnecessary confirmation.

"You Saints are all fucking impatient," he continued as he walked in.

Apollo would never tell him to mind his language, around anyone.

Not him.

Not Valen Kincaid.

Apollo was tall enough. Valen was taller.

Apollo was charmingly gorgeous. Valen was sinfully sexy.

Apollo used his polite words and wit and smile. Valen used very different words, razor sharp insults, and his fists.

Apollo melted every panty in a room by walking into it. Valen's mere existence had you willing to drop to your knees and beg for more.

I loved Apollo Callahan. I was promised to Apollo Callahan.

I loathed Valen Kincaid. I craved Valen Kincaid.

It was a conundrum to be sure.

While there were parts of who Apollo had become that I didn't agree with, that I didn't like, we'd been in each other's lives far too long for anything to make a deal-breaking dent in the love I felt for him.

On the other hand, I despised Valen. He was a brute. He was a womanising arsehole. He was one of the Saints. There was absolutely no reason to feel a shred of positive emotion for him. No reason other than he had sworn to protect Apollo with his dying breath.

Which made the absolutely idiotic, barely controllable lust I felt for Valen a slight thorn in my side.

"Your old man was looking for you," Apollo said as he passed Valen the bottle of Cognac, the movement of Valen's arm making the holster under his jacket visible for a moment.

Valen took a swig as his eyes scanned the room. The bottle was still at his lips when he saw me, and I could have sworn I saw the hate from there. Even in a semi-darkened room, hazy with vape smoke.

The way he froze at the sight of me. The way he took another long swig before handing the bottle back to Apollo. His eyes never leaving me. What I did see was the way his upper lip twitched like he was just itching to say something unpleasant to me.

I didn't know what it was about me. He was the only person I knew who hated me. Well, the only person who hated me for some inexplicable reason that wasn't simply because I was Apollo's girlfriend.

"Yo, did you hear me?" Apollo asked, whacking Valen's arm.

Valen nodded and finally pulled his eyes from me. "Yeah. Just seen him."

Apollo nodded as he took a drink. "Lovely. So, we done?"

Valen nodded. "We're done. Fender's got everything organised back at school."

Apollo smiled. "Good. Good." He looked over and found me. He kicked his head. "Come on, then. We, at least, get to leave."

Triss and Exie muttered under their breath, and I gave them an apologetic smile.

Exie waved a hand. "We'll no doubt be let off the leash in an hour or so."

Triss nodded. "Like keeping us here is going to actually make Archer Callahan more likely to do business with them," she scoffed. Most days, I felt like the way our fathers did business wouldn't make sense even if we were allowed to know about it.

"I'll see you back at school," I said.

They nodded resignedly.

"See you then," Triss said.

Apollo was waiting for me at the door to the billiard's room, his jacket over one arm, the bottle of Cognac in his hand, and his other hand outstretched for mine.

"Thank God, that's over," I said to him as I took his hand, and he drew me under his arm and into his body.

He kissed my head with a chuckle as we headed for the garage. "One litre of rainbow ice cream is waiting for you."

Chapter Four

Back at Saint Benedicts, it was a different story.

Valen opened the car door for me. It wasn't politeness, it was to remind me how powerless I was. I was nothing but a weak woman who wasn't to get her hands dirty to the point I couldn't even open my own door.

I glared at him as I stepped out of the car.

"You're welcome, *Miss* Vanguard," he said sarcastically with a ripple of a snarl at his lips.

"Ugh, thank fuck that's over," Apollo laughed as he climbed out of the front passenger seat.

Just like that, the flip was switched.

Gone was the golden child, Apollo Callahan, and in his place was the God of Saint Benedicts. The other man I hated.

The Saints took anything and anyone they wanted. Apollo Callahan was no exception. He'd been groomed from the moment we'd stepped foot on the hallowed grounds of Saint Benedicts to take his rightful place as God. A title handed down from one rich arsehole to another, Apollo had taken the mantel the year earlier. The strong, compassionate boy I'd known and loved had been slowly smothered into nothing more than a tiny, flickering ember by the entitled, ruthless man I saw before me.

Valen still had one hand on the car roof and one on the door, boxing me in.

I ignored the flutter of my stomach – and lower down – and frowned. "Do you mind?"

He sucked his teeth as his eyes dropped. From that vantage, he had a pretty decent view. "Not really."

Apollo laughed. "Valk, stop being a dick and let her go. Harlow's had plenty of that for tonight," he said suggestively. "She needs to go to bed."

There was always someone telling me what to do.

If it wasn't my father, it was Apollo's. If it wasn't Apollo, it was Valen. If it wasn't them, it was the staff at school. The only time I had a moment's peace was in my room with my roommate and best friend, Florence. Even then peace was a relative term, but that was my refuge and that was where I was going.

Valen looked down at me once more, his grey eyes boring into me. Searing every piece of skin they lighted on. Without taking those eyes off me, he removed the gun from his holster, like he was making a point, and emptied the clip. The nuns had put their collective feet down about weapons on campus. Guns were no-go, knives were easier to hide.

I had to force my breath to remain steady, to not give anything away under the watchful eyes of those gathered. Those, plus the ones who'd just joined us in the boys' dorm garage.

"And so, God walks among man once more," Fender cried, opening his arms wide to Apollo, who chuckled as Valen finally turned away from me and put his gun in the glovebox.

Fender. Another Angel. Followed by Marco and Gage. *Four Angels shall there ever be, to help uphold God's sovereignty.*

"You take care of things while I was gone?" Apollo asked Fender before clasping his hand in greeting.

Fender grinned. "We've got a nice one waiting for you," he answered, like I had no idea what they were talking about.

Cleanliness might have been next to godliness, but Apollo was anything but clean. His name meant 'destroyer' and it was the worst kept secret at Saint Benedicts that the Sinners called him the destroyer of girls. An utterly pathetic joke, but one I'd heard was true nonetheless. Though I'm sure they meant it physically, rather than whatever mental implication Apollo's actions actually had on those he used and discarded.

Apollo instructed Valen to move with just a look, then reached for me. He put his hand on my waist and kissed my cheek. Always my cheek as agreed. "I'll walk you back."

I smiled. "No need. I'll be fine."

He looked at me like he genuinely cared. And there was a part of him that still did. "You sure?"

I nodded. "Yup. All good. Four years really gives a girl the lay of the land."

He chuckled. "All right. See you tomorrow."

Another nod. "See you tomorrow."

He pressed another kiss to my cheek and started leading his Angels away. Valen alone paused before following his God. He threw me a look of utter contempt that I felt burn right through me. The only thing I could do was return it.

When I was alone in the garage, I breathed in deep. Then out. In. Out. When my heart had settled once more, I headed off for the girls' dormitory and the safety of my own four walls, such as they were.

The room wasn't much, but it was the closest thing to home I knew.

"Oh, you look nice. Have a good night?" Florence asked as I came in.

I shrugged. "It was fine."

"Where's prince charming then?"

"No doubt ball's deep in a Magdalen by now," I answered as I started getting changed.

We called them Magdalens. The whole school did. The girls who threw themselves at the Saints. Their conquests. The ones who made it to second – or more – helpings more than earned their name. A small sect in reality, but they were those girls either messed up by their fathers enough to believe they needed the validation of being fuckable by such 'superior' men, or who were looking for any social advantage that being even the future mistress of a Saint would afford.

Florence scoffed. "Lovely."

I finished getting changed, undid my hair and brushed the blonde curls out, and cleaned off my make up. I looked tired. Not just physically, but mentally. There was a weariness deep in my honey eyes as I looked myself over; I was built like a pixie as my dad had always said. It made it easier to play my part when I looked like I epitomised it.

When I joined Florence back in our room, I dropped to the

floor at the end of her bed and took the proffered chocolate biscuit.

Florence and I had been roommates since our first year at Saint Benedict's College. She was a beautiful, curvy girl with thick curly dark red hair and piercing green eyes. She liked to joke that her Scottish ancestors were to blame, although neither of us knew for sure if she had any. Thanks to her, my sexual awakening had occurred without any help from the opposite sex. She'd passed on the magazines, the books, shared the TV shows and movies with me from the day she found out about my…predicament. She'd firmly believed that, if Apollo wasn't going to teach me about the more pleasant things in life, then someone had to make sure I didn't hit eighteen with no idea what I liked or wanted.

She'd had my back for over five years. She accepted me for who I was; the princess in an ivory tower. She'd been my escape, even if only mentally. She'd also made sure my mind spent as much time in the gutter as hers, even if her body was the only one making use of the knowledge.

I felt movement and saw her looking at me askance from where she lay upside down on the bed, her head hanging over the end near mine.

"We've never really talked about Apollo…" she said slowly. "Not like that."

I shrugged nonchalantly. "Not like what?" I asked.

She grinned at me ruefully, knowing full well that I knew full well what she meant. "Fucking him."

I snorted and shoved against her shoulder playfully.

"I'm serious," she said. "Would you do it?"

I lay my head against the bed and looked at the ceiling. "I don't know," I told her honestly. "That would depend."

"On what?" she asked.

I sighed and looked at her again.

She'd always been so non-judgmental about my relationship with Apollo. She'd never pressed or pried about the intricacies of who we were to each other. Like the rest of the school, she knew that I was his girlfriend, that our parents were just waiting until we were old enough to start planning the wedding that neither of us really seemed to want, and that he fucked any Magdalen that would open her legs for him – which was all of them. What she knew, that the rest of the school didn't, was that he wasn't touching me any time soon, she just didn't know why.

Apollo and I were the only two who knew the full details about our relationship. Surely, after so many years of her standing by me unquestioningly, it was time I repaid her with some truths.

"Oh, this gonna be good, isn't it?" she said with a wide grin.

I laughed. "Yeah. It's going to be good."

She flipped herself awkwardly off the bed and came to sit beside me on the floor. She took my hand, wriggled to get settled then said, "Okay. Ready. Spill all."

I snorted. "I'm Apollo's…" I paused, not quite knowing how to phrase it.

"Girlfriend," she guessed. "Fiancée. Future baby mama. Cuckold."

I smiled at the last one. "All true, but I was going to say princess."

She rolled her eyes and looked at me like I'd lost my mind. "Yeh ha?"

"Princess. It's the best way we've been able to describe it."

"Ivory tower. Locked away. Yadda yadda. Okay. Keep going," she said with a sceptical nod.

"I'm the one he's…protecting."

"Excuse me?"

We'd never directly addressed it, but I'd always assumed she thought Apollo just wasn't attracted to me. After us seemingly being together longer than she'd known me and clearly not saving himself for anything, I didn't blame her.

I fought another smile. "I know how it sounds."

"Yeah, you do. And yet you're fine with it?"

"I wouldn't say fine, per se."

"Hmph. Keep talking and we'll see how fine anyone is at the end of it."

"It's all fake," I told her, feeling a weight off my shoulders. "It's just for show."

"What!" she cried. "I'd never have guessed!" She grinned at me ruefully.

"You can't tell anyone," I told her, but I didn't think she would.

She crossed her heart. "I won't. Despite the juiciness. Fake. This whole time?" she clarified, and I nodded. "Huh. I mean, the thought had crossed my mind, but I actually didn't guess. I can't say I'm surprised, though."

I smiled at her. "You just thought I was a soft pushover?"

She shrugged with a sad finality. "Every woman in our lives is. What else was I to think?"

That was scarily fair. The women in our lives were what our

world had made them.

"It's not quite that sad. But I am going to be his wife. I'm going to bear his children, and throw his dinner parties, and show off the picture-perfect family to land that deal in Japan," I said. Frenella and Mum had trained me well, beginning before the marriage contract but increased ten-fold since. Instructed me in everything the wife of a peer and a peer's daughter should be. What was expected.

"So, explain to me this fake thing," Florence warned. "If it's gonna happen, why fake it now? Are there rules?"

"Kind of," I admitted. "We haven't exactly sat down and made a list, but we're free to be with other people, so long as we keep it discrete–"

"Yeah, he's about as discrete as–"

"I know. But I'm going to be his proper, upstanding wife. I'm not the girl he bends over his desk and fucks until he absolutely ruins her. I'm not the girl he…" I searched for anything even remotely kinky, or dirty, or most likely fun. "The girl he chokes. The girl he fucks hard and fast until she's screaming his name. The girl he throws against the closest surface because he *needs her*, right then and right there."

"Oh," she chuckled. "And you definitely haven't thought about this at all."

"I don't think about…fucking Apollo," I said honestly.

"No," she said with a wicked grin. "No. That honour goes to someone else."

I frowned at her. The problem with sharing a room at boarding school with someone for over four years was that, if you were to ever talk in your sleep, even once, you can guarantee it'd be during term time, when they were in the room, while they were awake. And you can bet that if wouldn't just be a mumble, it'd be grabbing the bed sheets and moaning his name so there was absolutely no way she didn't know what you were dreaming. It was a testament to our friendship that that incident hadn't been as embarrassing as it could have been.

"I know!" she said, holding up her hands, one still holding mine. "I know. No one is allowed to know that the dreams you can in no way control are filled with a man you should in no way be thinking of."

"Boy," I corrected her.

She scoffed. "He is all man, sister." She nudged me. "Hang on, if you're allowed to see other people, why can't you *see* him?" She didn't need to so heavily emphasise the word for us to both know that's not what she'd meant.

I huffed, trying to put all thoughts on *him* out of my head. Little difficult if I had to explain myself to her.

Other than I hated him? "He's Apollo's…" I breathed out heavily, wondering how to best explain in that would make sense.

"Tame wolf. Hired assassin. Mindless drone," she offered.

I smirked. "They are blindly loyal to each other. It took less than a year for them to become like brothers," I told her.

"Brothers?"

I nodded. "In all but blood. As far as I know, he firmly believes I'm totally Apollo's."

"Ah," she said. "Which is why he beats any dude who looks in your vague direction even though you're allowed to see other people."

"That's my guess. And even if he did know I wasn't now, he knows I will be. If there was a single chance in hell that he'd think about me like that, he'd never touch me. His God's girl? Not a fucking chance."

"Okay, well, is it possible for you to look at any other guy and feel even a slight tingle in your pussy?" she asked.

I batted her. "I'm not quite so far gone over him that I can't even look at another guy."

"Aren't you? Show me all these guys you'd be happy to fuck," she begged. "Let me sort it out for you. I can be *very* discrete."

I had no doubt that Florence could be. Valen had whipped the true fear of God into the guys of Saint Benedicts but, if there was anyone who could get me laid behind his watchful eyes, it was Florence Walton.

But I sighed. "Okay, fine," I admitted, without having to admit that it was all Valen's fault. "I am yet to find a guy I'm interested in enough to go to the bother of it all."

Because it was true. Every time I looked at a guy in any sexual capacity, all I did was compare him to Valen fucking Kincaid. The harder I tried not to, the worse it was. And no one could ever come close to making me feel what Valen made me feel by just thinking about those disdainful stormy eyes. Combined with the effort in sneaking around behind Valen's back, it was all too damned hard. I had a vibrator. It got the job done. For now.

She nodded. "The laziness is strong."

"The laziness is strong," I agreed.

"So, we just have to get Apollo to want to ruin you?" she

suggested.

I laughed. "Yeah. It's not as simple as that."

"Ah, you're not attracted to him?"

I shrugged. "Not really. I'm not *not* attracted to him. I just… We don't have that kind of relationship." And we didn't. I thought of him as a friend – a good friend that I loved – but not one I felt like having sex with.

"Any interest in getting that kind of relationship?"

That was the million-dollar question. At the back on my head was the constant knowledge that Apollo and I had to change at some point. We were going to marry. We'd agreed. We hadn't said in so many words, but we knew that our relationship would have to change at some point so our marriage wasn't total shit. We'd just never talked about how or when that was going to happen. I had the distinct impression that I spent a lot more time thinking about it than he did. Maybe if I could be bothered going to the effort of getting laid, I wouldn't think about it so much either.

I nudged her gently with fondness. "For him – for them – passion and marriage are separate. Your wife needs to be kept sweet and respectable, worthy of mothering your kids. You have…Magdalens to curb your sexual cravings."

"You were going to say whores," she teased.

I nodded. "I was going to say whores."

Florence snorted. "He does know you don't just want vanilla missionary sex your whole life, right?"

I sighed and risked voicing a long-quashed but not extinguished hope. "Yeah, unless I can get out–"

"Or pull a Khaleesi," Florence offered.

"Go mad?"

"Was referring to the whole taming her husband with the power of her pussy thing, but you do you."

I smiled. "Barring either of those scenarios, I don't have a lot of choice."

"Okay." She nodded. "Then we go all Khaleesi on his cock."

I loved that Florence never pushed me. She never tried to make me feel bad. She accepted my acceptance, as far as I had actually accepted my fate. She knew I was watching for a way out, but she knew just as well as I how unlikely that would be. She knew why I put up with Apollo, his behaviour, his unfaithfulness, and the way he treated me. She knew there were bigger things here than just me letting a man walk all over me and treat me like crap. If I could stand up for myself, I would. When I could, I would.

"And how do we go all Khaleesi on his cock?" I asked, happy to talk through hypotheticals. "I love you, but I don't want to offer him a threesome with you."

"Just with me, or have you ruled threesomes out entirely?"

I smirked.

"Oh. Juicy. Do tell."

I shook my head. "No. Just… Once?" I said and she nodded eagerly. "I dreamt about them both having me at the same time."

"Heavens to Betsy," she breathed, fanning herself with her free hand. "The God and his avenging Angel?"

I nodded.

She nodded as well. "Yeah. I'd take that sandwich, please and thank you. Use me up and leave me ruined for all others!"

We burst into laughter. She was laughing so hard that when I elbowed her jokingly, she toppled over onto the floor, which only served to set us off even harder.

CHAPTER FIVE

After school on Monday, Florence and I did our usual choir practice, then she went off to the Art Studio and I went to find Apollo. It was habit for me. I did it every week. Had done for the previous four years. Three weeks into the school year, it wasn't an abnormality.

Still, as I opened his door, the noise should have warned me what I was walking in on. But my ears didn't seem very well connected to my brain, because I didn't stop.

And there he was, balls deep in yet another Magdalen. She was completely naked, splayed stomach down against his window as he took her from behind. He himself was in nothing but an open shirt and – I hoped – a condom.

She moaned and whimpered like an actress in a cheesy porno. Telling him how big he felt and how good he was.

As I stepped into the room, he groaned as he finished.

"Nothing like your arrival to make a man nut himself, Valk," he laughed as he pulled out of her.

He turned and all humour on his face left him as he saw my face.

"Fuck. Harlow," he started but I shook my head and high tailed it out of there.

It wasn't the first time I'd walked in on him, and I knew it wouldn't be the last. It was like I was too stupid to learn. I liked to think it was more that he was too stupid to not fuck girls in his own room where he knew I'd come find him. Maybe that was the point? Maybe he wanted me to see him. Maybe he didn't think it mattered. Maybe he had a bit of a exhibitionist streak and there were few people he could fuck in front of without giving the whole game away.

Even knowing that our relationship was fake, there was still something about it that hurt. And, stupidly, I let it. Every time. I let him hurt me, and then feared I should have known better. But I just couldn't give up on him.

As I hurried down the staircase, I wiped a tear from my cheek.

It wasn't that I felt he was cheating on me – we had agreed we could be with other people. It was that I worried we were losing the parts of our relationship – our friendship – that we had left. That he didn't care about me enough anymore to finish with his fucking around before we were supposed to hang out. That I wasn't enough to save him from himself and this world, and it was going to break Frenella's heart. And mine.

I heard him call my name and found him jogging down the stairs, bare footed with his shirt still undone but thankfully wearing trousers. Not that they left anything to the imagination.

But I just couldn't with him right then. Not when he was in his cocky, post-pleasured haze. I shook my head, turned and barged out the dorm front doors. Right into an immovable man mountain.

I didn't need to see more than his chest to know it was him. Valen.

At the shock of me barrelling into him, his hands went to my arms to steady us both.

"Idiot," I muttered.

It wasn't enough that Apollo knew I'd walked in on him and run away with tears in my eyes. Now, Valen knew it too.

"Harlow," Apollo said again as he caught up to me.

"Sorry I interrupted," I told him, trying to push past Valen. But he kept me firmly in place.

"It's fine. She was leaving anyway," Apollo said as though I'd actually been apologising. He touched his hand to my arm gently. "Did you want something?"

Not anymore. I shook my head. "No. I have to…do my homework."

Apollo looked me over like he was trying to work out if that was the truth or not. "We'll catch up later? Dinner?"

I sighed and plastered on a smile I knew didn't reach my eyes. "Sure."

Apollo nodded, looking a touch confused but clearly not confused enough to press. He kissed my cheek absently. "Good. Valk, walk her there," he said with a dismissive wave of his hand before he turned and started jogging back up the stairs.

Valen's hand on my arm tightened and he tugged me slightly in the opposite direction. I finally managed to rip my arm from his grasp and start stalking away.

"I'm quite capable of being in control of my own body, thanks" I snapped as I started up the stairs that led from the front entrance to the boys' dorm to the walkway that led to the girls.

Naturally, after such a pronouncement, my feet saw fit to betray me. I missed the step, overbalanced, over corrected, and started falling.

Valen was there to catch me. His strong arms flew around me and pulled me close to him. Our noses bumped as I came up hard against him and I was left looking into deep grey pools swimming with hate and contempt.

I doubted I could say the same about my eyes. I very much hoped they didn't show the wanton, dripping need that suddenly squirmed to life in the pit of my stomach, sending heat pooling between my legs.

My hands were on the very impressive biceps of God's tame wolf. My chest and stomach could practically feel the rigid contours of the six pack under his tee. My lips were dangerously close to finally tasting his.

"Yeah," he said, sarcasm dripping from him like the desire in my pants. "You're definitely in control of your own body."

I panicked that he knew. That he could see how much I wanted him. How much I'd always wondered what he'd be like. That I craved him. It was enough to make me question if that flicker in his eyes was the same feeling? Did he see it in me because he felt it, too?

Then, I realised he was just pointing out the irony of my previous statement.

Still, I didn't move.

Just as I thought this was a moment and he was going to kiss me, he said, "You want a picture? It'll last longer and you can put it in your spank bank."

I pushed away from him, wobbling before I got my footing. "You'd be the last person I'd think of while...spanking," I told him as I started back up the steps. Which was a blatant lie. He was the first.

"You wouldn't be able to handle me anyway," he said, his voice rough with dark humour.

I stopped and he ran into the back of me. I turned and found him looking at me in amusement.

"I doubt the big, bad wolf's bite is anywhere near as bad as he *thinks* his bark is."

He leant in close to me, our eyes a lot closer than usual due to my being higher up the steps than him. His eyes were hard. His jaw was clenched.

"I would ruin you," he promised, and an excited tingle shot through my spine.

"Doubtful."

He snarled and yet somehow it was still sinfully sexy. "I would break you. It's almost a shame you're not to be broken."

"Almost," I agreed with saccharine sweet sarcasm. "I always thought you liked the challenge of breaking them in. The *harder* the better." I looked him over. "Or are you going soft?"

"You want to throw around words like hard and soft, I'll take you back to Apollo."

I laughed. "Am I making you uncomfortable?"

He got right in my face. "If you need to let off steam, I'm sure he's ready for the next round by now."

"No doubt he has another Magdalen lined up."

His smirk was anything but nice. "I'm sure he'll let you join

48

in."

"Watch and learn? I don't think so, thanks. I might go find myself a real man." I paused so my next words hit him at home. "I certainly don't see one around here."

Valen growled. His hand went to my neck as he bared down on me. Something told me I was supposed to be afraid of him. But I wasn't. I liked it. I felt the challenge in my eyes. I saw what could have almost been an answer in his.

"You'll go back to your room or Apollo's. Up to you."

I held my chin high. "Third option. Bit out of left field. No."

"I'm taking you back to Apollo."

"Why?" I laughed. "It's not like I've got anything he wants. Not yet anyway."

Confusion flashed in his eyes. "I don't give a fuck if you two are having a dry spell. That's between you two."

"Is it still dry spell if there's *never* been any rain?" I asked him, my eyebrows raising.

While he was standing in stunned silence, I turned on my heel and walked away.

"You don't walk away from me," he growled, jogging to catch me up.

I looked down at my feet. "It seems I do," I said in mock surprise.

He grabbed my arm again and electricity shot through me at his touch. He pulled me to face him and, even with his eyes piercing hatred into mine and his face hard and unforgiving, I couldn't help my attraction to him. My stomach twisted itself into pleasant knots and I had to fight to keep my breathing even.

Almost like, the more he hated me, the more I wanted him.

We'd never argued like this, Valen and I. I barely argued with anyone except Florence, and arguments about which Salvatore brother was better hardly counted as a real argument. I'd been brought up to be the polite little society darling, always saying and doing the right thing, only ever leaving anyone with the impression that I was 'such a nice girl'. My insides had never matched my outsides, but I played my role like the good little princess I was supposed to be and hoped that I wasn't the cause of anyone's untimely deaths.

But, quite frankly, seeing Apollo in the throes of carnal pleasure and now being too close to Valen for too long was frying those brain cells that were usually so good at ensuring my survival. I was hot and bothered. I wanted release. I needed a cool shower and enough time alone to cum hard enough to satisfy my cravings, inevitably picturing the man with his hand currently wrapped around my arm.

"You do not want to test my restraint, Miss Vanguard," he hissed.

I smirked at him. "One day soon," I promised him, "I will be your goddess. And you will bow before me."

"I will never bow to you," he snarled.

I leant towards him, daring him to close the gap between us. "I'll have you on your knees, Valk," I purred. I took his chin in my hand with a brazen confidence I didn't remember ever acting on before as I leant my lips to his ear. "And you will worship me." I pulled back to look into his eyes.

He was breathing hard. I couldn't tell if he was trying not to kiss me or hit me. Wishful thinking made me imagine it was the former. I almost believed that there was as much desire in his eyes as I felt deep in my soul whenever I looked at him.

I wanted him. I wanted him so badly that I felt like it was going to rip me apart, shattering me into so many pieces no one would ever be able to put me back together. I hated him with every fibre of my being, but so intertwined with that was blatant want. Carnal need. I couldn't tell the two apart anymore.

"You're playing with fire, princess," he said, his voice was low, husky, almost strangled like he was losing the fight against suppressing some inner emotion.

Feeling emboldened by the sound, I nudged my nose with his. "Good. Because I like it hot," I whispered.

He growled as he pushed me away. "You wouldn't know heat if it engulfed you." His voice dripped with disdain, contempt, hate.

My heart thudded painfully in my chest.

No.

He didn't want me.

Of course not.

No one wanted me.

Not like that.

And they never would.

"Tell your *God* I'll be in my room," I said, dropping my eyes as I pushed past him, hoping I didn't look as crushed as I felt.

He didn't follow me. He didn't call after me.

As I turned to take the walkway to the girls' dorm, I surreptitiously snuck a look back to the steps, but he wasn't there.

He hadn't even bothered watching me walk away. That was how little I meant to him.

It was for the best, obviously.

I didn't like him. I just wanted him to do unspeakably pleasurable things to my body. There was no reason to feel dejected by his obvious rejection. But it wasn't just him. It was the stark reminder that my life was mapped. In a few years, I'd be Apollo's wife. I was watched over and protected. Everyone in our lives knew this. Even if someone did catch my interest enough to make me forget about Valen, no one would dare risk the wrath of a Callahan or a Vanguard, let alone a Kincaid.

"Are you okay?" Florence asked as I trudged into our room.

I nodded dejectedly as I face planted onto my bed. Well, not so much face planted as full body planted.

"Are you sure?"

I lifted my face from the bed only long enough to tell her, "I walked in on Apollo and some Magdalen."

"What happens when you two get married?" she asked, taking me totally off guard.

"What do you mean?"

"Well, does he still get to fuck around while you sit around having no fun?"

I snorted, but without humour. "I don't know. I doubt it."

"You mean you'd get to fuck around, too?"

Now I laughed as I rolled onto my back. "No."

"Because no one could compare to Valen and you can't have Valen," she said matter-of-fact.

"Florence!" I snapped.

Thankfully she dropped it, but picked up her previous train of conversation. "Then, he'd stop? Apollo fucking Callahan would actually be faithful?"

I shrugged. "I honestly don't know. I think so."

Everything I knew about the men of our world was that affairs weren't common, or at least common knowledge. Whether they got better at hiding them once they were married, in order not to shatter the flimsy pretence of wedded bliss, or they stopped, I didn't know for sure. My closest role models of my parents and Archer and Frenella suggested they did love each other. Eventually.

"From what I've gathered, it's kind of like a sowing his oats before settling down thing," I told her.

"So you need to get sowing your own oats." I looked at her with a raised eyebrow and she nodded. "Gatekeeper," she said like that answered her own question. "He has totally fucked you over."

"If only," I sighed, and we laughed.

"Can't have him. He won't let you have anyone else. It's so unfair."

I fake gasped. "You wouldn't be suggesting an equality of the sexes?" I asked sarcastically.

She grinned. "You could give it a red hot try."

I shrugged. "Yeah," I said, unenthusiastically.

"There's *really* no one you want to have a go at?"

I sighed. "Not really."

And there wasn't. I got horny like everyone else. I saw to my own needs as often as I felt like it – privacy allowing. I read the books. I saw the movies and TV shows. I watched porn.

Alarmingly regularly. I wasn't quite so naïve as the Saints believed I was.

"Even Valen?" Florence pressed teasingly.

I gave her a smirk. "Other than the obvious. But even if I had a chance in hell that he'd throw me on the nearest surface and fuck me absolutely raw… I don't know," I told her, dropping the jokes and being honest.

"Liar."

I smirked at her in an effort to suppress my full smile. "It's never going to happen," I told her.

"Which is why it's totally safe to admit that you want him bad."

"I hate him," I reminded her.

"So? Last I checked, you don't actually have to like someone to want to fuck them."

I nodded in resignation. "You really don't," I said.

She laughed and playfully threw a cushion at me. "You do want him bad."

I joined her laughter and admitted as much to myself as to her, "I really do."

We dissolved into giggles at the sheer absurdity of my situation.

CHAPTER SIX

Florence and I walked to the main building first thing Wednesday morning, books in our arms and minds on how to best fall asleep without Sister Felicia noticing.

"I still think googly eyes," Florence suggested. "Woman's eyesight isn't for shit. And I know about eyesight that's not for shit." She pointed wholly unnecessarily to her own glasses.

"Yeah, but she's a nun. She's got like, a sixth sense for this stuff. I reckon behind a book's enough. If you can con her with anything, keep it simple."

"I think–"

But I never did get to find out what Florence thought, because a shower of red, white and pink rose petals rained down around us. The scent was overwhelming. It was gorgeous. They brushed against my skin like the softest caress. I dared not take another step for fear of crushing their beauty.

"Well, you can't say he doesn't go all out," Florence commented dryly.

I nodded. "There are definite perks," I agreed.

Apollo walked out of the main building – conveniently

Callahan Hall, named after, yep, his family – and down the steps to me. It seemed he had no qualms about stepping on the hundreds of petals surrounding us like a blanket. I wondered how many Saintlings and how many hours it had taken to collect that many petals. It was just the sort of job Apollo would set for the youngest of the Saints. Once, that had been our job.

"My princess," he said warmly, with not an insincere syllable passing his lips. "You look beautiful."

I grinned. "I look the same as I do every day in my uniform."

Which was nothing special. Blue and grey plaid dress, grey socks and black shoes. My hair, as school policy demanded, was in nothing more than a simple ponytail. A ponytail I'd barely even brushed that morning. Were it just up to the Dean and his faculty, we'd have been allowed to express whatever style we wanted within a flimsy pretence of a school dress code. As it was, Saint Benedicts still answered to the church, and the church cared little for the frivolous whims of the wealthy and elite. They still paid by the bucket load to send their kids to Saint Benedicts, so it was all the same to the nuns.

"As I said, you look beautiful," Apollo said with a big smile.

I nodded, knowing better than to argue with him. "Thanks."

"Well..." he started then snapped his fingers.

A Saintling appeared out of nowhere, running like he was trying not to be seen, and held out a box to Apollo. With his eyes still on me, Apollo took the box and dismissed the Saintling.

"Happy birthday, Harlow," he said, offering the box to me.

Understandably, by now, there were a lot of people who'd stopped on their way to class to see what stunt God was up to now.

No doubt a fair portion of them were betting that this was the moment, that there was a giant diamond in that box. Based on Florence's face, she was on the fence. I gave her a surreptitious shake; if Apollo knew me at all, he wouldn't do that at school. Not first thing in the morning. Not before I'd had a cup of tea and a scone – because who woke up early enough for proper breakfast if they didn't have to? And not without warning me.

"You trying to prove something, sweetheart?" he asked with a wry tilt to the corner of his mouth. "Or are you going to take your present?"

I blinked, then forced a saccharine smile. "No, of course. Thank you."

"You know what she's like first thing," Florence said quickly.

Apollo looked at her and a silent moment passed between them. One of those ones that no one else saw outside our little bubble. Had I not known both of them better, I'd have sworn there was a spark between them. A battle of wills that could tighten into an unresolved sexual tension. As it was, there was merely a battle over me going on. Apollo thought he still knew me better. Florence knew she knew me better.

"I do," Apollo said smoothly, although we all knew he didn't.

Apollo and I hadn't woken up together since it was still acceptable for us to have sleepovers. That had been a good few years now and before we'd started at Saint Benedicts.

"Of course he does," I said, still smiling sweetly and I took the box from his hands. "Thank you, Apollo."

"Aren't you going to open it?" he asked, one eyebrow quirking in challenging question.

I had no choice now, did I? And woe to you, Apollo Callahan, if it was diamonds. I was already not choosing the man who was going to propose to me, but I was not being proposed to in the bloody schoolyard.

I nodded. "No. Of course."

As he grinned with wry triumph, I gingerly opened the little box. The fluttering of my heart stilled when I saw what was in it, but only just.

It *was* diamonds, but it wouldn't pass for an engagement ring. Not by a long stretch. This... This was a statement piece.

"Fit for my princess," he said, honestly meaning every single word and totally missing the point.

But, for him, it counted as trying so my smile for him was genuine. It wasn't his fault that his best role model for relationships was his father, or that this whole thing was fake and he'd long since stopped knowing me well enough to get me something I really wanted for my birthday. That last bit was probably as much on me as him. I wasn't sure I'd be able to buy him the perfect present anymore either.

It was a ring. There were diamonds. But it was a crown. Far fancier and over the top than something I'd pick myself, but I understood the sentiment.

Apollo took the ring from me, his fingers lingering on mine. I looked into his eyes – those deep sapphire pools of warm humour – and there was a part of me that fluttered. A part that skipped. A part that warmed. A part who loved the man in front of me.

Then, as he slid the ring onto my right middle finger, my eyes scanned the courtyard and I saw all the people watching. I remembered this for the spectacle that it was. The showman the Saints had made him. And I hated him all over again. I hated him. I hated us. I hated the life I was stuck living.

But I smiled. I took his hand. I let him kiss my cheek. I bowed and simpered and played it up for the applauding crowds because that was what Harlow Vanguard was expected to do.

"Happy birthday," he whispered into my ear, his words full of love and admiration.

"Thank you," I said, feeling more sincere.

He held up the hand with the ring on it and showed off to his worshippers.

"Thank you, Mr Callahan," came a stern voice, preceding Sister Agnes. "If you are quite done, there are classes to be had."

"Yes, Sister," Apollo said, using every ounce of his charm. "Sorry, Sister."

Her eyes dropped to the bling on my finger. She grew a disapproving grimace. "Because that is a gift and it is your birthday, Miss Vanguard, I will allow you to wear it for today. But today only."

I nodded, wishing she hadn't decided now to use up her once per term leniency. "Thank you, Sister."

She looked around and we needn't be told twice.

"I'll see you later, birthday girl," Apollo said, kissing my cheek again before rushing off to class with his Angels.

I noticed then, that Valen had been nowhere to be seen. Odd for him.

"This frivolous waste," I heard Sister Agnes mutter as Florence and I headed to class.

Florence grabbed my hand and inspected the ring as we walked.

"This isn't, like, *it*...is it?" she asked, sounding sceptical.

I shook my head. "No."

"Good. 'Cos, for a standard ring, it's pretty and all, but it would make for a fucking terrible engagement ring."

I snorted as I looked at her. "Awful," I agreed.

At that moment someone turned into me and our shoulders collided. Well, I say shoulders... My shoulder hit his arm. I looked up to apologise, but the words died on my lips.

"Valen," I said carefully.

"Princess," he said disdainfully.

I knew he'd overhead us. "Don't judge what you don't know, Valk," I warned him.

He put his arm out across my body so I couldn't walk away, and it came dangerously close to touching me. My eyes flashed up and we glared at each other. My eyebrows rose quizzically, calmly waiting for an explanation.

"Most girls would kill for that bauble on your finger. Most girls would *beg* for the honour." His voice was venom.

"I appreciate the sentiment, if that's what you mean."

His eyes narrowed. "That's not what I mean."

"Well, I'm hardly going to drop to my knees in gratitude in front of Sister Agnes, am I?" I told him.

I kept a straight face.

Valen kept a straight face.

Florence snorted and tried covering with a cough.

"He spent a long time picking that out for you."

I nodded. "And I appreciate it." I honestly did. "But that doesn't mean I have to want something similar for my engagement ring."

"You think you'll have a choice?" he sneered, a vicious glee in the depths of his grey eyes.

"If Apollo cares for me at all, then he'll consider my wishes."

Valen huffed a humourless laugh. "You think *he* has a choice?"

At least Valen didn't tell me Apollo didn't care. At least there wasn't a question about it. For all that my relationship with Apollo was currently just for show, he was the only one who got to benefit from it. I shouldered the weight of our parents' expectations. I felt like I bore the responsibility of maintaining the facade. I was the one who had to think about the future – what we'd be, what we'd do – and hope that none of my sacrifices had been in vain. As a part of me would always love Apollo, I had to hope that a part of him still loved me, too.

Valen picked up my right hand and inspected the ring. I couldn't tell if it was the first time he'd really seen it or if there was something about it on my finger that was confusing him.

I told myself my skin didn't tingle at his touch. I refused to acknowledge that my heart beat faster in my chest. I ignored the way my stomach flipped and warmth pooled between my legs. I just watched his beautiful face, holding my own for when he looked at me again.

"It looks better on you," he said finally.

His eyes flew up to check my response. There was that cheeky, mischievous glint in them.

"Than who?" I asked.

The corner of his lips tipped up in victory. "Have fun tonight," he said, like it was a threat.

He dropped my hand, but gently. The wanton thirst in me said his touch lingered, like he didn't want to let me go.

"Than who, Valk?" I asked him.

His grin deepened and he started walking away.

I turned to watch him go. "Than who?" I asked again. "Than what?"

"Ignore him," Florence said. "He's just trying to get a rise out of you."

I shifted uncomfortably, fingering the ring. "Well, it's working."

Florence grinned. "Down, girl," she teased. "Now, let me see this ring again."

She wasn't the last person to ask me that day, and it wasn't all students – read, Magdalens. The entirety of my birthday paled into insignificance under the shining beacon of Apollo's love for me dazzling on my finger. The ring was all anyone talked about.

In class.

In the corridor.

At lunch, where Apollo kept me firmly tucked under his arm and reminded me about the big birthday surprise he had planned for that night.

By the time Florence and I were back in our room to get me ready for the birthday surprise, I felt like just putting the damn thing back in its box and burying it with the rest of the trinkets Apollo had given me over the years.

"Holy fucking hells," I heard Florence splutter from my bed. "Have you seen the appraisal and insurance information?"

I shrugged as I wound my hair around the curling iron. "No. I don't bother. Why?" I chuckled. "Is it half decent?"

"That little crown your royal highness is so cavalierly carrying upon your dainty little finger?"

"Mmm?" I answered with a wry smile at her hyperbolic teasing.

"Twenty-five... Are you sure you're ready for this?"

"Just tell me already."

"Twenty-five thousand."

I turned to her. "What?"

She nodded, her lip caught in her teeth in semi-disbelief. "Plus."

"Shut the front door."

She shook her head. "I won't, but it's true."

I smirked at her, then remembered the price tag on the relatively tiny piece of jewellery on my hand. My mouth parted in a little 'o' and I breathed out heavily.

"That's... That is a lot," I admitted.

"Someone feeling a little guilty about their...extra curriculars for once?" Florence hinted, her eyebrows bouncing up and down suggestively.

I smiled wryly, but went back to looking at the ring.

Apollo and I came from families that Florence liked to say didn't only have more money than sense, but had so much that numbers lost all meaning. In some ways, she was right. In theory, I could have anything I wanted, so long as I could put forward a good argument for having it and didn't already have ten (unless it was clothes or shoes). My father would pay it. Anything for his little princess. But I'd had Florence's steadying influence most of my teen years. Her parents might have had plenty of money, but they'd been sensible and instilled a value for money in their offspring so they didn't fritter away their inheritance. What we called old versus new money.

Apollo hadn't had any steadying influences. He was surrounded by people who pandered and simpered. He threw away money like it was nothing. To a point. Never to this degree. Anything with more than five figures was calculated. Or drunk ordering. This sort of spending meant something. This sort of spending meant that Florence might have been right.

"It wouldn't have been the motivating factor," I guessed. "But it might have contributed. He's certainly making a statement, though."

"Shame you can't wear it in class," she chuckled, and I grinned.

"Yeah," I answered sarcastically. "Such a pity. I do, though, have to wear it ever other waking hour of the day."

"And you'll need to remember the code to the safe for when you take it off," she reminded me, and I cursed.

The safe that my father had bought me to keep my valuables in at school. I'd argued I could just leave my valuables at home where they were extra safe. Apparently, that wasn't the right mentality. Expensive jewellery was honestly more trouble than it was worth.

"I might need to get Valen to break into it," I muttered. "He may as well be useful for something."

"He'd be useful for a great many things," Florence said suggestively.

I gave her a disapproving glare that kept trying to be a smile. "Not that I'll ever find out."

My phone went off, and Florence threw it to me.

Apollo

Running late. Meet me in the quad.

I wasn't going to ask him what quad. We knew each other incredibly well. At least, I knew him incredibly well. If he was running late, he meant the quad outside the boys' dorm.

"Is he not even going to pick you up?" Florence asked, disgust evident in her voice.

"Of course, not," I answered, heavy on the sarcasm. "A God never goes to a princess, even if it is her birthday."

"If he doesn't get you like a million dollars in jewels, kick him in his."

I smirked at my best friend. "Yeah, sure. I'll do that right after I tell him exactly what I think of his phoney birthday dinner dates and wasting the Saintlings time on pulling the petals off I don't want to know how many roses for that idiotic display."

My finger twirled the new ring around my finger.

"You okay?" Florence asked gently.

Here was someone who did actually know me incredibly well.

I nodded. "Sure. Of course."

"With skills like that, it's no wonder Apollo still thinks you're nothing more than his innocent little princess," she said sarcastically.

I huffed a laugh. "Thanks."

"What's up?"

I shrugged. "I don't know. I just feel…confined. More than usual. Like the walls are closing in." I sighed. "Like time is running out."

"What time?" she asked.

"I don't know," I laughed humourlessly. "The time until I can't deal with this anymore, I guess."

No matter the consequences, no matter what Apollo and I agreed, I knew there would be a point where I couldn't do this anymore. Something would have to give. I just had to hope it wouldn't be my sanity or someone's life.

"So, Operation Khaleesi is on?"

I gave her a small smile. "Maybe I'm tired of doing all the work."

"And telling him that is out of the question?" she guessed.

"I can be Harlow with you, and I can be the princess with him," I told her. "There is no in between."

She nodded, understanding. "And he loves the princess."

"What small part of him loves me loves the princess. I can't risk losing that, Floss. I can't risk being tied to a man who has absolutely no love left for me."

Florence sighed resignedly. "Okay. I don't like it, but I accept it. As your best friend, it's my job to help you live your best life. If this is your best life, let's do it!"

"It's the best life I can hope for...for now."

She gave me a smile. "Then let's knock his overpriced socks off."

When I was dressed and primped and primed, Florence walked me to the quad, just to see exactly what had kept Apollo, and she wasn't to be disappointed.

The Saints were gathered in a circle in the centre of the quad around two bare chested fighters. One of whom needed no introduction. He was also the one who was giving the epic beat down. Why the other guy had bothered, I don't know.

There were always four Angels.

Four Angels shall there ever be, to help uphold God's sovereignty. It was more than just the unofficial Saint Benedict's motto.

It had been that way since we'd started at Saint Benedicts. Always four. You wanted a spot? You had to challenge another Angel. And that's exactly what was happening now. Had to be. It wasn't a ridiculously rare occurrence. Someone challenged an Angel probably once every couple of months, though most were pushed into it for the spectacle.

Few dared challenge the Angels' leader. It was virtual suicide. Of course it was. But this idiot had done it. It made this a real challenge. But why on Earth would anyone challenge a man who had been trained from birth to be the leader of the Angels of Saint Benedicts?

Because that was Valen Kincaid. Like Apollo had been trained to be its God, Valen had been trained to take his place at God's side. He was Apollo's avenging Angel, born for sin and so much more.

His body was magnificent. It should have been, the amount of time he was made to spend keeping himself in peak physical condition. It was his job to always be ready no matter what kind of threats were posed against Apollo.

Emblazoned on his back for all to see were the marks of his trade. His oath in ink. Two striking angel wings. A cross with the Callahan coat sitting in the middle of them. It was a barbaric and ridiculous hark back to days of a bygone era when that meant something to the world. But, while most parts of the world that cared were disappearing, enough was left for it to mean more than a bit of ink should. To me, all it served was to highlight every ridge and contour of Valen's highly muscled body.

His right arm was covered in more tattoos. In pride of place on his shoulder was a wolf. Howling. Valk. The wolf. A clever nickname based on the first letters of his name, though I understood the Kincaid's ties to Russia were flimsy these days at best. The rest of his ink, I'd never braved staring in his even semi-naked direction for long enough to discover. And I certainly didn't now.

It was amazing what doors money opened. When you had enough, you could find someone willing to ink a kid no matter what the law said. And the little I knew about the Kincaids, they started getting inked by thirteen. They didn't believe in starting them too early.

As Valen spun, there was the usual flash of silver on his chest. Like all the Saints, he wore a cross around his neck. It wasn't a cult thing. They weren't all identical. Growing up in families who'd grown up in a school run by nuns, it just kinda came with the territory. You didn't have to be a Saint to wear a cross, but you did wear a cross if you were a Saint.

Despite his opponent wielding a knife, surprisingly like he knew how to use it, Valen needed no weapon. Going without made it the closest to a fair fight the poor idiotic challenger could ever hope for. Even still, had I been the betting type – and many of those gathered were betting on the match – my money would have been on God's tame wolf. It was boring in how predictable the outcome would be.

My gaze flickered around the quad. In the distance, I saw two of the nus, heads bowed as though they were discussing the outrage of the spectacle. But they wouldn't come any closer.

Back when Saint Benedicts was going through its first expansion, two hundred and fifty-odd years ago, the alumni all agreed on one thing: if they were going to gift the school an unseemly amount of money, then their offspring were going to get perks they'd only dreamt of. And so, the new boys' dorm was made the purview of the lay staff, to be ignored and unjudged by the nuns and clerical staff. They didn't like it – never had, never would – but they abided by it. Thus, a fight on the quad outside the boys' dorm was, much to their chagrin, not something the nuns could do anything about. It wouldn't stop them gathering and gawking from afar, no doubt tittering to each other about the number of hail Mary's the boys were going to owe.

As my gaze kept moving, it finally fell on Apollo, who was watching me like he was just waiting for me to notice him. It was nice to think he'd been the one waiting for once. He gave me a small nod, said something to Fender at his side, held a hand up to someone else, then made his way through the crowd to me.

"There you are, sweetheart," he said, like he *had* been waiting for me.

"Here I am."

"You look nice." He turned his gaze to Florence. "Florence."

"Apollo," she replied, equally as forcibly polite.

There was absolutely no point in trying to make my future husband and my best friend get along. Quite aside from the fact it was never going to happen, I wasn't sure I wanted my two worlds – my two personalities – to collide.

"You ready?" Apollo asked me.

I nodded. "Sure."

He smiled, then called over his shoulder, "Valk."

My eyes slid to Valen. On his God's command, he stopped toying with the poor idiot who'd challenged him. Fat lot of good that knife was going to do him. Two more hits were all it took to send him to the ground. And he wasn't getting up by himself any time soon.

Without a second thought, Valen shook the sweat from his hair and grabbed the towel Fender was holding out to him. He wiped most of the blood off his hands, swapped the towel for a t-shirt and pulled it on. Then he was behind Apollo and bearing down on me like he hadn't, moments before, been beating a guy to within an inch of his life.

"Ready?" Valen asked, barely even winded.

Apollo nodded, his smile for me warm and mirrored in his eyes. "It's time to show my princess just what she means to me."

Oh, this was going to be good.

Chapter Seven

While Saint Benedicts had been built to be as inaccessible as possible – or as inescapable as possible – the modernisation of the world had made it far easier for people to get to, and students to get away from. Whether they were being allowed to or not.

The school itself was built cascading gently down the side of a hill. It was picturesque and beautiful, with a road that wound down and around to the nearest town, which tumbled further down the hill slightly less elegantly. Bieityn was home to some few thousand people and paid homage to the Callahan Estate. As a family who enjoyed the finer things in life, the Callahans had been good to the people of Bieityn, helping them to create up-market restaurants and shops, all kept open by the thick wallets of the Saint Benedicts' students' parents.

While I hadn't been told – I was never told – what the plans were for that night or where we were going, I had assumed that Apollo would take me to dinner at *Bieito*, the town's swankiest restaurant. A place where the Callahans were treated like the royalty they liked to think they were.

For as long as there had been crime, there were people trying to cash in on it. And the Callahans had been at it longer than most. Archer Callahan may not have had an official Title recognised by any country's government, that he so desperately wished for, but among thieves he was a lord.

As Valen pulled the car to a stop in front of the brightly lit windows of *Bieito*, I knew I was right. One of the maître d's strode towards the car and opened the door.

"Miss Vanguard," he said with a warm smile. "Happy birthday."

I nodded to him and forced a smile of my own. "Thank you."

"Park the car. Do what you like. I'll let you know when we're done," Apollo said to Valen before patting his shoulder, then getting out of the car.

Valen looked back to me. "Enjoy your dinner."

Everything he said to me was disdainful. It came across like a threat. Though what he could possibly be threatening in a simple, 'enjoy your dinner', I wasn't sure. Knowing Valk the way I did, he could make a threat out of nothing more than existing.

"Shall we?" Apollo pulled my focus and I looked out at him standing next to the maître d'.

Apollo looked fine in anything, but it never hurt when he made an effort. And I knew him well enough to know he'd made an effort. Just not the kind that would matter to anyone else but me.

He wore simple chinos and a button down shirt, top button undone. His hair was artfully messy and he wore brushed suede shoes. Nothing about him screamed money, nothing except the fact that he was eighteen and taking his girlfriend to *Bieito* for dinner on a school night.

He held his hand out to me and the warm mischievous look in his eyes promised me the world. And I knew he could give it to me. Had he actually been offering. But Apollo had never once thought of offering me the world, only the parts he was interested in. It was to be expected, but it was also a stark reminder that we had a long way to go before our relationship was anything close to resembling real.

I put such thoughts out of my head and put my hand into his. There were times to worry about my – our – future and times to enjoy the present, and this was most definitely the latter. While our relationship was currently for show, there were more perks than public displays of affection in front of the whole school. More private perks where I didn't hate him quite so much.

Apollo helped me out of the car and shut the door behind me.

"Your usual table's ready," the maître d' told him. Not me. Him.

Apollo nodded, his hand going to the small of my back as we were led inside. "Perfect."

The weather was still warm enough that the jacket I wore was decorum only. So we still had to go through the palaver of taking it off and checking it. But this wasn't the sort of place where you got a stub in exchange.

"Usual to start, Mr Callahan?" Apollo was asked as we went to our table.

"Yes, thanks," Apollo said with a smile. He looked at me. "Unless you want something else?" he asked me.

Surprised by the thoughtfulness, I shook my head. "Usual is fine."

Apollo cocked his head as he looked me over. "You sure?"

I smiled. "I'll have what you're having," I said, giving in.

He grinned warmly. "All right. The lady will have what I'm having," he told the maître d'.

He inclined his head. "Certainly, sir."

At our table, Apollo pulled my chair out for me and kissed my cheek before I sat down, then he went to his own seat. When I looked up at him, his eyes were warm and taking me in carefully.

"What?" I asked with a laugh.

He shrugged. "Nothing. You look really nice."

I shifted in my seat. "I don't look any different than usual."

And I didn't. I wore a simple scoop neck dress, fitted in the bodice, flared in the skirt, with short cap sleeves, in a soft rose pink. I'd added a strand of pearls at my neck, another on my wrist, and one more around my waist. My hair was in my standard go-to 'going out' curls and I had on my white pumps. It was an outfit he'd probably seen too many times for society's approval, but I liked it. I felt good in it. We'd had some of our best dates with me in that dress.

"No," he agreed. "You don't. You always look really nice."

I scoffed. "You might not think that when you see me first thing in the morning." When, not if.

His grin grew more rueful. "I'm sure I will."

Because it was a given it would happen one day. I didn't know when our relationship would progress from for show to something more real. When we left school? When he put an unnecessarily large diamond on my finger? When we'd signed the papers and I was officially Mrs Callahan? But it would happen. We both knew that and pretending otherwise wouldn't do either of us any good.

Apollo reached over the table for my hand and I gave it to him. He ran his fingers over my new ring and an uncertainty crept into his eyes.

"Do you like it?" he asked, his voice low, quiet.

I saw then that Florence had been right. There was a part of him – no matter how small – that was trying to compensate for his extra curricular activities the best way he'd been shown how. Not in the way most people would think, but because he'd chosen them over our friendship. As much as I hated that side of him – hated who he'd become with everyone else – there was still the boy I loved. Very, very deep down.

I nodded and squeezed his hand. "I really do," I told him with the most sincere, reassuring voice I had. "I love it. Thank you."

The relief flooded his eyes visibly. They softened instantly, the corners of his lips tipping up gently like he was about to smile. This was the side of Apollo I rarely saw anymore. This was Apollo without the mask. Not that he ever really wore a mask with me – he never hid his thoughts or feelings from me like he so often did with nearly the rest of the world, he wasn't just Archer 2.0 – but I watched him wear it for everyone else. I watched him put on the show. I had to help him put on the show.

But not here. Not now.

Now, it was just us. Just him and me and us. Free from watchful eyes. Free from people speculating about how solid our relationship – and therefore our fathers' contract – really was. We didn't have to be the perfect God and his perfect princess. We could just be Apollo and Harlow, the way we'd been as kids.

The most obvious sign was when the waiter brought us two beers.

Apollo rarely let himself be seen drinking beer. It was considered lower class. But when it was just us, before dinner, he liked a beer. And tonight, I was having one with him.

"Happy birthday, Harlow," he said as we clinked glasses.

"Thanks, Apollo."

He took a sip and somehow managed to dribble a little down his chin.

"Frist time drinking?" I teased and he grinned widely.

"Shut up," he chuckled as he wiped his face.

"I'll show you how to do it." I mimicked bringing the glass to my lips and taking an exaggerated sip, without spilling it, then put the glass back down.

He shook his head, still smiling. "Oh! Thanks. Now it's all so clear."

I laughed and the smile we shared was full of warmth and shared experience. There was so much between us. So much history here. So much potential. So much love. We just weren't in love with each other. Not like we were supposed to be. Not like everyone thought. Well, was supposed to think. I doubted the Magdalens he fucked thought he was in love with me. If they did, they must have thought he had a mighty funny way of showing it.

"I never pictured you as the having a beer kind of girl," he said to me, his tone musing.

I shrugged, as much shrugging off the reminder that he didn't know me that well anymore. "Call it Florence's bad influence."

The corner of his lips tipped up in a cheeky half-smirk. "All of

Florence's influence is bad."

"She's my best friend, Apollo."

"So?"

"So, you don't get to judge my best friend."

"Why not?" he asked, but his tone was light and teasing and I didn't take him entirely seriously.

"Because *your* best friend is Valen Kincaid."

Even saying his name felt dangerous to me. Even just saying his name, knowing he was in the vague vicinity, had my stomach fluttering and made me want to bite my lip. Like that was going to hide what I was thinking rather than broadcasting it to the world. Thankfully, my beer saved me from announcing to the world just what my smaller head was thinking about Valen.

Apollo chuckled as he sat back in his chair. He was as relaxed as I'd ever seen him. He wasn't keeping one eye on the room around him like he knew we were being watched. He wasn't worried about acting accordingly. He didn't need to find fault with the wait staff just because he needed to remind everyone he was superior. It was just us in our own little world.

"No, I suppose not," he conceded with a nod. "Valk and Florence. That'd be a pairing."

I wanted to say that jealousy didn't threaten to consume me, but I wasn't in the habit of lying to myself too often.

I covered with a sceptical laugh. "That would be like dumping gallons of petrol on an already burning church. Whoosh," I said, mimicking the explosion with my hand.

Apollo laughed. A full head back, belly rumbling laugh. "You're right. Even the cockroaches wouldn't survive that." He sobered somewhat, training his smile on me. "She's not too bad. Considering."

"Considering what?" I asked as I picked up my menu, a smile on my own face.

"Considering she loathes me."

"Oh, what's the matter?" I teased. "You just not used to girls hating you?"

"It's a novel experience, I'll admit."

"Well, I doubt she'll change her mind any time soon," I warned him.

He took my hand again and I looked at him.

"What?" I asked.

"Nothing. I just… I really enjoy these times we have together."

I pressed my lips together. Uncharacteristically on the tip of my tongue was a scathing remark about how we could have more. How we could be real. We could do this and so much more. He just needed to put some effort in. But, at the same time, I didn't want more. Not like that. Not now. Not yet.

The only reason I had to want it was that I knew it had to happen eventually. And so far, I couldn't see a way where we got from here to happily spending our lives together. Not without some effort on both sides, and less fucking around on his. But then, the reality of us changing now was just as scary as knowing we had to eventually.

"Me too," was all I could say.

He gave my hand a squeeze, then picked up his menu, completely oblivious to the push and pull that was constantly in my head and my heart.

"What are you having?" he asked.

I sighed as I looked the menu over. "I don't know. It all comes down to how much space do I leave for dessert?"

"Lots."

I lowered my menu slightly to peek at him over it. "Lots?"

He nodded, clearly very pleased with himself. "I paid an absolute fortune to make them serve rainbow ice cream tonight."

The idea that the most sought after restaurant in thousands of miles was serving rainbow ice cream made a very undignified snort threaten.

"You didn't?"

He nodded, with infectious glee lighting those sapphire eyes. "Oh, I did."

I leant towards him like we were sharing a secret. "Your dad would kill you!" I laughed.

The humour in both of us died a little when we realised that my words were just a little more literal than I'd intended.

"But Mum would be proud," he said and there was that glimpse of the sweet boy I knew.

Maybe he wasn't quite so deep down as I thought he was. Maybe I wasn't failing Frenella quite as badly as it sometimes felt.

Being a Callahan, Apollo didn't so much as have permission for us to stay out all night as no one dared tell him we couldn't. Even with all his entitlement, he wasn't stupid enough to keep us out past eleven. It didn't mean we weren't stupid enough to drink more than was perhaps sensible. The good thing about our country was the legal age for drinking was sixteen so, legally, no one batted an eye.

No one except Valen, who was in charge of helping my giggly arse back into the car at the end of an incredibly pleasant evening. I'd had such a good time with Apollo, that my half-drunk brain wasn't even that annoyed by Valen's existence.

"Thank you," I chirped to him, taking his hand as I climbed into the car.

I felt his hand tighten on mine and looked back at him. Something flashed over his face too quickly for me to catch, but I didn't miss the feeling of my hand in his and what it did to my insides.

It wasn't until my butt was safely on the seat and my legs fully in the car that Valen and I let go. Our eyes not leaving each other's. I didn't know what was going through his stormy grey head, but I just hoped that I wasn't completely giving away what he did to me. If he knew what went through my head when I thought about him, then I was completely screwed. And not in the pleasant, satisfying kind of way.

"Miss Vanguard," he said carefully before closing the door.

As we drove back to school, Apollo was glued to his phone. He'd had much more than me, but then his tolerance was also much better than mine. Still, I noticed the signs of the slightly drunk. He giggled once or twice, and he bit his lip like he had to concentrate on typing the right letters.

I'd have been a naive idiot to not know what he was doing. And while that was the persona I chose to show the world, I liked to think I was anything but.

So, I wasn't surprised when we pulled into the garage and Apollo slapped Valen companionably on the shoulder with a,

"Take her back for me, yeah?"

There wasn't even a look spared for me as he almost stumbled out of the car and disappeared towards the boys' dormitory. All I got was a, "Night, Harlow!" like he'd left me in front of the couch watching a movie when he couldn't stay awake any longer.

I felt heat prick my eyes and a lump threatened in my throat. I wasn't surprised that Apollo was off to lose himself in some Magdalen, but I was somehow also upset that he'd so carelessly do so after we'd had such a good night. It wasn't like I wanted him to drag *me* up to his room for a night of unrestrained pleasure, but it still hurt that he chose to get his dick wet over me again.

I took a deep breath and jumped when the door next to me opened.

"Let's go, then, princess," Valen said, his voice low.

I plastered on my 'I'm fine' face and got out, careful not to touch him this time.

"So sorry to keep you waiting," I said sarcastically. I threw him an icy stare for good measure, but it didn't fully hide the hurt in my voice.

He cocked his head, his eyebrow rising quizzically. As we walked, I felt his glare raise the hairs on the back of my neck, but it wasn't until we reached the shadowed courtyard next to the girls' dorm side door that he spoke.

"Apollo seems to be the only one *waiting* on you."

I slowed to a stop and he paused with me.

The tiredness in my voice came out more than I intended. "Firstly, how dare you assume anything about my relationship, Valen. Secondly–"

"Secondly, what?" he asked, as though daring me to defy him one more time.

I frowned at him and started for the door. "You assume I'm the one holding out?"

He scoffed. "Apollo's certainly not saving it."

I rounded on him, shoved him in the chest, and glared up at him. "So that means I must be?"

He looked down on me. In the relative darkness under the hanging wisteria vines, his features were shadowed, but I could feel our bodies brushing against each other. Warmth pooled between my legs and I ached for him. Florence had better be asleep when I got to our room because I was in desperate need of a date with my vibrator in our bathroom.

"If you know what's good for you, you will be," Valen snarled.

Oh! It annoyed me at the best of times that I had people dictating my life. Who I could talk to. Who I could see. Who I could *think* about fucking. None of it was my choice. I had to be seen as a good little princess and wait around for Apollo even if everyone knew he wasn't waiting for me. And Valen had made it his personal mission to keep me 'pure'.

I was done.

I was so ready to pick the first guy I saw and take Florence up on her offer of arranging covert shenanigans behind the big bad wolf's back.

I was also a bit tipsy and had the mad urge to run my hands over Valen's hard chest. Valen, who was a guy I could currently see...

FUCK!

My hand was actually on his chest.

I looked back up and saw something flash over his face.

In a moment of bravery, I left it there purposefully. "You don't tell me what to do," I warned him, my voice little more that a breathless whisper.

He took a step, forcing me to back into a section of wall and gently laid his hand over my throat. "If it serves Apollo, I will."

"Apollo doesn't tell me what to do. Who to want. *What* to want," I said, lifting my chin in defiance. There was a little too much meaning in my voice, but I didn't care anymore.

The sizzle of something very definite was swirling around us. I didn't just think but knew that he was teetering on the edge of kissing me. Here he was, telling me I'd wait for Apollo – the 'or else' being heavily implied – and we were so close to the exact opposite. I felt emboldened. I felt a thrill run through me. I didn't care if it was just the booze talking, I had never been more certain about the fact that someone wanted to kiss me. My heart thudded in nervous anticipation.

A moment passed.

Two.

Like Valen was trying to stop himself from saying something – doing something – he knew he shouldn't.

He held me against the wall, his hand dominating but exhilarating on my throat.

"You've wanted my cock in you since the day you laid eyes on me," he finally snarled like he just couldn't help himself.

So maybe he did know exactly what I thought about him all this time. Well, I wasn't going to be intimidated by the likes of

Valen Kincaid, no matter what he did to my insides.

"You've wanted your cock in me since the day you laid eyes on me," I countered.

He growled, low and primal. His hand tightened ever so slightly around me, like it was a warning. I just didn't think I was the only one he was warning. "Apollo know about that mouth on you?"

I licked my lip to draw his attention to said mouth. It worked like a charm. "He wants a good little princess? He'll get a good little princess," I told him, surprising myself with the venom in my tone.

Valen's nose wrinkled. His lips rose in a snarl he seemed trying to suppress. His eyes narrowed. "You watch yourself, Miss Vanguard."

He pushed off my throat none too gently and began stalking away.

But I felt brazen. I felt charged. Too charged. Energy zipped around me. My nerves were going haywire. My heart pounded in my chest. But I wanted to push him that little bit further. I wanted to watch him bite back.

"I'll do what – or who – I please, Valk," I said, my voice even, controlled, commanding.

He paused and his head twitched like he was fighting the instinct to turn around.

"You will do nothing of the sort," he said slowly and firmly.

I walked towards him as though I had not a care in the world. "I don't see how you'd stop me."

Again with that twitch. He wanted to turn. I wanted him to

turn.

I stood behind him and trailed a carefree finger down the back of his arm. "How would you stop me, Valk?" I pressed. "I'm dying to know."

He spun quickly. His finger lighted under my chin and tilted my head to make me look at him. He didn't touch me anywhere else, but my body thrummed, on high alert.

"He'd kill any man who touches you," he said, his voice ragged.

I cocked my head to the side. A challenge. "He doesn't get his hands dirty."

"I'd kill any man who touches you," he growled. He snarled roughly, then pushed through me and stalked from the courtyard.

The way he moved, you'd be forgiven for thinking he had to get out of there before he did something he couldn't take back. Before he did something he'd regret.

I breathed heavily.

Desire curled in the pit of my stomach. My clit throbbed. My nipples ached.

Because I'd seen the look in his eyes. It was personal. Not just obeying the command of his god.

I'd been right that day on the steps.

It wasn't just the booze talking.

Valen hated me.

Hated me as much as I hated him.

But he also wanted me.

Wanted me as much as I wanted him.

Chapter Eight

"Will you stop that?" Florence snapped, throwing a balled-up piece of paper from her desk to mine.

I looked at my hand and realised that I'd been incessantly tapping my pen against my book while I did my homework that Friday afternoon. I wasn't really even doing my homework. Not unless doing homework meant reading that one sentence for the thirteenth time and still not knowing what it said. I took a deep breath and tried to stop my heart beating as fast as I'd been tapping my pen.

"Sorry," I told her.

My mood made me more short with her than I should have been.

"Don't be sorry," she said kindly. "But if you want to talk about it, I'm here."

"You're a better friend than I deserve, Floss."

"Why?" she laughed. "Because you're a Saint and they're all mean and bossy and stuck up?"

I smiled despite myself. "Something like that."

The truth was, I had it in me. I had it in me to be mean and bossy and stuck up. Inside, I was snobby and judgemental. I enjoyed the finer things in life. I liked that I was born into privilege and all that gave me. I knew I was lucky, but at the same time I'd been brought up to believe it was my right.

I wasn't perfect. Not really. But Florence didn't expect me to be. She loved me for me, and that was something I knew I had to be worthy of.

As I looked at her, I opened my mouth, took a breath, and closed it again.

She smiled. "Come on, you've been in a mood since your birthday. And I know it's not just that precious metal weighing down your hand."

I dropped my pen entirely and swivelled my chair to face her.

"I'm going to marry Apollo, right?" I asked and she nodded.

"Right..." she said slowly, obviously waiting to see where I went with this.

"I hate who he's become, but I have to marry him."

"Unless we find you a way out."

I nodded and didn't correct her. "Unless we find me a way out."

"That's my understanding, yes. Why? Has something happened?"

I frowned as I tried to work out the answer to that. "I don't know..." I said slowly while I still got my head around it. "Maybe..."

"Eek!" Florence spun so quickly that she went too far and did a full rotation and a half before stopping to face me. "Did he finally kiss you?"

I shook my head. "Not with Apollo. If something happened, it wasn't with Apollo."

"Yes!" She threw her hands in the air and spun around quickly.

"You don't even know what happened," I laughed.

She pointed at me as the chair came back around again. "No, but if it didn't happen with Apollo, then it happened with–"

"Don't say it!" I interrupted, my hand reaching for her like I'd actually do something to shut her up. "Don't say it."

It wasn't like anyone was going to hear us, but I wasn't going to risk it.

"But I'm right? With...?" She waggled her eyebrows and kicked her head in the vaguest direction of the boys' dorm.

"*If* anything did happen, and I'm still not sure it did, then yes."

"Tell me what happened. If anyone knows whether something is *something*, it's me."

I had to give her that one. I'd never be so shaming as to call my best friend a slut, but she'd affectionately awarded herself the title on a few drunken occasions.

"Okay, so he was walking me back after my date with Apollo..."

Florence rolled her eyes. "Because *he* had to run off and fuck one of his Magdalens." I then watched her eyes narrow in thought.

"What?"

She shook her head. "No, nothing. Just... Sometimes, I think he uses those Magdalens because he thinks he's not supposed to touch you, but he's so into you that he needs release the only way a spoilt, rich wanker thinks he can get it."

"We're not really dating, remember?" I reminded her.

She shrugged. "Yeah, but there's got to be more to it."

It was certainly a theory, but not one I could see having a grain of truth.

"And those times you're more heavily grounded in reality?" I laughed, deciding to just go with it.

"Those times, I just see him for the pompous dick he is." She shook her head again, like she was trying to dislodge a stupid thought. "Anyway, you were telling me about this something..."

"The only way I can describe it is a sizzle..." I said slowly.

"Oh, the best kind of something."

"Is it?"

She nodded. "It is. How did it happen?"

I waved my hand vaguely. "We were talking about how he couldn't tell me who or what to want, and things took a... turn."

Florence scooted her chair towards me eagerly. "Ye-es...?"

"Well, next thing I know, he's got my back against a wall and he's telling me I've wanted his cock in me since the day I met him."

She blinked as she took that in, then nodded appreciatively. "The man has a way with words."

"Florence!"

"To be fair, though, true."

I frowned at her. "So not the point."

"I notice you're not disagreeing."

"Of course not. It is true."

She snorted. "Okay, then what happened?"

"I told him he's wanted his cock in me since they day we met."

Florence's eyes bugged behind her glasses, but she looked

proud as punch. "Not like you at all."

"No. And he noticed."

"What happened next?"

I shrugged and sunk into my chair, and talked her through the rest of it. "Before he left, he said he'd kill any man that touches me...like it was personal," I finished.

Florence started chuckling under her breath

"What?" I asked.

She shook her head. "Well, now we have a problem."

"Do we?"

She nodded. "Yeah, because it seems the big, bad wolf wants you as much as you want him."

Which is what I'd suspected, but it was nice to know it wasn't all in my head. Florence had a sense about her. Like she *knew* these things. Like some modern-day Cupid incarnate, she just knew who liked who, and whether it was just sex...or something more.

"But I'm promised to his God. My prince."

"And what does your clit say about that?"

"Some of us don't have the luxury of listening to our clits, Florence."

She snorted again. "Okay. But just say you did."

I knew what it would say: *Forget the prince, I want the big, bad wolf.* But I couldn't have the big, bad wolf. Of all the people I could get away with messing around with, Valen was probably the only one I couldn't. And even if I could, Valen Kincaid had the self-control of a monk. He might have wanted me, but he wouldn't be stupid enough – or be willing to betray his friend and

God enough – to actually touch me.

"I have no power over it, so it doesn't matter what my clit would say."

She sighed. "All right. Enough study. We need tea and cake."

I laughed. "I could be persuaded."

"Come on, then."

We were still in our uniforms, but we weren't nearly as pristine as we had to be during class times. It was one thing that set me apart from the 'normal' Saints. They were always dressed up whenever possible. Appearances being important and all. I was far too lazy to change multiple times a day, something for which I blamed my much more level-headed Florence.

So naturally, on our way to the campus cafe, who did we see coming our way but Apollo and Valen?

They, of course, had changed.

Apollo was in his usual pale chinos and button up combination. If I recognised that short-sleeve shirt right from that distance, it was his blue Ralph Lauren shirt. His hair swept back from his face, which was its usual combination of haughty and beautiful. He walked across the school – and through life – like nothing ever fazed him, nothing bothered him, and everything was owed to him.

Valen, meanwhile, was the typical stark dark contrast to Apollo's pleasant pastels.

He wore black trousers, and a dark denim shirt over a white t-shirt. The shirt sleeves were rolled up to his mid forearms, showing off the bottom of the tattoos that he never let show when he was in uniform. He'd also donned his typical accessories.

Leather cuff on one wrist. Watch with thick leather band on the other. Big black ring on the middle finger of his right hand. Silver ring on the middle finger of his left hand. And Saint Benedicts Saints' signet ring on the little finger of his left hand.

We all had a signet ring. It was one of very few pieces of jewellery we were allowed to wear during class time. The girls rarely wore theirs. The signet ring was more a bro thing, with them the ones who felt the need to proclaim to the world that the upper echelons of the elite had accepted them as one of their own. They were, after all, the ones with all the power.

Apollo was clearly in a mode. His swagger was a bright red warning light that he was puffed up on some high. No doubt he'd just had Valen stuffing a Saintling's head in a toilet or something. I wasn't privy (pardon the pun) to the entire catalogue of Saint hazing rituals. As the intended of the future-God, I'd been spared from anything but acceptance, though it often felt like I'd neither earned my place nor was I truly one of them; I was both inner sanctum and outsider. Without feeling like I properly belonged to one side or the other, I often felt lost as to my true place.

"He's looking at you," Florence hissed, elbowing me.

"Uh, no, he's not."

Because I was looking right at Apollo and he was focussed on a Magdalen across the grass. With an elbow into Valen's side, I could guess how their conversation was going. There was very little difference in height between the two of them, so they didn't have to bend far to confer.

"Not your pretend boyfriend, the other one."

My eyes slid back to Valen, with a vague sense of surprise that they'd ever managed to slide off him in the first place. And I found he was staring right at me, all while his mental focus was trained on Apollo.

"Shall we say about nine?" Apollo suggested as they got closer to us.

Valen nodded. "Fine." He stopped in front of me, and I felt my whole body warm under his stormy grey gaze.

Apollo realised Valen had stopped and turned to look at whatever had halted their progress.

"Harlow, hi," he said with a warm smile. His eyes slid to Florence. "Florence."

"Apollo."

My best friend and boyfriend exchanged a terse nod, then Apollo was smiling at me again.

"Where are you girls off to?" he asked.

I tried keeping my eyes on Apollo, but they kept shifting back to Valen's face.

His eyes were hard, and his jaw was harder, but I saw the heat in the depths of those soulful eyes. I saw it for what it really was. And it was only then that I realised that it had been there for a while, expertly hidden behind his hatred of me. Desire. Wanton lust.

Well, it was nice to know my feelings for him were mutual.

Not.

I could feel a new sense of anticipation shimmer around us. It set my body on high alert. Like I was waiting for him to touch me. I was ready for him to touch me. I could almost feel him. Where his fingers would stroke. What he'd explore. Florence and I had discussed the theory of a hate fuck numerous time – though never in direct relation to Valen – and I knew just by looking at him that he'd meet and surpass every expectation.

"We're getting cake," Florence answered, when it seemed I was incapable.

I nodded blankly, seemingly stuck in a silent battle of wills with Valen. I saw the challenge on his face; he dared me to do something about this new sizzle that sparked between us. Dared me to say something, do something, that made it real. Brought it out of silent assumption and forced us both to admit the last thing we ever wanted to.

Florence elbowed me. I blinked and forced myself to look at Apollo.

"Cake, yes."

If Apollo had noticed that I'd been unable to keep my eyes of his best friend, then he didn't show it. "Sounds good. We'd join you, but I have…somewhere to be, unfortunately."

I didn't know if it was just me, but Apollo seemed to be getting lazy with hiding his trysts. It was no small wonder the whole school knew about them. The nuns were probably even talking about them. That's how obvious he was getting. When I looked at Valen, he seemed to be thinking the same thing.

And there was something new in his eyes. Not new, just resurfaced. Contempt. A contempt that threatened to wrinkle his nose and raise a snarl at his lips. A contempt that set his square jaw hard.

He knew that I knew what Apollo had to go and do instead of hanging out with me and he… I didn't know what it was. It was like he… Surely he didn't care? But he thought I should say something? Do something? What exactly was I supposed to do? A powerless fake girlfriend tell a God who he could and couldn't stick it in? I didn't think so.

"That's fine," I said, turning a smile to Apollo.

I had to ignore it. I had to ignore what he got up to. I'd go mad if I let myself care about every single time he was with someone else. It was the strangest sensation. I didn't care so much for Present Harlow, but I cared for Future Harlow. For the one who had to be in a real relationship with him one day and who didn't know if he'd still be fucking around on the side.

"You guys have a good afternoon," I finished.

"You too, sweetheart," Apollo said affectionately, leaning over to give me a kiss on the cheek as his hand went to my waist.

I flicked a quick look to Valen and saw the disdain flare to life. The wrinkle. The snarl. The jaw twitch.

I didn't know how I knew, but I knew he wasn't jealous. He wasn't annoyed because Apollo got to kiss me and touch me and be close to me and he couldn't. He was annoyed *with* me. I just couldn't really see what, particularly now, he could be annoyed with.

Apollo pulled away from me with a gentle squeeze of my arm and whacked Valen's stomach.

"All right, let's," he said to Valen as he started moving away.

Valen's eyes stayed on me, narrowed in what felt like both a warning and a wanting.

A potent mix that I saw every time we crossed paths for the next week.

And, given that I was often by Apollo's side and Valen was always by Apollo's side, to say nothing of the fact that we both had classes in the same school and often together, we crossed paths a lot. A. Lot.

Every encounter left me feeling hot and bothered. The intensity turning up with each one. I already hated Valen, but I'd never hated him because I wanted him until that week. I'd never hated anyone because I wanted them until that week. Quite possibly because the only person I'd ever wanted that much was my fake boyfriend and future husband's closest friend and protector.

By the next weekend, I was itching to let off some steam. I'd avoided talking to Valen as much as possible, which wasn't difficult because we always tried to say no more than necessary to each other.

On Saturday night, there was a party in the woods, like there was wont to be. The nuns and teachers knew all about them and pretended wholeheartedly that they didn't. Most times, they were little more than alcohol-fuelled orgies. Couples separating over the course of the night, only to come back to the bonfire to recharge before another round, with the same person or not. The Saints did what the Saints did, and peddled the more recreational of their daddies' wares. Uppers. Downers. Undoubtedly roofies. I didn't know enough about drugs to begin to guess what they all were but, if it altered your mental state, it could probably be found passing hands at those parties in the woods.

Florence and I went to every one. Needless to say, she was the only one who'd ever done any separating from the bonfire. I was always watched carefully. Not that it was necessary, because very few people would have been stupid enough to approach me for more than a chat with the Saints and Angels watching over their God's intended, like he was being faithful.

Marco, Fender and Gage had been taking it in turns to have one eye on me all night. Valen had been doing a decent job at pretending he didn't have both eyes on me, but I'd glared right back at him, daring him to do something about whatever it was that was going on between us. Apollo had been out of sight on and off and I'd been drowning my boredom and annoyance in as many bottles as possible.

"Princess," Valen said, appearing at my side and I didn't even bother to ignore the thrill that ran through me.

If it wasn't obvious by his tone that he'd had a fair amount to drink, I'd have guessed it by the bottle in his hand. Valen's duties to Apollo meant he had two speeds; sober as a (decent) judge, or 'drink enough to maybe forget the horrors of my life this time'. The only in between occurred while he was in the process of drinking more than his weight in alcohol. And, the proficiency he had in downing booze, that process was fairly short-lived.

"Let me guess. While God's fucking his way through as many Magdalens as possible, you have the unfortunate task of making sure I don't have any fun?" I asked him.

"I wouldn't call it unfortunate," he said lazily.

"No. Any chance to obey your God," I said sarcastically.

"There are worse powers to obey," he answered smoothly.

Despite the fact that I could tell from his words exactly how bad those worse powers were and enough of the nature of what they expected from him, I wasn't in the mood for empathising. Besides, Valen didn't want empathy. For him, it was just fact. Just life.

"What a hardship for you," I muttered.

"Aw, you only say that because it's not your job to keep an eye on that arse in those jeans." His voice was condescending, but I saw through it now.

"Ah," I said, like I'd discovered his big secret. "That's not what's hard. Is it, Valen?"

"You want to watch yourself, Miss Vanguard," he growled.

"Tell me, Valk, if I was to go and throw myself at..." I searched the area for a decent candidate. "Arnie Brickworth over there... Would you be *obliged* to kill him?"

He took a step towards me, his chest brushing my arm. "I wouldn't call it obligation."

I looked at him sideways. "What would you call it?"

"I don't answer to you, princess." His voice was low, a warning.

"You will," I promised him. "So, you might as well start practising."

His hand went to my waist, and he pushed ever so gently as he stepped towards me again. I was forced to take a step back and his front came up hard against mine. His palm seared against my skin, despite the layers of clothes between us.

I had never cared less about a potential audience. Even with Apollo among them. I wanted Valen to press me up against the nearest tree and show me exactly how powerful the right hand of God was.

"I will not tell you a third time, Miss Vanguard," he said through gritted teeth.

"I will not watch myself, Valen," I practically purred. "But it seems...you will."

I laid a hand on his shoulder and pushed. He let me slip out and away from him, but I could feel his eyes on me as I walked away.

I went straight for Arnie. The closest guy who, when drunk, would be too excitable to let a silly little thing like the Saint Benedict's hierarchy get in the way of me directly flirting with him.

"Hey, Arnie," I said as I got to him, pressing my body to his. I kept one eye on Valen across the fire and saw the fury on his face. I smiled.

"Harlow," Arnie said with a wide smile as his hand went to my hip. "Uh, hey."

"Listen... What do you say to you...me...somewhere quieter?" I asked him, reaching my lips up most indecently to his ear.

The boys with him were in various states of panicked and encouraging. This was, after all, Harlow Vanguard. Most wanted. Least touchable. But then, people always wanted whatever they couldn't have. It had nothing to do with me at all.

Arnie's eyes slid from my face. Gone was the smile like he'd won a lottery. In its place was fear.

He took a very deliberate step away from me, but it still wasn't enough. I turned in time to see Valen throw his bottle down to the ground, where it shattered, and start to roll up his sleeves. For a moment, I was mesmerised by the ink winding its way up his right arm and disappearing under his sleeve. Then that arm swung at Arnie, and I stopped daydreaming.

His fist collided with Arnie's temple and Arnie went down like a sack of bricks.

I didn't have time to check whether Arnie was okay because Valen grabbed my arm and pulled me out of the clearing. Once we were far enough away that no one was going to find us by accident, he pushed me roughly and my back hit a tree trunk. He crowded my space.

I was very aware of the strength and power Valen commanded. He seemed to hum with barely restrained anger and violence. The air around us shivered with it, and it turned me on.

There was a part of me who didn't like that. Didn't like that I was attracted to the darker sides of him. The part that sometimes believed I really was sweet and naïve and innocent. And in some ways, I was. I might have thought the thoughts, but I'd never acted on a single one of them. I'd never been in any situation where I'd come close to doing them. I'd been kissed. Once. But then Valen had found out and there was zero chance of it ever happening again.

Then there was that other part of me. The more dominant part. The one that didn't care anymore. The one that had been caged too long. Needed freedom. Needed release. Needed something to change. Anything.

I was done being a captive in my own life. Done waiting patiently for a future I didn't want.

"How much does it kill you?" I asked him.

His hand smacked the tree trunk above my head. "Do not test

me, princess."

I planned to. "Wanting quite possibly the only person in the entire world you can never have."

He leant his lips to my ear. "You think very highly of yourself for a woman who lets her man fuck around."

I reached up ever so slightly to his ear. "On the contrary. I think very little of myself. Least of all that what I want matters to anyone else but me."

Valen pressed against me, and I felt his whole body was tense. I couldn't tell if he was holding himself back or holding himself in place. Perhaps they were one and the same.

"You are many things, princess, but self-deprecating and defeatist you are not."

"How would you know what I am?"

"It's my job to watch you."

"You mean, it's your job to make sure I stay pure and innocent while Apollo gets to wet his dick in any idiot who'll spread her legs for him?" The venom in my tone surprised me.

"I don't see you doing anything to stop him," he growled, like he took it personally.

I shoved against him, and he swayed right back to press me into the tree again.

"Apollo wouldn't care if I was spread, willing and naked, over his bed in offering," I told him. I sounded bitter. I was more bitter about the fact that I wouldn't have minded being spread naked and willing in Valen's bed at that point.

Valen's hand touched on my hip, softly at first then harder. Just as slowly, he ran it up my side and splayed his hand just under my breast.

"And still you want him," he said, but it was accusing.

"I *am* all but engaged to him," I reminded him. I'd meant to sound sarcastic, but all that came out was my anger for Valen.

His body pressed into mine deeper. I felt my breath come faster. My heart hitched in my chest. My clit tingled.

It was dark. We were both drunk. No one knew where we were. And we felt on the cusp of tumbling into something dangerously amazing.

His nose dipped to my jaw, and he released the faintest groan, like desperation mixed with resignation. His breath on my skin sent goosebumps flaring. My nipples tightened.

My hand went to his chest. I didn't push him away. My hand fisted his shirt like I was holding him in place. My body pressed back into his as well as it was able.

I was on the precipice of nervous anticipation, but my heart was steady. Thudding evenly in my chest like this was right. This was natural. Normal.

Valen ran his nose over my skin and his lips skimmed my throat with the briefest of kisses. My head tipped sideways to give him better access and his hand on me tightened. His other hand went to my other hip and his body shifted as he almost thrust against me. He was hard. Very hard.

My hand closed tighter over his shirt, and I leant my head against his.

We were breathing the same air. We existed in the same space.

And I didn't want to be anywhere else.

Suddenly, a howl rent the night.

It was a very poor, drunk human imitation, but the bursting of the bubble had shivers running up my spine and I jumped. Valen's hands tightened on me again, but it was almost supportive and steadying this time.

The howl stopped, followed by Marco's voice, "Valk, Valk, Vaaalk!"

Valen's head rubbed softly against mine as he muttered, "Fucking fucker…"

With what seemed like an effort, he pushed away from me and turned to face Marco, who was sauntering into view like he was dancing his way through the woods with nary a care in the world. He looked like some sort of fae gone wrong. No, not wrong, just less the Disney version and very much the darker, drunken, traditional fae image. He had a bottle in one hand and a knife in the other. He vibed danger and, like all the Angels, treacherous temptation. It was almost lucky that Valen was there so Marco paled in comparison, even to my drunken and highly sexually excited brain.

"Well, what do we have here?" Marco asked happily, waving his bottle around.

"What are you doing?" Valen asked, his voice low and gravelly.

"Me?" Marco asked innocently as he slid the knife back into its sheath. "Nothing. I'm just off on a stroll through the woods on this pleasant evening. Making sure no one's getting into trouble. But I see the princess is under control."

They squared off against each other and I watched the silent exchange pass between them. I didn't know what it contained, and

I didn't need to know.

"She needed a reminder of her place," Valen said carefully.

Marco nodded. "I saw." He looked past Valen and waggled his finger at me. "Naughty. And we can't have that. But, if the punishment is complete, I am going to need the wolf for something less…savoury."

Valen's whole stance changed. "What?"

"God fancies himself the vengeful sort tonight."

Valen looked back to me. "Go back to the fire."

I frowned. "I think I'm done for the night."

"Get back to the fire."

Valen's voice brooked no argument. It was bossy and forceful, but different than usual. It sounded important. Not just a useless order that I was just expected to blindly obey so he could flex his superiority.

So, I nodded. "Okay."

"Find Florence and get back to your room," Valen added.

"What's—?"

"Just do it, Harlow!" he snapped.

I blinked at the force of his voice, but I nodded again. "Okay. Okay."

Valen started pulling his gun from its holster, seemed to rethink and held it out to Marco. Marco took it and, like they could read each other's mind, handed over his knife.

"See she gets back. Stay with them if you need to."

Marco nodded, tucked the gun in his waistband at his back, and saluted his lieutenant.

Valen stalked off through the night, leaving me cold and

shivering without his warmth.

"Come on, then," Marco said cheerfully.

"What's happened, Marco?" I asked him, starting to follow him back to the fire.

"Nothing you need worry your pretty little head about, missus. Valk will sort it like the good little tame wolf he is."

I felt like there was a message there, but I'd had too much to drink and was still replaying those last few moments with Valen in my head to really pay attention to him.

Marco helped me find Florence and saw us back to our room, where of course I told her everything that happened.

Whatever had happened after Valen walked away would forever remain conjecture. The only hint that something had gone down was the cut and bruise that Valen sported on his cheek the next day and the way his glare seemed stormier than usual. Apollo looked a bit worse for wear, like he did after a night of heavy drinking, but was otherwise as pristine as ever.

Chapter Nine

If I'd thought there was a sizzle of unspoken energy between Valen and me the week before, it was only amplified after Saturday night. But after whatever else had happened on Saturday night, it wasn't just amplified but even more hate-fuelled than it had ever been.

As I walked through the school corridors, he always seemed to be there. Finding any excuse to push past me like I was always in his way. His body clipping my shoulder every time. No explanation. No harsh words. Not even a backwards glance. And I'd know, because I gave him a backwards glance every time. And he never did.

Whether I was in Apollo's lap and he was sitting across the room from us, his eyes followed me. He tried not to. I could see it in the frustration on his face when I looked at him and saw him watching me. The times he growled as he stood up and swept out of the room, kicking or hitting or throwing something as he went.

I could see Apollo watch him carefully as he went, a question on the tip of his tongue but never asked.

They might have lived life for the decadence and the violence, but there was no denying they cared for each other. They were honestly like brothers, in all but blood. There was a bond between them formed by the knowledge that they had to trust each other, that they were born for each other, that if they had no one else in the world they had each other.

What did it say about me that I was promised to one and pined for the other?

The rest of the week was much the same. The major difference was that the wound on Valen's cheek went from red to purple to green to yellow. It was the easiest way to keep track of the passing of the days as I tried not to think about him any other way. Reminding myself he was little more than a house-trained animal, living for nothing but the word of his God, was supposed to help me not fantasise about him pressing me into that tree and not being interrupted by Marco. It seemed to do the opposite. The harder I remembered what I hated about Valen, the more I fantasised. The more I saw the want in his eyes when he looked at me.

Confiding in Florence was one thing, but nothing she said could calm the storm Valen had raised in me. By Thursday, I couldn't go to bed without Valen invading my waking dreams. And the more I fought it, the more he stayed.

So, long after the rest of the school had gone to bed, I could be found in the rec room, my nose in a book as though I was actually reading it. Naturally, I needed to read every word three times and took in maybe one in ten. But it was better than the alternative.

The alternative which had me hearing noises in the middle of the night.

I looked up from the book and saw a shadow by the flickering fireplace. It was barely Autumn, but we were in the mountains and the place was big and draughty.

My heart thudded in my chest as, even though he was only lit by the dance of the dying flames, I recognised him.

"What are you doing here?" I asked softly.

He shrugged and took a step forward. "It's a free country."

One sentence and I was already annoyed by him. Annoyed and turned on.

"Only until you get caught."

"A Kincaid is never caught."

"No?" I asked, like I had any idea. "Not with Callahan money behind you, I suppose."

He growled. "And what does that mean?"

"Just that I imagine you can get away with anything when the people paying your bail have deep enough pockets."

"Kincaids don't need handouts."

"No, I'm sure you earn every penny," I scoffed sarcastically.

"You shouldn't speak of things you don't understand, princess," he warned.

"No? Well maybe someone should fill me in then," I snapped, standing up. "This princess doesn't need protecting."

He strode towards me, fuelled no doubt by anger, to stop a hair's breadth from me.

"Perhaps it is less about protecting, and more about appearances?" he suggested.

I scoffed again. "Sure. It's fine that I know the Callahans and Kincaids get up to shady shit, but if I know exactly what it is, I'll walk. Like I have a choice."

He pressed me into the wall behind me. His head bowed towards mine. He crowded me without touching me, but I so wanted him to touch me. My skin felt alive, like every nerve was ready, waiting and willing to be the first to register his touch.

"You might forgive a lot, princess, but there are some things you might not."

"I think you'll find I forgive much less than you think, Valk."

"You've got a funny way of showing it."

"You seem to be forgetting how little power I have in my life."

"So, you sit idly by and let Apollo do what he wants? You don't even try? I would have thought you were better than that. I expected you to be better than that," he spat. Once again, like it was personal.

"Now who's talking about things they don't understand?"

"I understand, princess. I understand about having your back to a wall–"

"Ironic given the current circumstance, don't you think?"

He leant his body into mine, his face a scowl.

"You seem to like having my back against walls, Valk. What's a girl supposed to think about that?"

"That she should remember her place and stop aggravating me."

"Exactly what aggravates you, Valen?" I asked sweetly. "Could it be how badly you want to bury yourself in me."

"Exactly what do you think this is going to achieve, princess?" he asked through gritted teeth. "You're playing with fire."

"Good," I told him, reaching my face to his. "Maybe I want

fire. Maybe I want danger. Maybe I want something more than my life now."

He looked at me like he'd never seen me before. But I didn't think that was a good thing.

"You're better than this, Harlow. You have to be better than this," he whispered like it was a prayer.

"Why?" I asked. "Because then you wouldn't want me anymore?"

"Who says I want you?" he snarled.

I didn't feel like I needed to explain it in words, but words had the power to push him over the edge. And, right then, that was the only power I had.

"That rod in your pants tells me everything I need to know." My teeth caught my bottom lip and we stared into each other eyes.

He growled again, low, then spun me quickly and pushed my front into the wall. I could feel him hard behind me as he pressed into my arse. He loomed over my left shoulder, the full force of his body leaning into mine. He grabbed a handful of my hair in his hand and turned my face towards him.

"Is this what you think you want, princess?" he spat. "You want to be roughed up? You want to play dirty? You think if you do, Apollo will notice you? You think you'll stop being the obligation, the sad naïve simp always following him around. So desperate for him that you'll sit by as he fucks girl after girl…after girl."

I struggled against him, enjoying the fight.

"You think you know me?" I snarled, though not nearly as impressively as him.

He held me firm, his cock in my back getting firmer and firmer with each movement of my hips.

"I know you," he said. The disdain in his voice told me exactly what he thought of me.

I rubbed my arse over his cock as best I could with him pinning me, and he growled, pressing up against me harder.

"You scared you'll like it?" I asked him.

His growl this time was…different. Less angry, more…instinct.

He still had one hand in my hair, but the other now trailed down between me and the wall. He didn't stop until he'd found the heat between my legs. I can't say he forced my legs apart because they softened to him all on their own.

His fingers skimmed me lightly and I shivered against him. For good measure, I bucked for some wriggle room.

"You scared you'll like it?" he purred in my ear.

Goosebumps skittered across every single part of my body. I felt my breath coming more heavily and I fought to keep it steady. God, I hated him, but I wanted him more.

"Scared's not the word I'd use," I replied disdainfully.

In one motion, he'd turned me again, picked me up and slammed me against the wall with my legs around his waist. We were head height. His hand slowly, purposefully eased against my throat again.

"Maybe you should be," he said, more a whisper on a forgotten wind than words.

"Admit it," I plead.

"Admit what?" he scoffed.

I put my arms around his shoulders and tightened my legs around his waist. I leant my lips to his ear. "Admit you've wanted your cock in me since the day we met." I took his ear lobe in my teeth and tugged gently.

There went another barely suppressed snarl. "So, what if I have?" he spat, pushing me back only far enough to look in my eyes.

My heart jolted in my chest and my stomach was all butterflies. Not because of some stupid teenage crush finding out he felt the same. Because someone did want me. Me. Not what my family could offer them. Not because they were supposed to. I was wantable. Desirable. Lustable. Even if it was a guy who hated me.

I curled a piece of his hair around my finger. "Then do it," I challenged.

He dropped me as though he was shocked, but his arms were there almost absent-mindedly to steady me as I got my feet under me again. "What?"

I nodded and slid away from him. "I get it," I said as I started to walk away. "The big, bad wolf is all bark and no bite."

My laugh was cut off as he scooped me into his arms and placed me on the pool table like I weighed nothing. He settled between my legs like he'd been born to be there. He looked me over and there was something in his eyes. Anger. Denial. But blazing, white-hot, was a burning desire I'd never seen in them before. What I'd seen up until now as want was nothing compared to this...this brazen need.

He pushed his hands up my legs, pushing my skirt out of the

way as he went. When he got to the sides of my panties, he grabbed them in one hand and pulled hard. His other arm wrapped around me, and his body was there to stop me falling off the side of the pool table. But the manoeuvre had done its job. I was no longer sitting on my panties.

Valen's eyes were pinned to mine as he pulled them off me, only ever getting as far away from me as necessary, and discarded them I didn't care where. He undid his trousers with one hand as his other stroked my clit with his thumb.

I breathed deep and even, trying to still the butterflies and the nerves on the edges of their seats. It was difficult with the rising pleasure emanating from my clit as he circled lazily. But as I looked into his eyes, I saw he was breathing just as deep as me. Just as even as me. Just as forced as me.

He took a step towards me and pulled me roughly to the very edge of the pool table.

"I'm going to fuck you, Harlow," he promised as his thumb flicked my clit faster. "I'm going to fuck you until you forget your own name. I'm going to make you cum so hard, the only name you'll remember is mine. Understood?"

I nodded. "Understood."

He plunged into me in one quick swift motion and I cried out, clinging to his back and burying my face in his shoulder against the shock and the sudden pain. Then he paused.

"It'll pass," he whispered softly. "Breathe and relax."

I took a deep breath, then another, and another. Slowly, I relaxed around him and the throbbing was less painful and more enticing. He didn't move again until I'd pulled away to look at him.

As he drew back, he coaxed my knee higher around his hip and the discomfort eased even more.

"Fuck," Valen groaned, thrusting slowly and steadily.

He palmed my breast as he dropped his forehead to mine. He held me to him like he was clinging to a life raft. I looked up and our eyes met. Something passed between us as he drove into me. There was hate – so much hate between us – but something else as well. Fire. Desire. Crackling attraction that threatened to overwhelm me until I really did forget my own name.

He felt...amazing now the worst of the aching discomfort had subsided. Far better than my wildest dreams. Far better than I could ever hope to expect from Apollo. And far better than even eight inches of perfectly moulded silicon.

As my breath caught, a moan escaped me. I could see the victory in his eyes.

"Does the good little princess like that?" he asked, his voice husky.

I nodded as I bit my lip. His eyes followed the movement. He groaned in satisfaction as he pulled me closer to him. I wrapped my arms around him, my face burying in his shoulder for a very different reason this time as I moaned loudly against him. The way his body muffled my cries made me bolder, louder.

"Oh, fuck," he muttered.

"Does the big, bad wolf like that?" I asked him, unable to stop myself smiling.

He took my jaw in his hand and made me look at him again as he thrust deeper into me. At the look of humour in my eyes, there was a flicker in his.

"I've told you not to test me, princess," he said, barely keeping the humour from entering his voice.

"And I've told you, you will bow to me, Valk."

He wrapped me in his arms and his lips went to my ear. "We'll see who bows to who," he purred, thrusting into me with a strong, powerful rhythm.

At that point, I wasn't overly concerned with who bowed to who. There was time enough to worry about that later. I just wanted to live in the moment and enjoy the feel of him, the reality of him.

In hindsight, I should have cared that we were in a very public room in the middle of our school and anyone could have found us. But I didn't. I was exhilarated. I cared about nothing. I felt free from my cage for the first time since I'd realised there were bars around my life.

"First time or not, you'll cum for me," he said, his voice hard in my ear.

His hand slid between us, finding a way in despite the awkward angle. I breathed in hard and arched against him as his finger found my clit.

All I could do was nod to him as he thrust faster.

"You like that?" he asked.

I nodded again.

"Tell me."

"I like it." I whimpered as his fingers worked me faster. "Oh, Valen. Don't stop. Yes!"

"Say my name," he commanded. "Say my name as you cum."

My arms gripped him harder as I felt it building. Despite all my practise and my best efforts, I'd never managed anything that even resembled the storm he'd built up in me. And it was lashing against its bonds, desperate for release.

"Right there," I panted, my head falling back as we moved in glorious synchronicity.

I forgot all sense of pain, of being stretched, or discomfort as my orgasm beat against the confines of the dam that held it back. Like a tidal wave of pleasure threatening to wipe out everything in its path. All the hate. All the confines of my life. As though true freedom, like my release, was moments away.

"Valen," I moaned as the crescendo rose. "Valen!"

I was so close. It was just there. Almost in reach.

His hand snaked into my hair again and he grabbed a handful, forcing me to look into his eyes. He thrust into me harder, deeper, faster.

"Cum for me, princess," he commanded.

I licked my lip and smiled. "You scared you can't hold on?" I teased.

He tugged on my hair. Hard. "Don't push me," he warned.

We stared into each other's eyes, his a storm to match the one raging in me.

"Why?" I asked, then gasped as he drove deep into me. "What will happen if I push you?"

"You don't want to find out," he said as I came completely undone for him.

"Fuck!" I breathed as the dam broke, the pressure floored me, and my entire body shook with the force of it. "Valen..."

He squeezed my breast harder as his rhythm increased. Faster and faster like he wanted to bury himself deep inside me, and leave his mark on my very soul.

He groaned softly in my ear as his body tensed, holding me close as he came. He pressed a lingering kiss to my neck then breathed in deeply. He wasn't the only one breathing deeply.

We leant against each other, fighting for breath, for a few moments before he withdrew and tucked himself back in his trousers.

"You knew," I accused, still panting.

"Knew what?"

"Knew it was my first time."

He shrugged. "You said Apollo had never touched you."

"So that means no one else has?"

His half-smirk was all cocky arrogance. "You're a good little princess," he reminded me.

"And you still just…went for it."

He looked me over. "Didn't see you complaining."

He scooped up my ripped panties from where they'd fallen and touched them to his nose.

I nodded to him. "Thanks." And held my hand out for them.

He shook his head and slowly brought them away from his nose. "These are mine, now," he said as he put them in his back pocket.

I scoffed as I smoothed my skirt over my knees like that would help in the naked feeling, or the cum dribbling down my leg.

"Suit yourself. And I wasn't complaining. I was…"

"What?" he scoffed. "Thought I'd be gentle, make it special?"

"You don't have to be a dick."

"That's what you want from me, princess," he said, leaning into me again. "You want me to fuck you with all the hate we have for each other."

If it was anything like that had been? Yes. Yes, I did want that very much. That and quite possibly much more.

"Pleasure doing business with you," I said sarcastically as I slid off the pool table.

He caught my wrist as I passed him and looked me dead in the eye. "Apollo never knows."

My heart thudded. "Of course not." Then, to cover, I scoffed. "Once never hurt anyone."

His hand slid over my stomach and his lips dropped to my ear. "You tell yourself that the next time you need my cock between your legs."

My heart thudded again. For an entirely different reason. "There won't be a next time."

"There shouldn't be, but I guarantee there will."

I pushed him away and walked out, determined there was never going to be a next time.

Annoyingly, when I crawled into my bed soon after, it was much easier to fall asleep than it had been all week. I still dreamt about Valen, but I minded ever so slightly less.

I'd also completely forgotten about the book I'd been reading when he'd walked in…

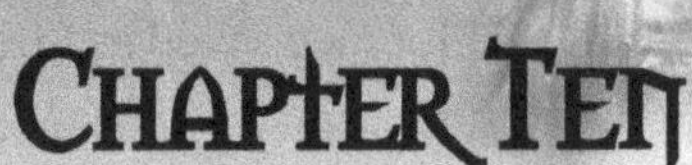

CHAPTER TEN

The next morning, I didn't have much choice in going about my life like nothing had changed because my alarm didn't go off.

Instead, I was rudely awakened by Florence shaking me roughly, with a, "Jesus, Mary and Joseph, Harlow Vanguard. There's late and then there's you," like she was a cardboard cutout of her overly proper and lovable mother.

I pulled myself awake. As I sat up, she threw something at me. I dragged it off my face and found she was throwing bits of my uniform at me.

"What are you–?" I mumbled.

"Get dressed. There's missing breakfast and there's missing morning mass. Sister Agnes is going to kill us."

I nodded, still blinking sleep out of my eyes and brain. "Sure."

I hurried to get changed while Florence flapped around the room in panic and kept marking every minute that went by. I had no chance to think of anything except trying to remember how to dress myself so all the layers went in the right order. It embarrassingly took a few goes, which only stressed Florence more.

"Come on," she whined. "I know you've not been sleeping well, but come the *fuck* on, Bridget!"

"Pants," I said, realising I needed to change my pants, which made me remember that Valen had stolen a pair last night.

"What?" Florence asked as I froze. "Have you forgotten where pants live? Where they go? Between your fucking legs, woman. Come on!"

"Right…" I muttered, pulling my focus to the current problems and finishing getting ready.

By the time Florence was pushing me out of our room and bundling me to the chapel, I was pretty sure I was fully dressed, my hair was up although totally not brushed at all, my bladder was empty, and I'd wiped a bit of toothpaste over my teeth.

"You'll do!" Florence said. "No one cares what you look like. It's the last day of term. You'll probably start a new trend."

I snorted, but then realised she might have been right. There was a time in Year Nine when I'd started winding ribbons through my plaits, and it had caught on to the point people were still doing it.

During mass, I fell asleep on Florence's shoulder and, whenever she jolted me awake again, was too tired to notice whether people were staring at me or not, whether they cared what I looked like or not. On the way out, I took a surreptitious look around and only received the usual smiles and nods and greetings. If I looked as bad as I felt, then no one did care.

As we walked into the main building for first lesson, I caught my reflection in the door and saw that it wasn't that no one cared what I looked like, it was that I'd actually managed to make myself look somewhat decent. At least decent enough to pass during class time. I was quite proud of myself.

Florence's panic had passed after none of the sisters had pulled us up on tardiness and we were now safely off to lessons, so she was chatting away about something. I was only half-heartedly paying attention to her, giving her the 'uh huh,' 'yup,' and 'really?' she was looking for.

But I paused as I saw who was up ahead. A very definite 'yip' sound escaped me and that got Florence's attention. She searched to follow my gaze and saw it fixed on Valen.

"Like you don't love any chance for him to intimidate you," she scoffed, nudging me forward with her shoulder.

My feet moved against my wishes.

Yeah, I loved Valen intimidating me. But that was before he'd fucked me. That was before I knew – *knew* – all my fantasies were pale imitations of how good the real thing was. I wasn't a total idiot. I had a suspicion why the real thing was so much better than the fantasies, because there was more to real life than the perfect planning of a fantasy. Emotions swirled – be it hate or not – and they heightened everything. They changed everything from the almost sterile, calculated, designed atmosphere of a fantasy.

Knowing all that, I didn't know how I was going to be able to even look at Valen ever again without everyone seeing how much I wanted to have it all again. But it was never going to happen again. I couldn't let it. Not when he was so certain it would. I had to prove him wrong. I couldn't let him be right. I had very little power in my life, and that was one thing I hoped I wasn't too weak to keep control over.

We were getting closer to Valen, who seemed to not have noticed me yet.

He was walking with Marco, another Angel – one of Apollo's lieutenants.

Marco had the dark hair and pale eye combination that seemed prevalent among the angels. He was a good-looking guy in his own right, full of cheeky mischief and busy fingers. He never sat still and always looked at you like he knew your deepest secrets. Marco was a big guy – taller than Valen – but somehow still looked small in comparison to the hulking presence that was Valen Kincaid.

Valen's…aura emanated power and a deadly darkness that threatened to swallow anyone stupid enough to get close enough. Many Magdalens had been lost to it. Marco's was good, but not that good. Not to me, anyway. I knew Florence thought the opposite, though, and each to their own. The world would be a fucking stupid place if we were all attracted to the same person.

Following the social mores of the high school corridor, I made to avoid running directly into Valen and Marco, and sidestepped. Problem was, Valen sidestepped as well. Seemingly as natural as anything, but the fact it was right into my path made me think it was anything but an accident.

We stopped right in front of each other, me forced to crane my neck to look up at him. I let my eyes take the scenic route, though. Up over his school trousers, enjoying the way the dark grey material clung to his muscular thighs. Over the shiny black belt at his waist. Up the white shirt that was absolutely not see through, but I could easily picture the body underneath. Past the collar with the open top button and loose tie. And finally into his face.

That face that I knew better than my own. The square jaw, the full lips, the near-black hair that hung into those storm grey eyes that raked over everything with keen disinterest and boredom. Like he was better than everyone and everything in any room he was in. Not the way Apollo was. Not like he ruled over everything, but rather like it was all trivial to him.

"Move," he told me, his voice a low warning.

My heart pounded and my clit throbbed, but I held my own.

"You move," I countered.

"Don't test me," he said, dragging it out like there was more he wanted to say.

"Harlow," I said.

His eyes narrowed. "What?"

"In case you forgot," I added.

His eyebrow quirked and he licked his bottom lip slowly. "Excuse me?"

"In case you forgot," I repeated. "Because I certainly didn't." I paused. "Forget my own name, I mean."

Understanding flashed in his eyes and his upper lip twitched like he was repressing some choice words. His eyes slid over to Florence as though he was considering what was safe to say in front of her.

"Next time," he said to me, and I felt his words caress me like a shiver of expectation with unbreakable promise.

I steeled my gaze and kicked my chin towards him. "Move."

He took a step towards me. He honestly couldn't be closer to me and it still be decent for the school corridor.

"Next. Time," he said again, enunciating carefully.

He said it like it was some new personal mission of his. Like it was a personal affront that I remembered my own name. Like he'd die fulfilling his promise if that's what it took.

I stared him down. Finally, he emitted a low, rumbling growl before he finally went around me.

Once he was gone, I released a breath I hadn't realised I'd been holding and suddenly noticed that the corridor was relatively quiet. People had seen, though I doubted they knew *what* they'd seen. I ducked my head and hurried towards my class. Florence sped to keep up with me.

"Um, what was that?" she asked.

I shrugged. "What was what?"

"Er, just the blazing, flaming sexual tension I could legitimately grab and motorboat it was so visceral."

I threw her a look, knew by the expression on her face that she wasn't going to give it up, rolled my eyes and dragged her into an empty bathroom. I double checked all the stalls were empty.

"Holy shit," she laughed. "You didn't?"

"How did you know what I was going...?" I shook my head.

Of course, she knew. She was my best friend.

I held up a hand to stop her talking. It didn't stop her.

"Holy *fucking* shit," she chuckled. "That's why you were spotting!"

I blinked at her. "What?"

"This morning," she said. "That's why you were spotting."

Comprehension dawned.

She'd come running into the bathroom that morning when I'd

yelled in surprise at the blood on the toilet paper, then gone right back to stressing about being late. In the two years since I'd started my three-monthly contraceptive injection, I hadn't had a single period, let alone spotted, so it had been quite the shock. Now, it all made sense. I doubted a real life penis was the same as moulded silicon if you went ahead and rammed it on up there.

"It all makes sense," Florence chuckled, then bumped me with her shoulder. "Although, I'm a bit miffed you didn't tell me earlier."

I laughed. "There wasn't a lot of time."

She nodded. "True. Just so long as you *were* going to tell me."

"Of course, I was going to tell you. You're my best friend."

"Next time, I expect instant news. Preferably during. Even better, before."

I had to laugh at the way her mind worked, but that was as far as my humour ran.

"It was one time. It's not happening again."

"Uh huh," Florence said. "And are you telling me or you that?"

"Everyone," I said in exasperation. "Whoever wants to know."

Florence looked around quickly, all humour forgotten. "You're not actually thinking about letting other people know about this?" she asked.

I huffed as we made our way out of the bathroom and back into the hallway. "No. Of course not. No one can find out."

She nodded. "No. Good. Just checking. I didn't think you'd actually lost your mind."

"Harlow!" I heard Apollo say as he came up behind me and wrapped his arms around my waist. His nose nuzzled my neck and he hugged me tight. "How are we?"

I felt my eyes widen in silent plea to Florence, but she pressed her lips together and shook her head.

"Uh, good. You?" I said, turning in his arms and plastering on a smile.

He nodded. "Good. Great. Holidays tomorrow."

I laughed and hoped it only felt awkward to me. "That it is."

"Home tonight. Looking forward to it?"

Home. Not quite, but close enough really.

"Uh huh." I nodded. "Should be good."

"Like always."

"Like always."

Apollo's hand slid into mine and we started walking. "Where are you two off to now?"

"Religion," Florence answered, sounding a bit miffed with him. "And hello to you, too."

Apollo squeezed my hand. "Oh, Flo, we don't say 'hello'. That's like our thing."

Florence looked at him shrewdly. "You're in a good mood."

"Shouldn't I be?"

"I don't know. Valk lace your morning coffee with something a little stronger than usual?"

Apollo turned like he'd seen Valen before finding us. "If he did, he should have kept some for himself. He's extra pissy today."

"Yeah, no shit," Florence huffed a laugh.

"You saw him?"

"Of course, we did. No one misses Valen Kincaid."

"He seem more out of sorts than usual to you?"

Florence threw him a glare as they walked side by side down the corridor, me on the other side of Apollo.

"Mr Lone Wolf is always out of sorts. Maybe he broke a claw?"

Apollo chuckled. "Yeah. You're probably right. His dad probably got in touch."

I didn't even like Valen, and my blood ran cold at that thought. Cillian Kincaid only ever got into contact with his son for one reason. Those worse higher powers that he'd spoken of on Saturday. It was a major reason to put him in a mood. I didn't know all the ins and outs of the Kincaid family dealings, but I knew enough to know that someone was probably going to lose their life.

"Harlow?" Apollo tugged my hand and I realised we'd reached Florence and my classroom.

I blinked. "Sorry."

"She's not sleeping," Florence said pointedly.

"Everything okay, sweetheart?" Apollo asked, rubbing my back.

I nodded. "Yeah. Just…you know…last year and all."

He gave me a warm, encouraging smile. "I get it. Everything's coming to an end."

"Don't put it like that," Florence snapped, whacking his shoulder.

Apollo grinned cheekily at her. "Well, it is."

"Yeah, but we don't want a reminder, idiot."

"Miss Vanguard. Miss Walsh?" the sister said from the

classroom. "I trust you'll be joining us today?"

"Yes, sister," I said with a smile. "Sorry, sister."

"And you have a class to get to yourself, Mr Callahan?"

Apollo gave her one of his charming smiles and any idiot could see she was trying not to soften at the sight of it.

"Of course, sister. I won't hold you up."

"Good. And I trust Miss Vanguard will be able to stay awake for more than five minutes?" she asked as Apollo kissed my cheek and squeezed my hand.

Apollo chuckled in my ear. "Be good."

"You be good," I replied, knowing that he wouldn't be.

"Not if I can help it."

He threw one more charming smile and wave to the sister, then sauntered off. Florence and I hurried quickly to our seats.

For the rest of the day, I could feel Florence burning next to me like a giant flaming question mark. She was itching to know more, especially with us being separated at the end of the day. But she didn't have a death wish, so she knew she'd have to wait until we were one hundred percent alone with no chance of anyone overhearing us. And that wouldn't be until the end of the day.

At Lunch, Apollo's arm was around me, but his attention was on anything but me as he talked with Winchester and Wyatt about nothing I was paying attention to. Valen walked over to the group, and I'd already locked eyes with him by the time Florence elbowed me.

I elbowed her right back. "Subtle," I muttered.

She shrugged. "What? There was a bee."

I looked at her in fond exasperation. "A bee?"

She nodded. "Yes. Or maybe it was an elephant. A great big elephant. *Grey* elephant."

"Okay," I snapped. "I get it."

"Everything all right, ladies?" Apollo asked, turning to us.

I nodded. "Yes. Yep. All good."

But after the first 'yes', Apollo had the information he needed to decide not to follow up, and his attention turned to the approaching Valen.

"Valk, man, you ready for a week off?" he asked with a grin.

"Got plans?" Marco asked, looking between them as he shoved some sandwich into his face.

Apollo leant back, his hand pulling my shoulder with him and I was brought into his body in a warm snuggle. It was a stance we'd affected many times over the years. It was as normal and natural and casual as breathing. My body instinctively leant against his and put my hand over his stomach. It didn't mean that my head wasn't a befuddled mess of awkwardness.

"Nothing but me, my best mate and my perfect girl for a whole week," Apollo said happily as he fiddled with his ring on my hand.

It was clearly happy families time. It had been all day. Showing off his perfect relationship with his perfect girl for all the world to see. It wasn't that I didn't like his attention or the time we spent together like this. In some weird way, I cherished it. Cherished some sort of semblance of our old friendship. But it was also getting tiring. Anyone with a brain would have worked out that our relationship was a sham. It just seemed like there weren't very many brains going around. That, or the whole school thought the same way about me as Valen; that I was a simpering idiot who just let her man fuck around because I was – what? – too weak and gormless to do anything about it?

The realisation that that could actually be the case made a shiver of sadness run through me. I tried covering with a cough and resettling against Apollo, but when I looked at Valen I saw him watching me carefully. There was no doubt he'd noticed, but what had he thought of it?

"Until the Halloween party," Marco added, with an excited wriggle-dance move.

Apollo's grin widened. "Until the Halloween party," he agreed.

"You still good for us to come over on Saturday to help prep?"

Apollo nodded. "All good."

And, by prep, they did indeed mean drink while ordering some staff around and maybe doing a bit themselves. At least, Florence was also coming on Saturday so I wouldn't be alone the whole time.

"And have we all got our costumes sorted?" Marco asked.

Apollo gave me a squeeze. "All sorted."

Florence and I exchanged glances. All I'd been told was that Apollo was dealing with a couple's costume this year and I was just going to have to wait and see what it was when it was ready for fitting in the holidays. The concept filled me with a bit of dread, but I was also mostly pleased I didn't have to do anything about it. Apollo had been on the organisation end for plenty of things for me in the past – not including the crown that still weighed heavily on my finger – and it had all turned out fine. If

Archer had given his son one good thing, it was good taste in jewellery, clothes, and style.

"You coming as your usual?" Apollo continued.

Marco nodded. "Nah, the Angels decided that the three Musketeers was a little overplayed. We've got a better idea this year."

Apollo turned a quizzical look on Valen. "A better idea?"

Valen blinked, long and slow, and gave a single nod. "You'll see it next weekend."

"Are you going to be at the Callahan's all holidays?" Florence asked Valen, not very nonchalantly at all.

Apollo nodded. "Yep. Aren't you?" he clarified with Valen.

Valen gave a much more curt nod. "In and out. Few jobs for my family."

"In and out?" Florence said casually. "No doubt."

Valen's eyes narrowed and turned to me. I gave a little start and leant further into Apollo, who absently gave me a kiss on the head as he talked with Marco. His hand entwined with mine like it was second nature, but there was no other outward sign he even knew I was there

When Apollo and I had agreed to this – to faking it – we'd decided to only do enough to support the ruse. Anything outside that, he didn't want to take up any more of my time or energy than he already had to. But that, what he considered to be giving me space, seemed to have become more akin to dismissive neglect in the last year or so. I knew I was losing Frenella's little boy – and my best friend – but I didn't know what to do.

A week at 'home' with him now wasn't exactly as exciting as

it used to be. It had been a downward slope since the day he met Valen. And now I'd fucked Valen, I was pretty sure it was going to be ten times worse.

"Well," Florence huffed a laugh to me quietly. "Your holidays are going to be great fun."

I frowned at her. "Shut up."

Chapter Eleven

By Monday, I'd fallen back into the same old routine at the Callahan Estate.

I'd spent most holidays with them since before I'd started at Saint Benedicts. All but a few weeks of Summer and some of Christmas. It was like a second home. I supposed it was to get me used to it. Keep an eye on me. Like a modern day hostage situation; bring the girl up in her intended's kingdom.

I was heading down the stairs, on the phone to my mother, who was checking in as she actually did relatively often. During term time it was mostly email and text, as we both had busy schedules. And, by that, I meant that she wasn't usually free between four and seven in the evening when I was.

"You still haven't sent me a decent picture of your ring," she accused, but good-naturedly.

"I'm sure I did," I told her with a wry smile.

"You didn't. I'm looking through the…" She paused. "Oh, no. There it is. Why didn't I see that earlier?"

I wasn't going to tell her it was because she'd never bothered to learn technology properly. I wasn't going to say anything even remotely derogatory to or about her, because she didn't have to be good at that stuff and I loved her.

My father might have been organising my future wedding for the sake of a business contract, and it might be normal for him because it wasn't that different to how his marriage came about, but my mother was me…just twenty-odd years older. She knew and understood my situation better than I did and, though we'd never directly, outwardly spoken about it, I knew she was in my corner and I had to appreciate that.

"At least it sounds like you had a good birthday. Did you and Florence do anything?" she asked.

I nodded, despite knowing she couldn't see me. "She made me a cake and snuck a three-litre bottle of 'Elle and Lui' in for us."

Mum chuckled, managing to tinge it with a touch of disapproval. "Well, I'm sure I did worse at your age," was all she said.

I opened my mouth to reply, but froze when I saw three men striding purposefully across the foyer in the direction of Archer's office. My blood ran cold, and I nearly lost my hold on my phone. Valen was following two other men. Two other Kincaids.

I might have been kept in the dark about the reality of the men's business, but I wasn't that twelve year old girl hiding on the stairs anymore. I knew what kind of men the Kincaids were now.

Ahead was Cillian Kincaid. Patriarch of the Kincaid Family. Though, family was perhaps a misnomer. Blood was less important than loyalty to the Family – the capital 'F' type. It just helped that most of the Family were in fact blood relations.

He was a big man. Tall and wide, with ash brown hair and an ugly scar running down his cheek and disappearing into his shirt collar. He wore a suit, like they always did. The goal *was* to fit in. Shame then about the light splattering of blood contrasting the pristine whiteness of his shirt. That wasn't going to stand up in polite society.

Next to him, a step behind, was Kane Kincaid. If his father hadn't put ice in my veins, Kane would have. He always had. Now twenty-six, he wasn't quite as tall as his younger brother or his father, but he was big enough. Where Valen was dark hair and pale eyes, Kane was light hair and dark eyes; ash blond hair and piercing green eyes. He always watched me for a moment too long. He didn't just strike the fear of God into me like a good Kincaid was wont to do, he also gave me a creepy shiver up my spine.

Kane's eye caught mine with an unsettling wink as the three of them stalked across the marbled floor and I was so busy proving he didn't bother me that I almost glossed over Valen. But as soon as I turned my eyes to the youngest Kincaid, they weren't in any danger of leaving.

His suit was ripped. The blood splattering Cillian was nothing compared to what covered Valen. He looked like someone had Carrie-d him; pouring a whole bucket of blood right over his head. I couldn't tell if he was injured under it. I didn't know if it was his blood or not.

My heart jolted painfully and my hand gripped the banister harder. He was watching me and I saw his tongue dart out to lick his lip, heedless of whether he was licking blood or not. He lifted a finger and pressed it to his lips with a dark warning in his eyes.

"Harlow?" I heard Mum's voice crackle through the static in my head.

The three men disappeared into Archer's office and I finally breathed again.

"Sorry," I said with a nervous chuckle. "Spaced. What were you saying?"

"Nothing important," Mum said and I heard the smile in her voice. "I'd better let you get back to Apollo. Say hello to him for me, won't you?"

I nodded. "Of course."

"And tell him I'm waiting on a chat."

I rolled my eyes, glad she couldn't see me. "Will do."

"Love you, Harlow."

"Love you, too, Mum. Say hi to Dad."

"I will."

She hung up and I breathed out heavily.

I would have got back to Apollo, but I didn't know where he was. If three Kincaids were arriving covered in blood, then bets were he was with Archer in his office. The holidays were a great time for Apollo and me to just exist away from expectant eyes, but it was stupid to think they weren't also a time for Apollo – and Valen – to be learning the tools and tricks of his father's trade. And, with less than a year before graduation, Apollo's lessons were getting more serious.

Apollo was Archer's only child. One day he would rule the Callahan empire with an iron fist to match his father's. Another day, further away, my son would take the reins. And if I didn't have a son? Archer would be furious. And my daughter would be married off to whatever family's heir wasn't already promised to someone else. I'd already considered just adopting a boy and getting rid of all the pressure that weighed down the edges of my mind.

I had no idea how long a debrief lasted these days. It probably depended on what job Archer had employed the Kincaids for. So I decided to just head to the kitchen and see what flavours of ice cream were left over after two days of me stress bingeing.

As I passed Archer's office door, I can't say I didn't pause. Half thinking of trying to see what was going on behind it. My hand even inched towards the doorknob. But I wasn't that kind of girl. I didn't know anything about espionage and creeping around, and remaining undetected. Knowing my luck, I'd just end up falling through the door and everyone would look at me expectantly, waiting to laugh at me until I'd left.

No. Better to keep moving and not even think about trying.

Just as I took a step to keep going, a large body barrelled out of the office door and rammed right into me. I lost my footing and fell to my butt, sliding a little on the smooth floor.

I looked up and saw Kane Kincaid looking down at me.

"Little princess," he said, a sinister tilt to his lips.

I couldn't have got up if I'd wanted to. Kane's gaze pinned me with nothing pleasant. I swallowed hard and just hoped he was going to go back into the office and leave me be. My skin got a creeping, crawling sensation. I knew the Kincaids were dangerous people, but Kane was the only one around whom I felt actually in danger.

"Harlow," I heard Apollo say as he hurried over to me.

Even with my intended, my intended's father, and his own father watching on, Kane didn't back off. Like he was waiting. Always like he was waiting. *Waiting for what?* My heart thudded in my chest and my breath came short.

"You know what they say about eavesdroppers," Kane said.

"Nothing compared to murderers," I said, far less impressively than I'd intended, but at least I'd said it loud enough for everyone to hear.

Kane's eyes flashed with something that made me wish I'd kept my mouth shut.

"The little princess seems to be growing a backbone," Cillian boomed in his thick Scottish accent. "Perhaps she'll make a decent bride after all, Archer."

"Harlow has many admirable qualities," Archer said smoothly. Somehow, he sounded like a proud father figure at the same time as the only admirable thing he cared about was the functionality of my ovaries.

I felt my cheeks flush and let Apollo cradle me against him as he helped me stand.

I couldn't look at Valen. I wouldn't. I refused to even think of looking for comfort anywhere but where I was supposed to. And that was with Apollo.

"Why don't you head back to your room?" Apollo whispered encouragingly in my ear. "I'll find you later."

I nodded against him. "Okay."

He kissed my cheek and nudged me in the direction of the stairs.

"Kane, get your fucking useless arse out of here," Cillian snapped.

"Apollo," Archer said carefully.

It was all done as though everyone was keeping me in the dark about their true nature. Like I couldn't see the blood on their clothes. Like I couldn't guess that Archer had paid the Kincaids to kill someone – multiple someones even.

Protected.

Appearances.

I didn't care what it was. I wouldn't be my mother and I wouldn't be Frenella. I wouldn't stay powerless.

But, I turned and I went back to my room as Kane left and Archer's office door closed behind me. Now wasn't the time to fight, but it was coming. I wasn't going to be the princess locked in the tower forever. No prince was coming to save me. My prince had more interest in keeping me locked away, even if he didn't realise that's what he was doing. I had to save myself. I just had to wait for the dragon – or, wolf – to fall asleep and drop its guard.

When I got to my bedroom door, I didn't go into it. I didn't feel like it after all. Instead, I headed out the back of the estate. I found the winding gardens and wandered along the paths, my hands skimming the leaves as I went. The sun was almost set and it was getting chilly, but I didn't mind so much. I knew I didn't have much longer before I had to go in and change for dinner. It was nothing big, just a few clients of Archer's coming over and we all had to dress up and play nice. Dressing up and playing nice was my life, it seemed.

Still, as used to it as I was, I lingered in the garden.

Suddenly, there was a hand on my arm and the owner was pulling me to face them. I reacted on instinct, my other hand raising to hit them away. He caught my wrist well before I made contact and glared at me with icy hatred in the depths of his grey eyes.

"What are you doing?"

I looked at my still-raised hand. "How was I supposed to know it was you?"

"If he'd come back, you think that would have stopped him?"

I blinked and looked back into his eyes. "What? If who came back?"

Valen growled. "Apollo's looking for you."

I wasn't going to be distracted. "If who came back, Valk?"

He took a step forward, forcing me to take a step back. "You shouldn't have provoked him. What the fuck possessed you?"

I still didn't know what he was talking about. "Who? When?"

He raised his hand like he was going to put it over my throat again, but just ended up cupping my jaw. "Just keep being the good little princess you're supposed to be, and we won't have any problems," he said scathingly.

"And what if I don't want to be anymore?"

A touch of humour lit his eyes. "I know I'm good, princess, but I didn't realise I was that good. Beg me nicely and I'll let you have my cock one more time."

I shoved him away from me. For once, he took a step back.

"You think you were that good?" I scoffed.

His head twitched like he was keeping his choice words at bay. "I know I was that good."

"The only one I see desperate here is you, Valk," I told him. "Still wanting the one thing you can't have."

"And, yet, I had it."

"And the knowledge you'll never have it again will eat you up inside," I snarled.

The corner of his lip twitched into a momentary half-smirk. "I'm fine just walking away, princess. Can you say the same?"

"Yes," I said, turning away to do just that.

But he took my hand and drew me back to him. My traitorous body went utterly willingly to melt against him.

"You can lie to Apollo, but you can't lie to me."

"Who's lying to who now, Valen?" I asked, feeling him hard against my hip. "You couldn't walk away for all the Callahan fortune."

His lips twitched again, but it was a snarl this time. "Maybe not," he conceded begrudgingly. "But neither could you."

I forced myself to smile. "I don't need the Callahan fortune, Valen. I have the Vanguard fortune."

And, as rich and powerful as the Callahans were, the Vanguards were older, richer and more powerful. We just didn't like to throw our power about quite so obviously as Archer. We were subtle. Practised. There was old money and new money, then there was older money. Callahans might have been old money, but Vanguards were much, much older.

There was the slight issue of Apollo being the one to inherit the Vanguard fortune, but that didn't seem relevant just then.

"Admit it," he plead.

"Admit what?" I asked, not liking him turning the tables on

me.

"Admit you still want my cock in you."

I set my jaw before answering. "So, what if I do?"

He leant his face to mine. "Then take it."

I smiled widely. "Unlike you, I have some restraint."

He scoffed. "You think you have restraint?"

I nodded. "Yes. I do."

"And you think I don't?"

"Yes." I nodded again. "I do."

His face hardened. "We'll see whose restraint is better than whose."

I pushed away from him. "Yes. We will."

He didn't try to stop me and he didn't follow me as I headed for my room to get changed. The name of the game now seemed to be make Valen regret his words. I'd show him exactly what he could be having, what I was withholding. I'd break his famous restraint if it was the last thing I did. And I had the perfect dress for it.

I think I probably had more clothes at the Callahan Estate than I did at my parents' house. Most of my purchases were made in or around Bieityn or online and shipped to the Callahans'. I was there the most and it was close to school, so it seemed a no brainer.

I was dressed and ready in record time. Seeing no one on my way to my room or the way back down, I knew I was running late. But dinners like this always started with drinks and discussion, so late was relative.

As I walked towards the Parlour, I felt a hand on my arm and found myself pulled into the side hall.

Valen boxed me in against the wall. He was changed, but in a long-sleeved tee and jeans, not being needed at the dinner.

"What do you think you're doing?" he growled.

I blinked, playing happily naïve. "I don't know what you're talking about."

He ran his hand up my exposed thigh as he leant into me. "This dress."

"What about this dress?" I asked.

The dress I'd chosen specifically to tease him. To tantalise him. To show him what he was missing out on. It was a deep blue two-piece. The top was a low-cut sweetheart, skimming the fullness of my breasts and making them look perkier than usual. It was cropped, showing off my waist. The skirt started at my belly button and draped elegantly to the floor, all but the thigh-high slit up my right side. It was classy and sexy. Something I'd never actively tried before. I'd never had a reason before.

He looked up like he was praying for patience and leant forward to whisper in my ear, "Do you think you're clever?"

I smirked. "Something the matter, Valk?"

His fist crashed into the wall by my head as he pulled back to look at me. He was scowling bloody thunder. I could feel his body almost humming with barely contained anger and restraint.

He splayed his hand on my arse cheek and squeezed. The groan that escaped his throat was barely loud enough for me to hear, and I knew I wasn't supposed to.

"Who let you come down here like this?"

I pretended to look around. "It seems like you're the only one with the problem here, Valen."

He took my hand and lay it over the very firm bulge in his pants. "I have a problem with it, all right."

I reached up and nipped his earlobe playfully. "I could take it off?" I suggested.

He slammed me back against the wall, leaning his nose against mine. The was a shimmering haze of lust surrounding us. I didn't care that I was supposed to be entertaining Archer's clients and showing off the perfect future in-law. I didn't care that Valen was supposed to be in his room and out of the way, being little more than hired help when it came down to it. I was in danger of falling for my own ruse, but right then I'd fall happily.

He ran his fingers over my clit teasingly, so softly that I came alive but would never be satisfied without more. And, by the humour in his eyes, that was the exact point. My hips rolled all of their own accord and the corner of his lip twitched victoriously.

"I told you once wouldn't be enough," he said as he rubbed me. "But if you want more, you'll have to beg for it."

I pushed his hand away. "You'll be the one begging, Valk."

The twitch at the corner of his lips this time was less humoured. "I will never bow to you."

I took a step towards him, getting into his space for once. "The only place you'll ever want to be is on your knees at my feet."

His hand went to my throat gently. "Not before I have you on your knees at mine."

"Take your hand off me," I warned him.

"Please?" he teased.

"I won't tell you twice."

A flash of desire lit his eyes at my defiance. A flash that I felt in my clit. I wanted him to throw me against this wall and show me exactly how bad I was being. He wanted that, too.

"I'll find her," I heard Apollo's voice and panic gripped my heart.

Valen growled in annoyance and pushed away from me. He stalked off in the opposite direction, in no rush to not be seen with me, but still avoiding Apollo finding us together.

"What are you–?" Apollo's voice cut off.

I turned and found him with his arm out and his mouth agape, like he'd frozen.

"What?" I asked, not really taking in the look on his face.

"You…" he breathed as I walked towards him.

"I, what?" I asked.

His hands went to my waist as I stopped in front of him and he looked me over. I saw him lick his lip slowly. Finally, his eyes found my face again and he smiled.

"You look gorgeous."

He took my hand and pulled me towards the Parlour.

"Thanks," I told him.

Just before the door, his arm went to my back and he indicated I precede him. Ever the gentleman.

As Apollo led me through the room, I realised his hand was lower than usual. Appropriate. Still very appropriate, but a whole hand's width lower. When we got to the bar – smaller than the one in the ballroom – his other hand slid over the gap of bare skin at my waist sensually.

"This new?" he asked.

"My stomach?" I joked.

He laughed and leant his nose to my ear. "No. The dress."

"It is. You like it?"

With the safety of the bar behind us, his hand slid down to cup my arse cheek. "Very much. You look good."

"Drink, Mr Callahan?" the bartender asked.

Apollo's attention was off me and on the bartender like flipping a switch, all hands back to where they were supposed to be. Apollo's face was suave and calm, not at all like a man who'd just had his hands on his girlfriend's arse. She says like she'd know what that was like.

After that, we were drawn into the politics of appearances and there was little time or space to really even think about what had just happened. But I had to wonder if, in trying to get one boy's attention, I'd accidentally secured another's.

Chapter Twelve

During the next two days, Apollo and I spent almost all waking hours together.

It was like we were ten again. Only with just a little more suave and sophistication. Just a little.

On Wednesday morning, he knocked on my bedroom door and sauntered in as I sat up, desperately blinking the sleep out of my eyes.

"Good morning, Miss Vanguard," he said chirpily.

He was already dressed. Nothing fancy, just trousers and a sweater over a long-sleeve tee with the sleeves semi-rolled up.

"Ugh, and what if I'd had a man in my bed?" I muttered, not yet awake enough to have put my filter in place.

I looked at him quickly as he dropped onto the bed beside me. But, if he thought that was a telling thing for me to have said, he didn't mention it.

"Then, there'd be two of us," he said with a wink, like he knew that would never happen.

I held the covers up over my appropriately clothed chest. "Well, what if I'd been naked?" I tried.

His grin widened. "I've seen you naked."

I rolled my eyes and batted him. "We used to share a bath when we were five," I answered.

He chuckled roughly. "We could share one now."

I looked at him, not quite sure if he was serious. From the look in his eyes, he wasn't quite sure if he was serious or not either. He patted my leg and stood up hurriedly.

"Come on," he said, kicking his head towards the door. "I heard tell it was eggs benedict morning."

I smirked. "You didn't."

He shrugged and it was adorable. "I might have."

When I'd first found out we were going to Saint Benedicts, I'd decided that eggs benedict would be my favourite breakfast, because what else would they serve you every morning at a school called Saint Benedicts? I'd figured, if I was going to have to eat them almost every morning for five years, then I may as well love them. Needless to say, the staff at Saint Benedicts did not feed us eggs benedict every morning, but I had become quite the fan.

"It's all about the hollandaise," we said together.

"And Mrs Mack said she's been working on an even more perfect recipe," Apollo said with a knowing grin.

I pretended to swoon. "Ugh, you know the way to a girl's heart."

His smile grew more rueful and sweet. "Really? I mean, of course I do. I've known you all my life."

"There were at least three years before we met, I'm sure."

He laughed. "Sure. You tell yourself that counts. Get dressed. I'll be out here."

He stuck his tongue out at me then slid back out my door.

Being away from school – from the Saints – gave me that warm happy feeling again.

Apollo was never again going to be that sweet little boy who'd follow me around his father's house like a love-sick puppy. But maybe, just maybe, there would be hope for us yet.

"Finally," he sighed dramatically when I emerged from my room.

"I've been five minutes," I said as we started for the stairs.

"More like five hours," Apollo teased. "You were so long, I'm going to have to shave again." He ran his hand over his perfectly smooth jaw.

I snorted. "Pfft. You barely have to shave at all."

"Excuse me," he laughed as he elbowed me companionably. "I make very good…stubble," he finished lamely.

"I think the word you're looking for is bum-fluff," I laughed.

He ran his hand over his jaw again. "It is not bum-fluff."

"I'll bet *I* have to shave more than you do," I said.

"Oi!" he laughed and I started running for the stairs. "You take that back!"

We laughed as he chased me and I felt free and easy, like it used to be.

Then I saw who was coming up the stairs and pulled up hard. Apollo crashed into the back of me, but we grabbed hold of each other and no one tumbled down the steps.

"Valk," Apollo said. "You in or out?"

Valen was scowling bloody murder – which was probably what he'd been doing – and looked little more than warmed up roadkill. But there was no blood and his clothes seemed in as many pieces as they were supposed to be. His knuckles looked pretty roughed up, though.

"What the fuck do you think?" he replied, his eyes falling to Apollo's arm around my waist.

When he looked back up, I wasn't sure what that look on his face was, but I felt a twinge of something when I realised it wasn't jealousy.

"So, you won't be joining us for an eggs benedict breakfast, then?" Apollo asked.

As if it was possible, Valen's frown deepened. "Do I need to dignify that bullshit with an answer?"

"Let's pretend you're human for a moment, eh?" Apollo joked, giving me a squeeze.

Valen's eyes dropped to my waist again, then back up. "What's *up* you this morning?"

Apollo shrugged. "I'm in a good mood, is that going to kill you?"

Valen's eyebrow rose. "It might."

Apollo laughed like Valen had been making a joke on purpose. "Okay. Fine. Will we see you later?"

"Doubtful. I'm needed."

The tightening of Apollo's arms almost felt like he was in need of comfort that time. But his answer gave nothing away. "You're going to sleep the whole day away?"

Valen just growled at him and started heading up the stairs.

"Go and get your beauty sleep, then," Apollo told him.

Valen looked at me pointedly when he replied, "Some of us

need it."

"Moody fucker," Apollo laughed as Valen disappeared.

Apollo took my hand casually and we traipsed down to the breakfast room.

"And I suppose this is your doing?" Frenella asked warmly when she saw me.

I looked at the table and saw far too much eggs benedict for any one family to eat.

"That would be your son," I told her as Apollo helped me into my seat.

Frenella, ever the doting mother, gave him a beaming smile. "I've tried to bring him up well."

Apollo ducked over to kiss her cheek before taking his place next to me.

"You've done a lovely job," I assured her. "He's very thoughtful." *For the most part.*

"I was thinking it's about time to have your parents over for another dinner, Harlow," Archer said to me from behind his newspaper as Frenella asked Apollo something about Valen.

"Oh, yes," she said, her focus off her son's best friend in favour of more pleasant topics. "That would be lovely. It's been too long since we've seen Sissy and Rex."

"Yes," Archer continued. "It's about time Rex and I smoothed over some finer details."

"Not everything's about business, Archer," Frenella chided.

Archer bent his newspaper to look at his wife. "Everything is business, Frenella," he said. "They're in their final year of school. It's only a matter of time now. Which reminds me. Apollo?"

"Yes, Dad?"

"We'll need to meet to discuss your…" Archer spared me a quick glance. Part of me wanted to say it was apologetic, but I knew it wasn't. "Conditions. I'm sure Rex has been redrafting his weekly since Harlow's first period."

I choked on my tea, but no one else seemed bothered about the mention of my menstrual cycle.

Of course, no one needed to consult me regarding my conditions for the marriage. No one cared what I wanted to get out of it or what I wanted full stop. I suppose I had to at least appreciate the fact that, while we were contractually obliged to marry, there had been no time limit set. We weren't waiting on my eighteenth birthday, or my twenty-first. I suspected, were I to hit twenty-five and there still be no ring in sight, they would have had something to say. But at least that was one less pressure.

"What did you two have planned for today?" Frenella asked, as though to diffuse the situation.

She hated any talk about business, believing what she'd been brought up – told – to believe; that it was the purview of the men locked away in their offices. She couldn't help being a product of her time or her upbringing, but that didn't mean I was happy being a product of mine.

"We've got a fitting for our Halloween costumes and then we were just going to hang out and watch some movies," Apollo answered.

Naturally, I hadn't been aware of any of that, but I'd had worse plans made for me, and worse were still to come.

"Oh, that sounds nice. What are you going as?"

There was a silence and I looked up to find Frenella watching me. Apollo had a cheeky smile in his eyes. One I couldn't help returning.

"I don't know," I answered. "Your son's keeping it a surprise."

"It's going to be good. I promise," Apollo said.

"Yeah?" I asked. "It better be *ah-mazing*."

Apollo's nose wrinkled in humour. "Watch out, your Florence is showing."

I stuck my tongue out at him and he laughed. As I went back to my breakfast, I saw Frenella watching us with a happy look on her face. She honestly believed we were the perfect couple. Madly in love. Totally devoted. Couldn't live without each other. The stuff of legends.

I wasn't looking forward the day she realised it was all bullshit.

† † † †

Late that night, Apollo and I were sitting in the rumpus room watching our fourth movie. I sat curled under his arm, with my head on his chest. I'd been doing the heavy lifting on three packets of cookie dough, and Apollo was doing the heavy lifting on a bottle of scotch. Not exactly the most cultured of pairings, but it worked.

About half way through the movie, Valen stalked into the room and dropped onto an armchair with a weary sigh. There was a new gash at his left eyebrow and he seemed to be favouring his left side. He wore grey tracksuit pants and a white short-sleeve tee that showed where his hair still dripped water from his shower.

"You look like shit," Apollo chuckled.

"Yeah?" Valen answered icily.

"Yeah. And this is after you showered?"

"You should see the other fucker."

"Why? Where's he?"

"Shallow grave."

Apollo laughed. "Job well done, then."

"Job done," was the only agreement Valen seemed willing to make.

"Stitches?" Apollo asked.

"Couple, probably. I'll deal with it tomorrow." He sank back in the chair. "I just want to fucking relax."

"Tough one?"

"Fucker wouldn't stay down."

Apollo leaned over and passed him the bottle of whiskey he had beside him. Valen took it from him with a nod, but Valen's eyes were on me.

"Your dad charging extra?" Apollo asked.

"If he doesn't, I will," Valen said, finally taking his eyes off me.

"Who was it for?"

"You know I'm not meant to talk about it."

"Come on," Apollo coaxed. "It's me."

"And Miss Vanguard."

"Oh, Miss Vanguard," Apollo laughed mockingly. "You *can* call her Harlow."

Valen took a long swig of the bottle. "That's not my place and you know it."

Apollo scoffed. "All that shit's years away."

"For you, maybe."

Apollo seemed to recognise that Valen wasn't in a mood for light-hearted teasing. He didn't poke him further, just let him be and we all settled in to watch the movie. But, it seemed, Apollo's night had been tainted. Not long after, he stretched dramatically and yawned.

"I might pack it in," he said. "You in for the rest of the night, Valk?"

Valen only nodded.

Apollo kissed my hair and slid out from under me. "Night, Harlow."

"Night, Apollo."

He gave me a smile, spared a concerned look for his friend, then headed off to bed.

Valen and I sat in silence for the next half hour or more until the movie finished, like we were both too polite to interrupt the other one. Only, we both knew that neither of us were that polite. Not with each other.

When the credits rolled, we still didn't move. Finally, when the silence was making my skin crawl, I cleared my throat.

"I guess I'll... Uh, also..." I said pathetically, then got up to leave.

Before I was out of the room, Valen had me pinned to the wall. His eyes were stormier than I'd ever seen, like proper turmoil raged inside him. I wasn't naïve enough to think it was all over little old me.

Then, I took one look at the cut at his brow and the one on his lip, and something in me melted. Melted for this boy who'd been forced to become a man so fast. I remembered the first time I'd caught wind of the possibility that Valen had killed someone. I'd been fourteen and not believed a word of it until I'd seen him in this very rumpus room, bruised and bloodied near beyond recognition. He'd looked like he'd had to fight for his very life and Apollo had spent a week nursing him. These days, I doubted anyone but his own family could come close to putting Valen Kincaid in serious danger.

I noticed his eye twitch and he sucked in a sharp breath, and I realised that I'd put my fingers to the split in his lip.

"Valen–"

"Would you run if you could now, princess?" he asked.

"Did you really kill someone?" I whispered.

"You'll have to be more specific."

"Tonight. Did you kill someone tonight?"

He looked at me like he was debating how to answer. Would he be glib? Would be lie? Would he be brutally honest, thinking it would scare me off?

"Would that stop you wanting me?" he asked.

I licked my lip as I thought how to answer. "Do you want me to stop?"

He leant his forehead to mine, and gently nuzzled his face over mine. "I should. I should want you to stop, but I don't. I can't."

"Why?" I asked, so quietly because I was afraid of the answer.

"Because I want you, Harlow. I need you. I had a gun against at my head tonight, and all I thought about was you. Burying myself in you one last time before I died. I couldn't die without you knowing what you do to me.”

“What do I do to you?”

He groaned. Desperation. Want. Need. Frustration. In answer, he took my hand and lay it over his cock. His very hard, ready cock. I inhaled and looked deep into his eyes.

I knew he saw the desire in me as clearly as I saw it in him.

“You want me to fuck you, princess? You say the word and I won’t hold back. Understood?”

I nodded. “Understood, Valen.”

He groaned again, but it was appreciative this time. His head moved like he was about to kiss me, but then he thought better of it.

“Not here,” he muttered like he was telling himself.

He took my hand and pulled me to the closest room, which happened to be his. He threw open the door and picked me up as he turned to close it again. My legs went around his waist and he smiled, only for it to turn to a grimace.

“Good girl,” he said.

“You okay?” I asked.

He nodded.

“Is this an appearances thing?” I asked.

He gave me a look like I should really know the answer to that.

I took his face in my hands and he paused in locking his door. His eyes met mine and I saw the storm soften slightly.

“I don’t need protecting,” I told him.

“I’m not–”

“And I don’t give a fuck what you get up to for your Family.”

He took a deep breath, then huffed a rough, humourless laugh.

"You might just be the death of me, Harlow Vanguard."

"Yeah, I might if you don't hurry up and fuck me."

His groan now was all appreciation and all pleasure. "Fuck, that mouth on you."

"Does the big, bad wolf like that?" I teased.

A cheeky darkness came over him. "I like it very much."

He wasted no time in propping me on his desk, sliding skirts up as he dipped his lips to my neck. I held onto him tightly as he pushed my panties out of the way, pulled himself out of his trousers and slid into me.

There was nothing slow and steady about it. No battle of wills playing out. Rather, it was like we both needed something and the other was there, offering it freely. We said nothing – exchanged no insults or challenges – but the occasional exhalation of the other's name on our lips as they skimmed necks and cheeks and jaws.

My pleasure built quickly, only to find an icy bucket of water dumped on it as a knock came at Valen's door.

"Valk?" Apollo's voice followed it.

Valen groaned. As he slid out of me, he pressed a kiss to my jaw just below my ear and muttered angrily.

"Valk?" Apollo said again.

"Just…" Valen snapped. "Wait. Unless you wanna see me with it out."

Apollo chuckled. "Your dad not leaving you any room to satisfy your urges?"

"I wouldn't blame my dad," Valen muttered to me and then finally registered the panic on my face.

He looked around, then nodded towards his wardrobe.

"I'll get him out of the way," Valen whispered.

"Look, I can come back if this is going to take a while?" Apollo said.

"Five seconds, fucker!" Valen snapped.

Just before I was out of arm reach, Valen grabbed my hand. I looked back at him and saw the regret on his face. I just didn't know whether it was regret we were interrupted, regret that Apollo almost found out, or something else entirely.

He didn't open the door until I was safely hidden in the dark wardrobe.

"What do you want?" Valen huffed.

"I wanted to check you were all right," Apollo said.

"You fucking didn't."

Apollo's laugh was anything but humoured. "All right. Maybe I wanted to check we were both all right."

"Why?" Valen's concern was obvious in his voice. "What's happened?"

"It's Harlow."

"Harlow?"

"Now, you call her Harlow," Apollo huffed a laugh.

"What's wrong with her?"

"Nothing," Apollo said. "That's the problem. The very opposite. Everything's right with her."

"All of a sudden?" Valen asked suspiciously.

"All of a sudden." Apollo's laugh this time was self-conscious. "I don't fucking know what I'm doing."

"What? You're suddenly in love with her now?"

"I've always loved her, Valk."

"What?" I whispered in time with Valen's question.

"I've just never been in love with her."

"Until now?"

"Maybe I could be."

"Fucking…" Valen muttered. "We're too fucking sober for this conversation. I'll get drinks. Smokes are on the balcony."

"You keep them out there?"

"You know how your mum feels about us smoking in the house."

"Oh," Apollo teased, his voice getting quieter as he supposedly moved to the balcony. "And you listen to my mum?"

"She lets me sleep on her nice linen," Valen said, his voice getting louder. "I'm nice to her."

"Idiot."

The wardrobe door opened, and I saw Valen wave me out.

"What the fuck?" I asked him as he surreptitiously bundled me out of his door.

"I don't know," he answered.

"You guys talk about me a lot?" I accused.

"This is the first time," Valen answered, looking at me hard.

I looked at his bedroom door like I could see Apollo through it. Apollo who had gone to his best friend to talk about how he felt about me. I didn't know what or how to feel about that.

"And it will be the last," Valen added.

I put my hand on his chest to stop him leaving. "We…"

The corner of his lip tipped up. "You want more?"

I opened my mouth and then closed it. I didn't know what I

wanted.

Being near Valen, breathing him in, feeling his tight body under my hand, my clit tingled and I wanted him to finish what he started. Whatever power he had over me, it was stronger than whatever was going on in Apollo's head right now. That feeling that we needed something from the other was niggling at me annoyingly. I couldn't shake it.

Valen caressed my cheek and tipped my face to look at him. "I'll come see you when he's asleep," he said softly.

I nodded, then darted away to my room before Apollo could come and see what was taking Valen so long about getting a couple of drinks.

I tried to distract myself with books and games and even showered. But, if Valen came to me later that night, it was after I'd fallen asleep, too exhausted to keep myself awake to wait for him any longer.

Chapter Thirteen

I was a mess. I couldn't even think about Valen without my clit tingling and my stomach twisting in desire. The things he'd done to me. The things I knew he could – would – still do to me. If only I let him.

By Sunday, I'd mostly discounted whatever he and Apollo had talked about on Wednesday night as nothing more than a follow on from Archer's announcement at breakfast. Of course Apollo was thinking about us when his father was making him. Deep down – way deep down – Apollo was a good guy and he'd want to be in love with me if he could. How unfortunate then that we couldn't just be in love with whoever we wanted.

One thing it had made obvious was that I couldn't keep up whatever I was doing with Valen. I'd have to stop at some point, so it might as well be now. While I could still walk away with some dignity in tact. Not that my clit much liked that decision.

Thankfully, Florence was there and trying to take my mind off it all as well as she was able as we got ready for the Halloween party.

"One more vine?" she asked me from over by the mirror.

I looked at her. "Huh?"

She looked back at me and saw me with my fingers on the doorknob. She grinned. "Where are you going?"

"To get us some drinks. Fuck knows I need many."

She snorted. "You don't need any to end up in a cupboard with Valen," she reminded me. "But many may lead you to other places with him."

My fingers fell. "Because that's just what I need…" I muttered.

She laughed. "No. But we do both need drinks. And you can go and perve on Valen while you're there."

"That is definitely, totally not…" I sighed. "Exactly what I was going to do. Ugh. What's wrong with me?"

"You're finally getting some and it's *ah-mazing*," Florence laughed.

"Shut up."

"Drinks," she reminded me as she went back to arranging her hair for her costume.

Mine was still sitting in its bag on the hook of my wardrobe door. I'd not even looked at it yet since it had arrived from the tailor, and told Florence she wasn't allowed either. Still, the boys were usually half-dressed – and half-drunk – by now so I might get an idea of what was in store for me if I saw Apollo.

As I walked out of my room, I bumped into Marco.

"Heya, missus," he chuckled as he jumped out of my way, and I did a double take.

His hair was sticking straight up. He wore all black; jeans, short-sleeved tee, boots. His eyes were outlined heavily with black eyeliner. And his hair was blacker than usual.

"Marco," I said with a nod.

"Can I get ye anything?" he asked, his accent always stronger when he'd been drinking.

"Just getting a drink for me and Florence."

He grinned cheekily. "Ah, the delectable Florence. And what's she coming as tonight, might I ask?"

I looked him over, not even sure that counted as a costume. "And what are you? A My Chemical Romance reject circa 2004?" I snarked.

His grin widened. "Oh, sass," he cooed. "God said you were getting a spine. It does look lovely on ye, missus."

"Watch yourself, Marco," I warned him.

He looked me up and down. "And what are you tonight?"

"Undressed," I told him as we made our way to the rumpus room.

That floor of that wing housed my, Apollo's and Valen's rooms – thankfully all with ensuites – a spare room, a bathroom, and a lounge complete with kitchenette for drinks and snacks to save us trooping to the main kitchen constantly.

"Cheeky," Marco warned. "I don't think God will look kindly on people seeing his missus in all her glory."

"I assure you, there is very little glorious about me."

"Ah, that's not true. Ye're a right princess."

I paused to look at him as we stopped by the fridge. "Was that a compliment, Marco?"

He gave me a cute grin and kick of his head as he looked at his shoes. It was all for show, but it did the trick. "I'm a nice boy, really."

"That, you are definitely not," I laughed. "And I won't be fooled into thinking otherwise."

"Marco," came the smooth, deep tones of Valen Kincaid.

My heart thumped in my chest, and I so badly wanted to turn around and look at him. But that way lay danger and I wasn't going to let myself give into him again. I didn't think I'd be strong enough.

"Boss," Marco said flippantly.

"Your turn."

Marco gave me a nod and a wink, which I returned with a smile, and sauntered off.

I gave it a few moments, lingering about getting Florence and me a couple of drinks out of the fridge to avoid running into Valen. I languidly grabbed two bottles of cola, picked up a bottle of fernet, and turned to head back to Florence.

Except, Valen was still standing there.

I dropped the fernet in surprise, thankful for the thick carpeting saving the bottle from breaking. As I took Valen in, I didn't even have any words. It wasn't anything new to me, but things had changed between us now and I couldn't help my reaction to him.

He was the same old Valen, just in nothing but a low-slung towel, water droplets still clinging to his body like they were loathe to let go. I didn't much blame them. His hair hung into his eyes, but I knew he was watching me.

He said nothing.

I gave him a terse nod, picked up the bottle of fernet and hurried back to my room where Florence had clearly been in the bag on my hook.

"Oh, snap," she said, looking at me.

I took in the dress and smiled in satisfaction. "Oh, snap indeed."

"Tell me Apollo didn't come up with this."

I shrugged, faux coy, as I put the drinks down. "Half of it."

"Half of it?"

I nodded. "I might have got them to shorten it at the fitting."

Florence gave me a very proud smirk. "Shorten. Tighten. Lower?"

"Maybe."

"For Apollo or Valen?"

"Why not both?" I asked her.

"Oh, you're gonna give me a run for my money," she said.

We steadily made our way through the colas and the bottle of fernet as we finished up with our hair and makeup. By the time we were both dressed and ready, I felt eerily calm despite the amount – or lack thereof – of clothes in which I was about to walk out of my room and down to a party full of our school mates.

"No going back now," Florence said.

"Nope."

"They'll probably never look at you the same."

"Good."

She nodded. "Okay, then. Good. Let's do this."

We headed for the terrace where the party had been set up. Braziers roared to keep everyone warm, which was good because, despite the chill in the weather, most people were a sexy version of something.

I saw Apollo talking to Tyson and made a beeline for him. People noticed me as I walked past. I didn't care about the whispers or the cat calls, encouraging or not. I was living with a little freedom, and I loved it.

Apollo's eyes finally fell on me and there went that jaw drop again. His eyes nearly bugging out of his head. I'd never seen him have that reaction to me before. He always looked at me with warmth and affection, but never that. Never actual – possible – desire.

For a moment, the feeling was mutual. He looked brilliant in his ripped shirt and tight royal blue trousers. A gorgeous Prince Adam he did make.

"Harlow Vanguard," he said appreciatively, taking my hand and making me spin for him.

"I…might have made a couple of changes…" I said with a smile.

He pulled me close. "I'm glad."

"Yeah?" I asked.

He nudged my nose with his. "Yeah."

As clichéd as Beauty and the Beast was, it wasn't something we'd done before. And I'd certainly never turned up in front of a party full of our school mates in a bright yellow dress with a tiny but full skirt with a cinched waist, and the material skimming over my breasts. Florence and I had even got some brown hair chalk to temporarily colour my curls appropriately.

Apollo drew me close to his body as he looked Florence over. "Some sort of faerie…?" he guessed and she smiled.

"Persephone. Queen of the Underworld."

Apollo grinned. "Of course. I'd expect nothing less."

Florence flitted around the party, but Apollo kept me with him. Always a hand on me, lingering. His lips near my ear. Telling me how beautiful I looked. I felt it. For once in my life, I felt as beautiful as people told me I was. Because I knew Apollo and he didn't just tell me I looked good to be polite. He was more likely to do the opposite. But it was more than that, there was beauty in the small amount of freedom I'd made for myself.

The party was in full swing. Apollo was talking with other Saints, but the Angels were nowhere in sight.

Suddenly, a thunderous noise crept up and overtook the music coming from the speakers. The whole party turned around, looking this way and that, trying to work out where the noise was coming from.

Finally, four motorcycles could be seen coming across the lawn.

"Your mum's going to be pissed," I said to Apollo and he just grinned.

"She'll get over it."

"Did you know they were doing this?"

He shook his head. "No, but trust my Angels to make an entrance."

Marco must have got his hands on a smoke machine because fog surrounded the riders as they pulled up to the side of the party, making them look eerie and mysterious. The engines shut off and the four men dismounted as one unit, to walk towards everyone. Their forms emerged from the fog and we could all take them in properly.

"Well, fuck me sideways," Florence muttered as she looked them over, and I was tempted to agree with her.

The four Angels were none other than the Four Horsemen. Each one in little more than heavy boots, a pair of tight jeans and a piece or two of armour, leaving their torsos naked and on full display to be ogled and worshipped by the lesser beings among them.

Gage was Famine. His jeans were pale brown and he alone wore no armour. His face and body had been painted like he weighed half as much as he did, little more than skin and bone. His hair hung drab around his face. But he still looked good.

Fender was Plague. His jeans and armour were neon green. He wore shoulder and forearm armour in a shiny bright green with a brace of rats dangling from his belt. His whole body shimmered a ghostly, pearlescent green-white.

Marco was Death. He still wore the black jeans, but gone was the tee. His armour clung to one shoulder, and he wore leather wraps around his forearms. His face was painted in a bewitching skull design, and great black wings sprouted from his back. The way he carried himself, you knew he was proud of their costumes.

And Valen.

Valen was War.

Apt considering the way he made me feel inside.

His jeans were deep red, like blood. His armour was only on one shoulder, with a strap to hold it in place over his chest, and he wore similar leather wraps, in red, on his forearms like Marco. His hair had been coloured a vibrant red and styled spikey and jagged. His eyes were outlined in heavy, smudged black and every single scar on his body had been outlined and highlighted.

I knew I shouldn't have liked it, but I did.

A cheer rose up and Marco threw his hands in the air in victory. The cheer doubled in volume. Marco lapped it up as he and the other Angels walked over to their God.

"Definitely not the Musketeers," Apollo commented dryly, hugging me tight.

Valen's eyes skipped right over me like he was looking for something, but I didn't know what. Or who. He just muttered something unintelligible and stalked off through the party.

"You look lovely, missus," Marco said to me.

I smiled. "Not as impressive as you. Angel, indeed."

He laughed. "And do my eyes deceive me or is that fair Persephone I see in front of me."

Florence gave him a once over. "That's Queen to you, Death."

Marco's grin was made all the more wicked by his face paint. "Death bows to you, my queen."

Oh, I was not being involved with that any more than I needed to be.

With Apollo distracted by the other Angels, I took the opportunity to slip away and get a drink. As I was waiting by the bar, Valen appeared beside me. Heat emanated from him, and I so desperately wanted to run my hands over the rigid exposed contours of his body.

"I thought it was bold of Apollo to be fondling a brunette in public."

"Excuse me?" I asked indignantly.

"You coloured your hair."

I huffed. "So did you."

"It's temporary."

"So is mine."

"Shame."

"You like it brown?" I asked, but he ignored it.

"And, what the fuck do you call this?" he asked as he flicked the bottom of my skirt.

"A costume, Valen," I told him.

"You quite happy exposing so much of yourself?"

"Are you?"

He ignored the meaning of my question and turned it back on me. "Happy with you exposing that much? No."

I looked him in the eye. "Apollo doesn't seem to mind."

He stepped closer to me. "No. Because God hasn't stopped to consider that anyone else will even *think* of touching what's his."

"Oh, and you do. Don't you, Valen?" I taunted. "You want to touch it so very much."

He growled, low. He looked around quickly, grabbed my arm and pulled me inside. He kept right on pulling – in no way hurting me – until he had us in one of the most out of the way bathrooms on the second floor and had the door closed and locked behind us.

His hands went to my waist and his nose was by my temple. Something about it felt more reverent than usual. I could feel how tense he was. Again, like he was either holding himself back or in place, or both. My heart skipped in my chest and my stomach fluttered.

"I will have you screaming my name," he breathed into my ear. "I'll make you cum, but even then I will thrust deep into you.

Relentlessly. I will be so deep inside you that you'll never forget the feel of me. And I won't stop until I've given you every ounce of pleasure your body can handle. Understood?"

It was tempting. There was no denying it. My clit throbbed angrily. I didn't know if it was angrier at him for promising it and not giving it right away, or with me for what I was about it do.

"Understood?" he asked again when I said nothing.

I couldn't give in to him. I wanted so badly to have him fuck me senseless, but I couldn't. I had to be stronger than this apparently insatiable lust I had for him.

I shook my head. "No."

He pulled away sightly. "No?" he asked, obviously surprised.

I nodded, feeling slightly more emboldened. "No."

He sucked on his teeth and took a noticeable step backwards. "No," he mused, like it was foreign concept to him.

"Look, I'm sure it's a novel theory, but–"

"I would do a great many things to you, princess," he said, his voice low and angry, his face like thunder. "I would cross a lot of boundaries to hear the breathy moan of my name on your lips as your pussy tightens on my cock. But 'no' is not one of those."

Holy shit. But wait, what?

If I hadn't felt nearly mad from denying myself him before, I certainly was now.

As he looked at me, his expression changed. He stepped towards me again and took my face in his hands.

"I won't hurt you, Harlow," he said softly, then his eyebrow quirked and there was mischief in his eyes. "Not unless you asked."

I licked my lip and breathed heavily. "I shouldn't want you," I heard myself whisper.

The mischief was gone again. "I shouldn't want you."

The air around us seemed charged. Like one move and we'd be zapped by invisible electricity. My heart thudded in my chest. I felt my hand touch his chest. It fisted around the leather strap across his skin.

I couldn't tell if I pulled him to me, but it felt like he came of his own accord.

Our lips met, almost hesitantly at first, softly. Almost like he was waiting to see if I'd pull away. When I didn't, his hand slid to the back of my head, and he pulled me to him in a close embrace. I wrapped my arms around his broad shoulders and kissed him back. It wasn't what I'd expected. It wasn't blazing white-hot passion, but it was full of need. Desire swirled around us as we stumbled backwards.

He propped me onto the counter behind me and pressed into me close.

It hadn't occurred to me before then that we'd never kissed. Not as in each other's lips. He'd kissed my body. I was sure I'd kissed his. But this was the first time we'd properly kissed.

Hands roamed over each other's body with no particular destination or purpose. Even as our kiss deepened, the goal wasn't how many orgasms in ten minutes.

"Fuck," he groaned against my lips. "Why are you so tempting?"

"Why are you?" I countered.

He slowly drew his lips from mine, leant his forehead to mine and breathed out deeply. I looked into his eyes and had no idea what I saw there. Almost as though he had to stop himself from saying any more, he kissed me again.

I took his hand where it lay on my waist and slid it up my thigh and under my skirt.

Call me weak, but there were ways he could ease this unrelenting need in me without me letting his cock in me. Even if that was actually what I wanted.

Valen's fingers trailed over me lightly. Not in a teasing, denial sort of way, more like foreplay. I rocked against him, encouraging him. Without breaking our kiss, he slid his hand into my panties and didn't stop sliding until his middle two fingers were buried deep inside me. I was so wet for him that there was zero resistance.

He thrust almost lazily as he kissed me deeper, his tongue sweeping into my mouth in a similar rhythm to his fingers. I moaned softly against his lips.

His thumb found my clit, grazing it softly as his fingers kept up their slow and steady pace inside me. My hips rocked with him.

It was slow. It was sensual.

My orgasm crept up on me and enveloped me like a big warm bed at the end of a really hard day. And the whole time, Valen's lips barely left mine. Not for more than a moment as they explored my cheek or down my neck.

He stroked me softly and gently as I got my breath back, teasing out the last strings of pleasure as they zinged heat around my body.

Suddenly, there was a buzzing at my leg. I looked down and

realised it was coming from his pocket.

"Always interrupted," he murmured a kiss against my temple as he pulled his phone from his pocket. He read over the text and sighed. "Marco's insisting on a photo shoot," he said, disgust evident in his voice.

I laughed, then bit my lip to stop it as he looked up at me sharply.

"Sorry," I said. "But…you do look…awesome."

He shook his head as his fingers trailed down my cheek and he looked at me tenderly. "You're beautiful, Harlow," he said, his eyes never leaving mine.

I felt like, maybe, he wasn't just referring to my outsides.

"Valen, I–"

He shook his head. "Not now," he pled. "Just let me have now."

I wasn't exactly sure what he meant by that, but I nodded.

He gave me a sad smile, pressed a lingering, longing kiss to my lips, then slipped out of the bathroom.

With a sigh, I slid off the counter and turned to the mirror. My makeup was a little smudged, but it could have been worse. Considering how much body paint was going around that night, it definitely could have been worse.

For example, once I was cleaned up and back at the party, I noticed that Florence had a little more shading going on than previously and Marco's skull looked like it needed a trip to the dentist.

Chapter Fourteen

The next morning, pretty much the whole of the top two year levels were the worse for wear. Those few who hadn't come to Apollo's party weren't the type to drink even if they had come.

Apollo, Valen, and I had got a Callahan car back to school that morning, arriving just in time for morning mass. Apollo didn't take his sunglasses off until we were sitting down in our pew, and Valen didn't even bother. Sister Agnes almost told him off, but seemed to think better of it on second thought.

As I sat down next to Florence, I could feel her buzzing with questions. She knew I'd snuck off with Valen, of course she did, but we'd yet to have time to really talk about it.

The rest of the party had passed in a blur. All I could remember was lots of laughing, always smiling, Apollo's hand on me constantly, his lips at my ear, and the ache in my feet suggested there had been a lot of dancing involved. I couldn't remember Florence getting on the bus to head back to school. I was fairly certain I'd tried to convince her to stay with me, but she'd never like the Callahan Estate. She said it was full of ghosts, whatever that meant.

Choir practice was the first time we'd really been together without either Apollo or one of his Angels being within ear shot. It was like Marco knew we had something to talk about and was trying to stall us as long as possible.

"So?" Florence whispered while we were supposed to be singing the aria.

"So, what?" I whispered back.

"What happened?"

"What do you think happened?"

"You fucked him?"

Exie turned around with a raised eyebrow and Florence flashed her a quick grin. As much as I liked Exie, she was just another Saint to Florence, and I didn't blame her. Exie hadn't bothered to get to know Florence either.

"Well?" Florence pressed.

Just as I opened my mouth, Sister Felicia tapped her baton on the music stand in front of her and the music came to a stop.

"If we're interrupting you, Miss Walton, Miss Vanguard?" she said.

"No, Sister," Florence said. "Sorry, Sister."

"Good, because–"

At that moment, Brighton's hand flew to his mouth and he ran from the room. It had been happening on and off all day. One kid had even thrown up all over the floor of the dining hall. The teachers and nuns had been doing their best to ignore it. As Sister Felicia did now. Almost.

"There are worse interruptions," she said coldly. "Would it prove less distracting if you were to come to the front, Miss

Vanguard?"

I ducked my head. "Yes, Sister," I answered as I squeezed my way to the front, changing places with Exie.

So, it wasn't until after Florence had finished in the Art Studio that we had a chance to talk. I knew how much she was looking forward to it, so I made sure to leave Apollo in time to be walking through the front doors to the girls dorm at the same time as her.

"You have so much to spill," Florence told me as we headed up the stairs.

"I don't think I have anything of interest," I teased.

"You cannot leave me hanging. I live vicariously through you, Harlow."

I laughed. "You do enough *living* for the both of us."

"And, yet, I need to know what happened."

"When?"

"Last week. Last night?"

"And what about you?" I accused.

"What about me?" she tried.

I scoffed. "You and Marco?"

As we dropped onto our beds, she waved her hand dismissively. "Me and Marco is far less interesting than you and Valen."

"That's a hundred times not true."

"It so is. You've wanted him for years and now you finally get to do him. And you do, like all the time!"

"Well, I didn't."

She frowned. "You can't lie to me. I know you did."

"Not last night," I amended.

Her frown deepened, but there was keen interest there. "What do you mean you didn't last night? What did you do?"

I ran my tongue over my teeth, not sure why I was suddenly so hesitant to tell her. I didn't want to hide it. I felt like it had more to do with me not wanting to know it meant something.

"He kissed me," I said quickly.

She rolled her eyes as she rolled onto her stomach. "Uh huh. Boring."

I shook my head. "No, I mean he kissed me."

She looked at me, one eyebrow raised in question. "He kissed you?" she asked, like she still couldn't see what was so great about it.

I nodded.

"He kissed you..." Her eyes widened as she worked it out. "For the first time?"

I nodded again.

"You mean, he's fucked you stupid but never kissed you before last night?"

Yet another nod.

"Huh," she said, sitting back up again.

"Huh, what?" I asked.

She looked at me like she was thinking. "And you didn't do anything else?"

"He...got me off. It was..."

"Different?" she guessed.

"Yeah."

"How was he this morning?"

I shrugged. "Hungover like the rest of us."

He'd been in a mood, more sour than usual, as if that was possible. He'd done nothing but grunt and snap at Apollo. Just before we'd got into the car, Apollo finally realised he'd taken it too far when Valen took a swing at him. Lucky for Apollo, Valen had also pulled his fist up short so as not to actually make contact. As far as I knew, Apollo and Valen hadn't spoken since. They'd been together all day, just not spoken.

She nodded. "He was putting them away last night."

"When did you see him last night? I thought you were too busy sucking face with Marco?"

She grinned. "I'm a woman. I multi-task."

"I'm a woman and I don't multi-task," I muttered.

"I seem to recall his intake got rapidly faster the lower Apollo's hand got on your arse."

I snorted. "What?"

She nodded, adamant. "Yep."

I shook my head. "No. No. Because that would imply that Valen cared, and he doesn't."

"Doesn't he?"

"He did knock out Arnie..." I mused. "But that was for Apollo."

"Was it, though?"

"Of course it was."

Florence shrugged. "It's new ground. You're fucking Valen–"

"Past tense."

She looked at me like she knew I was full of shit. "And Apollo's getting snugglier."

"Snugglier?"

"Don't tell me you haven't noticed."

I looked down at where I was playing with my shoelace. "No. I mean, I guess I have..."

"How are you feeling about it all?"

I let out a huge breath. "I haven't really given myself much time to think about it."

"Do you think you should?"

"I don't... Should I?"

"I don't know. I'm not your bloody conscience. I'm legit asking if *you* think now is a good time? Does it matter that Apollo's... I don't know, paying attention?"

I chewed my lip and fiddled with my shoelace some more as I thought about it.

Did I need to think about what was happening? Apollo was taking notice, but I'd also told myself rather sternly that I was done with Valen. I was fine with casual sex – after all, the boys certainly had plenty of it, so why shouldn't I – but there was casual sex, and then there was hate fucking a guy you couldn't stand.

"I don't know," I told her honestly. "But I know I have to be stronger than my want for Valen. I've got limited power in my life. The least I can control is my own libido, surely."

Florence snorted. "Yeah, good luck with that."

I frowned at her. "Not helping."

"That," she said, pointing at me, "isn't my job. Go on, then. What about Apollo?"

"What about him?" I asked.

"Well, what do we think about him waking up?"

I sighed and flopped back on my bed. "I don't know about that either."

"It's what you wanted, isn't it?"

"Sort of," I said lamely.

"Help me out here, Harlow," she begged. "I'm in your corner, I'll support whatever you need, but I just don't get it."

"I guess it's what I wanted," I said. "I'm expected to marry him, so I know we have to go from fake to real eventually. I just don't know if I want it now."

"You worried he won't be faithful?"

I laughed. I had to. "No. Oddly, that's not high on my priority list."

"What, then?"

"We just don't have that relationship. I don't see him that way."

"But you've thought about it?"

"I guess. He's hot. It doesn't gross me out or anything. I just..." I sighed. "I don't know what me in a relationship of any kind looks like. I feel like I haven't got me figured out, so how can I have Apollo and me figured out."

"Well, let's figure you out!"

I smiled at her. "And that's the problem. What's the point in figuring me out if I'm just going to be Apollo's princess anyway?"

"Okay...?"

I took a big breath. "I love my parents. Sure, they're basically pimping me out, but I love them and they love me. I don't want to let them down. So, I've accepted I'll marry Apollo one day. Our mums are legit just excited about it. I don't want to crush their hopes and dreams." Plus, there was the whole people dying issue, but I couldn't bring myself to voice that with Florence.

"What about your hopes and dreams?"

"I don't have any."

"What?"

"What's the point when my destiny is set?"

"But you've always talked about getting out. You're just waiting for a way."

My laugh was anything but humoured. "Yeah. And part of me wants that, but no part of me has ever believed I can find it. I have to marry Apollo. And I just hope that, before that day, we fall in love. It's like I'm waiting for him to notice me but, at the same time, I don't want him to."

"Why?"

"Because that's the day my life ends. It's also the day it finally begins."

"So, what *are* you going to do?"

"In what way?" I asked.

"Well, if Apollo's paying more attention, are you going to stop fucking Valen?"

"I'm going to stop fucking Valen, but not for Apollo."

She scoffed much the same way she had when I said it before. "Okay. Let's pretend for a moment that's true –"

"Florence..." I warned her.

"Harlow..." she mimicked. "I'm being realistic here."

I raised my eyebrow at her. "Are you?"

She nodded. "Yes. Why do you have to stop fucking Valen?"

I sighed. "Because I hate him."

"That just seems like more reason to keep doing it."

I smiled despite myself. I wouldn't admit out loud that part of me thought, if I kept going it, I'd never be able to stop. By admitting it out loud, I could no longer deny it. And I had to stop some day. Some day I had to be faithful to Apollo. So, why not stop now when I had a chance of succeeding?

"What are you going to do about both of them?" Florence asked when I didn't respond.

I huffed. "Do I have to anything about either of them?"

"Yes. You do. You can tell yourself you're not going to hook up with Valen again, but we both know that's shit. The way Apollo's going, you might end up hooking up with him. Are you prepared? Are you going to do both of them at the same time?"

"Literally?"

She laughed. "I would pay to see that." She frowned. "No. Not see. That's not my thing. I'd pay to hear about it. But, no. Like juggling them both."

I shrugged. "If I was stupid enough and unable to control myself enough to end up being with Valen again *and*, as unlikely as it seems, Apollo somehow actually wanted the woman he's supposed to marry..."

"Then?"

It was weird how easily the answer came to me.

"Then, without any kind of promise of something different... Without some sign that Apollo was going to give up his Magdalens... Then, yeah. I'd juggle them both."

Florence and I looked at each other surprisingly seriously for a second, then both laughed.

"Okay, nympho," she teased lovingly. "Good to know where we stand."

I nodded. "It is, isn't it?"

She gave me a wide grin. "It seems I rubbed off on you."

"Yeah, you're not the one that rubbed off on me," I told her cheekily.

"Valen is a very good colour on you," she commented.

"Yeah?" I asked as I got up and pulled out a book to start on my homework.

"Yeah," she said. "Very good. You're so much less..."

"Not sure that's a compliment," I told her when she didn't elaborate.

"Much less resigned."

"Leas resigned than what?" I asked. "To what?"

"Your fate."

I looked at her sceptically. "I'm still very much resigned to my fate."

"True," she conceded. "But you've also been absolutely *had* by Saint Benedict's most infamous walking wet dream."

"I thought you weren't interested in him?" I sassed.

"Oddly, that doesn't stop him being the most wanted man on campus."

"I thought that was Apollo?"

Florence scoffed. "Oh, please. We go home to men like Apollo...right after we've been hammered by guys like Valen."

"This is your Beast and Gaston argument all over again, isn't it?"

"What?" she asked as she came over to our desks. "Am I

wrong? You get Gaston to pleasure you until you can barely stand *then* go home to Adam. Beast can get in on that Gaston action as far as I'm concerned."

I laughed. "Is that your way of saying something?"

Florence's hand went to her mouth and she chuckled. "Oh, yeah. Apollo was Adam last night."

I nodded at her pointedly.

She chortled to herself. "Mayhap it is foreshadowing?"

"Foreshadowing what?"

She shrugged and tapped the side of her nose. "Your future, Miss Vanguard."

For a moment – one, single panicked moment – I worried she was right. Then, I remembered this was Florence Walton. She didn't have powers of foresight and, while she might have known who liked who and whether it was more than sex, there was nothing more between me and Valen than just sex.

After her grand declaration, Florence went on with her homework and I failed to get on with mine. At least, I didn't tap my pen incessantly on my books this time, so she had no idea that I was trying hard not to stress about whatever situation I'd found myself in.

Chapter Fifteen

"Claudio is an idiot," Florence called from the bathroom.

"I never said he wasn't," I replied with a smile as I swung around on my chair aimlessly and waited for her to get back.

"Absolutely no trust in his love."

I nodded to myself.

We'd been studying *Much Ado About Nothing* in English, and Florence had some very strong feelings about how it would have all turned out if only people talked to each other and trusted each other. But then, she was always annoyed with Shakespeare. We hadn't met anything about Shakespeare that she didn't take exception to. Had I not known her inside and out for the previous four years, I might have said she possibly had an aversion to the notion of romance. As it was, I knew her very well and was very right it saying that she did believe in love, but she also believed we had a whole lifetime to find it, so who the hell was in a rush to put a label to things?

"It's a play, Floss," I reminded her with a smile.

"Honestly," she huffed. "Can't have a good romance without a misunderstanding, can you? It's nice to know it's been that way for centuries. Sorry, Jane, you didn't invent it after all."

I laughed. For all her anger with Shakespeare, she did love Austen. I didn't blame her.

"Is it just me, though, or is Benedick kinda hot?" she asked absently.

"He's definitely fictional," I answered, still spinning my chair.

"I know Don Juan's meant to be all that, but I love me a guy with a bit of sass."

As I span, I saw Apollo at our door. He leant against the door jamb and grinned. He knew when Florence was on a tirade, and he was as amused by it as me.

"Do you think Apollo's more a Claudio or a Benedick?"

"I don't think it's safe to answer that," I told her and Apollo cracked his cheeky smirk at me.

She popped her head out of the bathroom and frowned at Apollo. "There is such a thing as knocking, you know."

He shrugged and pushed off the door. "It was open."

"So, you didn't feel the need to announce yourself? Two of us live here, you know."

"I am *well* aware," Apollo told her.

"What are you doing here anyway?" she asked, her eyes narrowing behind her glasses in suspicion.

"What are you doing with the bathroom door open?" he countered.

"None of your business."

"Again with the open doors." He shrugged. "If you want secrets, you should keep the door closed, Flo."

"It's Florence," she told him, then looked at me pointedly.

"And, we will remember that."

I frowned at her. The last thing I needed was Apollo thinking I had secrets. I wasn't sure how he'd feel if he found out about Valen and me. We might have been fake dating, but that didn't mean he wouldn't feel something about his future wife and his best friend sleeping together.

"You never told us what you were doing here," she reminded him.

"Hanging out," he answered, throwing me a smile.

"Oh no, you're not," Florence objected with a huff. "I don't want to have to deal with you two being all lovey dovey while I'm dealing with Shakespeare."

I kept my smile to myself at the evidence Florence would never let on she knew the truth behind me and Apollo.

"I thought teenage girls ate Shakespeare up?" Apollo chuckled.

Florence rolled her eyes. "Yes, because thirteen-year-old girls making poor life choices is a romance to which we all aspire," she said sarcastically, then fake gagged.

Apollo gave her a nod. "All right," he said. "Good to know. Less deaths. No suicides. Ixnay on the poison. What about comparing them to a rose?"

"What *about* comparing them to a rose?" Florence asked, still highly suspicious.

"Can I compare Harlow to a Summer's day? Am I to believe if she were named other than she was, she would be as sweet? Shall I be prepared for the course of love to not run smooth? Nay, does my Cupid kill with arrows or traps?"

Florence looked at me, then back at Apollo. She was trying very hard not to be impressed. I could see it in the way her mouth twitched. She was torn between trying not to give him any encouragement and trying to pout, and all she was doing was failing not to smile.

"You're confusing your sonnets and your plays," was what she finally said.

"Now, you're mad I know *too* much Shakespeare?" Apollo laughed.

"No one should know that much Shakespeare," Florence told him.

"Well, I'm obviously not the only one."

"Next you'll be quoting our Lady Jane," Florence scoffed sarcastically.

"There is a stubbornness about me that never can bear to be frightened at the will of others," Apollo answered.

I looked at Florence blankly, but she was gaping at Apollo. She snapped her mouth shut and narrowed her eyes.

"A truer attribution has never been appropriated," she told him and he grinned cheekily in reply.

"Selfishness must always be forgiven you know, because there is no hope of a cure."

"Oh my God. Stop," Florence breathed. "Don't you normally have…other things to do on a Wednesday after dinner?" she asked.

I knew she didn't mean 'things' but, if Apollo worked it out, he didn't comment.

He shrugged. "I made myself available."

"For what? Taking Harlow to a late-night movie?"

Apollo smiled at me. "If she likes."

"Just where are these late-night movies?" I asked him.

"My room?" he said, with just a little bit of suggestion in his voice.

I couldn't help but smile. "You propose to take me to the boys' dorm this close to curfew?"

He grinned at me, and it was actually very endearing. "I'm Apollo-fucking-Callahan, sweetheart, I can do whatever I like."

"Love the optimism. Get it out of here, Harlow," Florence said to me, but I saw the humour in her eyes.

I sighed, and huffed a rough laugh. "You want to watch a movie with me on a Wednesday night?" I asked Apollo.

"I don't much care what we do, I just wanna hang out with you."

Well, I could hardly say no to that, could I? Even if I could, I didn't want to. It was nice to be wanted, even if it was just a movie. But then, Apollo and I did movies well.

"And, what happens if we get caught?" I asked.

"Firstly, we won't," Apollo answered easily. "Secondly, if there was a chance in hell that anyone would pay enough attention to the boys' dorm... It's me. I get away with whatever I want."

"At least, you know what you are," Florence muttered loudly.

Apollo chuckled. "As do you."

"What's that supposed to mean?" she asked.

Apollo looked her over. "You just do you, Flo. It's a good look."

She frowned. "Wish I could say the same."

This probably need not go on any longer than it had to.

"All right, just let me change and we can go," I told Apollo.

He held a hand out for mine. "No need. You look–"

"Be very careful how you finish that sentence," Florence warned.

"Comfy," Apollo laughed. "You look comfy."

And I was comfy. Slouchy trackies, slipper boots, a baggy hoodie that might have been his once, no makeup, and my hair in a messy bun. I was the very definition of comfortable.

"Don't say that like it's a bad thing," I said with a smile.

He shook his head. "No. No. It's definitely not that."

The look in his eyes told me he was being sincere. He honestly didn't care what I looked like – what I wore – he just wanted to be with me.

I held my hand to Florence, who threw me my phone. As I put it into my pocket, I shrugged at Apollo. "All right, be it on your head," I said.

"It's a risk I'm willing to take," he said, reaching for my hand again.

I took it and looked at Florence. "I'll see you later."

She nodded. "Don't do anything I wouldn't do."

"I didn't realise such a thing existed," I teased her, and Apollo snorted like he was trying not to laugh.

She narrowed her eyes at him, but smiled at me. "It is a very small list, true," she admitted.

"Bye," I said.

"Have a good night," she called to me before turning to Apollo. "Treat her right!"

Apollo bowed. "Always."

I saw the look on Florence's face. She didn't believe him for a second. Of course, she didn't. She didn't think he'd ever treated me right. But he'd never promised me anything, so I wasn't really sure that he'd treated me wrong. To me, those were two very different things.

Apollo swung my hand casually as we walked to the boys' dorm.

"What do you want to watch?" he asked me, sounding like the happiest guy in the world, utterly content with where he was, who he was with, and what he was doing.

I shrugged. "I don't mind. You didn't have a plan?"

He gave me a coy smirk. "Not really. I just felt like seeing you, and the rest has just kinda fallen into place. Or not," he chuckled. "As the case may be."

We got back to his room without seeing many people. What people we did see didn't look at us twice. Why would they? It was just Apollo and his girlfriend. They were known to walk around holding hands. That we were headed to his room at almost curfew also wouldn't have given them a second thought. By and large, the assumption was that we had sex. Whether they thought I was absolutely shit in bed and that's why he fucked around, or whether he just had serious kinks I wasn't into, I didn't know and I didn't care to. Let them think what they wanted. Nothing they thought changed the reality of the complex situation Apollo and I had found ourselves in.

I dropped onto the couch in his room as he hunted down the remotes.

It was a warm room and I'd always felt comfortable in it. The carpets were blue and golden yellow, the wood a rich walnut, and all the accents were in golds and blacks and whites. His was a room designed for entertaining. Around the fireplace were large plush couches, one facing an enormous TV on the wall. There was an actual bar and fridge. Behind a half-wall partition was his bed and desk, and the doors to his bathroom and wardrobe. Like his room at the Callahan Estate, it was lived in. Piles of clothes and books, pictures and posters, the random paraphernalia that accumulated in a lived in space. He'd never been into tidying and who needed to when you had people for that? True, at school, it was the Saintlings who tidied up after him, but it still meant he didn't have to do it himself.

Apollo got us some drinks and snacks, and I settled against him as I always did. His arm was around my shoulder and we fell into the old familiar routine, sitting in comfortable silence as we watched a movie. Neither of us felt the need to break the silence until a Christmas scene came on.

"I *cannot* wait until the Christmas holidays," he said excitedly.

"Really?" I laughed, thinking it an awfully random thing for him to say.

He nodded. "Really."

"We're not even a week through this term."

"I know." He nodded again. "Aren't you going to ask why?" he promoted when I didn't.

I smiled at him. "All right. Why?"

"Because I'll get you all to myself."

"And what do you call this?"

"I call this counting down the seconds until you have to leave me," he said, and his tone was almost sorrowful.

"That's almost cute," I told him, and he kissed my cheek enthusiastically.

"Would you change it?" he asked suddenly a few moments later.

"Change what?" I asked.

"Propriety. Appearances. Our world thrives on them. Would you change it if you could?"

I looked him over, thinking it a rather weird question. There were a great many things I'd change if I could.

And there went that word again. Appearances. Valen had used that word. It meant more to them than it did me, obviously. But one had to wonder who it was affecting more.

"What do you mean?" I asked carefully.

Apollo's hand slid up under my jumper and gently caressed the skin of my stomach. "If we didn't have to worry about those things, you could, for example, stay the night without worrying about what people would say."

I had a feeling they'd be more complimentary about me spending the night than any of his Magdalens. But then, I'd never heard of one staying the night before. Did staying the night mean something else? Something more? Or was it just harder to convince people that nothing scandalous had gone on?

I wasn't sure what Apollo wanted. I didn't know what I wanted. His hand was warm on my stomach, and I didn't hate it there. So, not knowing what else to do, I aimed for a joke.

"Are you propositioning me, Apollo?"

Thankfully, he laughed as his nose brushed along the shell of my ear. "I like spending time with you. I really enjoyed last holidays."

Apollo's nose trailed over my neck, my jaw, my cheek. It was soft and it made my heart beat faster in my chest. I lay my hand on his cheek and he looked at me through hooded eyes. There was that look again. Like he wanted me. Actually wanted me. I felt myself swallow hard. Was this it? Was this the moment our relationship changed? It's not like we'd never kissed before, but that had been the curiosity of the pre-teen in us and had only happened a couple of times. I suspected he'd had quite a bit more practice since then.

But nothing happened.

Apollo's phone buzzed and I felt him shift against me. He cleared his throat and kissed my cheek.

"It's getting late, you should probably get back," he said before pulling away from me.

Seriously? Was he seriously kicking me out because of a booty call? Had he organised it? And was this before or after he so *desperately* wanted to hang out with me?

But I wasn't going to say any of that because I didn't want to open that can of worms. I didn't want to have a conversation about what we were doing. Or, more obviously at that point, what we weren't doing. I still didn't know how I felt about us actually doing that. I hadn't wanted him to stop touching me, but I wasn't sure that meant I wanted him to keep touching me.

Apollo sent off a message and I had no choice but to nod and stand up.

"No, sure. Class tomorrow and all that."

"The fuck do you want?" came a very angry voice at Apollo's door.

"Valk," Apollo said with a smile. "Can you take Harlow back to her room for me?"

Valen looked at me like I was less than a bug on the bottom of his shoe. "You brought her here, why can't you?"

"Because I'm asking you."

Valen's lip rippled with a barely repressed snarl. "I'm busy, do it yourself."

Apollo frowned at Valen, and I didn't blame him. Valen had never outright said no to Apollo for anything. Valen was known to avoid me at the best of times, but this was something else.

"Yeah, all right..." Apollo said slowly, not sounding pleased but not arguing.

"It's fine," I said. "I'm a big girl, I can walk myself."

"You sure?"

"What other option is there?" I asked.

If Apollo realised I was giving him a chance to step up, he didn't take it. Instead, he nodded.

"Okay, good."

"If you don't need me..." Valen said pointedly.

Apollo shook his head and Valen stalked out.

"Good night," I said to Apollo, walking out before he had a chance to reply. It didn't take a genius to notice he didn't follow me.

"Oi!" I hissed at Valen once Apollo's door was closed behind me.

Valen just growled and headed for the stairs. I ran to keep up with him through the darkened halls.

"Fine!" I snapped. "I guess I'll just see if Arnie Brickworth's still awake!"

Okay, I'd wanted a rise out of him, but that may have been taking it too far.

Valen whirled on me and shoved me back against the wall. His face was dark and thunderous. His jaw clenched and he was breathing heavily.

"You go back to your room," he ordered.

This wasn't the party in the woods. There was no hidden meaning. There was no necessity. He just wanted to order me around for the sake of being bossy.

"Are you going back to yours?" I countered.

He huffed. "I don't answer to you, princess."

"So it seems. You don't answer to me. You don't talk to me. You don't even look at me if you don't have to."

"I hate you," he seethed.

"Is that all?"

"Yes."

"I thought you could hate me and still want me."

"Not anymore."

I couldn't pretend that didn't hurt. "Why?"

"Because I have to."

"Why now? What's changed since last week?"

Last week, when it felt like we were the only two people in the world who could give each other exactly what the other one needed.

"God's woken up, princess. He finally realises what he has." He looked me over. "How happy you must be. You've finally got what you always wanted. God's attention."

I shoved against him. He swayed away for good measure, but as he swayed back he came closer. His hand went to my hip. The flutter in my stomach didn't stop me feeling angry with him.

"Of course. Because you know what I've always wanted," I said sarcastically.

There was a wicked gleam in his eye and a cheeky tilt to the corner of his lips. "I know plenty about what you want, princess." His nose dropped to my ear and my heart stuttered to life. "I feel very confident in saying I know exactly what you want...given how easily you melt for me..."

"Ugh!" I pushed against him again, but he didn't move. "Well, clearly God has some learning to do if he's still wetting his cock in any idiot who'll spread her legs for him."

"Why should I give a fuck who he sticks it in?"

"I don't know, Valen," I sassed. "Why should you? You're only avoiding me because of him."

He snarled. "I don't expect you to understand."

I was tired. I was upset. I was angry.

Here these boys were, dictating my life. Again. They got to do whatever they wanted while I was denied one simple thing I wanted. It was one thing. Was it really so much to ask to have one thing for myself?

"No, Valen," I said quietly. "No. I don't understand. I don't understand why Apollo gets to fuck around with as many girls as he wants and I... I can't have the one man – the *one* man – I want."

When I shoved against him this time, he didn't hold his ground. He stumbled backwards like I'd actually surprised him for once. But, I didn't care. I'd said too much.

Idiot.

I ran out of the boys' dorm, tears hot in my eyes. It wasn't fair. None of it. And I didn't know what they wanted from me.

Apollo had spent the night like it was a date, like maybe we were making progress. Whatever that meant. Florence had been right when she'd said he was being more attentive. Valen was certainly right when he pointed out I had Apollo's attention. And yet he still kicked me out for a Magdalen? To add insult to injury, Valen wasn't going near me because he thought Apollo had suddenly decided to claim me?

I wasn't standing for it.

When I got back to our room, Florence was still awake.

"How did it...?" Her question died on her lips as she took in my face. "What?"

"Those boys are going to pay," I said, my voice like acid.

"Okay. Loving it. Why?"

I closed our door behind me and felt my teeth grinding.

"Apollo had the audacity – the *fucking* audacity, Florence – to kick me out so he could have a Magdalen visit."

"He didn't!"

"He did."

"Arsehole."

I nodded. "Yes."

"And the other one?"

"He apparently *only* hates me, because he has to now that

Apollo's paying attention."

"...to a Magdalen?"

"To me. Apparently, despite the fact Apollo's off fucking whoever he likes, Valen denies he still wants me."

"Oh, juicy. What's the plan, then?"

"Revenge."

"Love it. Tell me more."

We were up way too late plotting my revenge. I wasn't the only one falling asleep in morning mass. Apollo, bless him, thought it was because he'd kept me up too late. I wondered how long he'd kept the Magdalen up...or, rather, how long she'd kept him up.

CHAPTER SIXTEEN

Trying to style a boarding school uniform for the purpose of seducing-slash-punishing a guy like Valen Kincaid took some effort and no small amount of creativity, and still the results were mediocre at best.

"I mean, look," Florence said on Friday morning, "we could celebrate the fact you were out of bed before eight?"

"Is that seriously how much faith you have in this enterprise?"

Looking at myself in the mirror, I was about at her level of optimism, but one of us needed to look on the bright side. I wasn't quite sure *why* it was so important to me to prove Valen wrong. It was just incredibly important that I kept some control and power in my life, and it felt like that was the only way to do it. Prove Valen wrong. Prove he wanted me. Me. Not just the idea of me or my inheritance.

"If this was me, it'd be easy," Florence said. "I 'accidentally' put your uniform on in the morning after a night of heavy studying. Small slap on the wrist, sent back to our room to change at morning tea, and hope the intended prey noticed the goods while it lasted. But you're like three sizes smaller than me, that strategy's not gonna help you."

No. But the idea had me thinking.

"No, but Exie is at least a size smaller than me..." I mused.

Florence's eyebrow rose, but she said nothing disparaging about my friendship with Exie.

"Come to think of it," I continued. "Triss wants to major in fashion..."

"*I* can cut up your uniform, babe," she reminded me slowly.

I nodded. "You can. You could cut it and paint extraordinary designs on it. What you couldn't do is put it back together without it being obvious that's what we did."

Florence huffed indignantly. "Yeah, all right, then. So, what's the plan?"

"Step one is do our best today. Step two is go all out at the Death Harvest tomorrow night. Step three is get Exie's and Triss' help for next week." I grinned at her. "Tomorrow *will* include your painting expertise."

"Oh," she cooed. "Colour me intrigued."

"Picture me with tattoos...then go to town."

Florence looked confused for a moment, then a grin slowly spread across her face. "Okay." She nodded. "Ohh-kay, girl. I feel you. You wanna give Valen the bad girl. Show the girl inside on the outside for once."

"Are you done with the excessive exposition, or can we get to morning mass?"

She looked me over. "You look good, but you don't look good enough to be excited about morning mass, babe."

I pointed at her victoriously. "Ha! You think I look good."

She rolled her eyes. "Of course I think you look good. You always look good. We could go to morning mass in pillowcases and we'd both look fabulous."

I looped my arm with hers as we walked out of our room. "Fuck, yes."

Sometimes, all you needed in life was a friend like Florence Walton.

Did we have flaws a plenty between us? Yes. Were we still figuring out life but liked to pretend we had it all down? Of course. Did we like to think we were mature and sophisticated, but in reality were still very much barely eighteen and high school students? Damn straight. But we loved each other and we supported each other, even if we'd look back with huge regrets in twenty years.

Was there a part of me that thought we'd look back on this escapade as the idiocy of our teenage years? Fucking-A. But we were doing it anyway.

We hadn't made too many changes to my uniform, how could we have? But we'd done what we could.

We'd rolled the waist of my skirt over a few times so it was shorter. The back of my shirt was scrunched in what few random hair ties we could find – hiding under my cardigan – so the front clung tightly to my curves. Florence and I had raided both our collections of bras for ALL the padded cups and push up bladders to give my chest some extra va-va-voom. I felt like, if I bent over, my boobs would strangle me and my buttons were straining, but damn I looked good. Pin-up model good. It wasn't a look I wanted to sport every day, but it was bound to get Valen's attention. I'd exchanged my usual tights for stockings and wore a matching black garter to keep them up; Florence was convinced that boys went mad over the sight of a garter.

The girls didn't seem to notice. Why would they? The aim here was to be subtle enough that the Sisters couldn't tell us off. Not even all the guys noticed. Marco noticed though. He was the first one.

As he saw us from across the quad, I saw his eyebrow raise ever so slightly. There was no reproach on his face. It was interest. Not interest *in* me, rather in what I was up to. I saw him nudge Valen gently. Valen didn't pause in his conversation with Apollo, but his eyes found me and he frowned heavily. He frowned, but I saw his tongue dart out to lick his lip. I hoped it was because he liked what he saw.

If Apollo noticed anything, he didn't mention it. As we all fell in step together, he took my hand. I expected him to keep talking to Valen, but he turned his attention to me.

"Good morning, darling," he said, kissing my cheek.

"Good morning, Apollo," I said.

He stifled a yawn. "How'd you sleep?"

I looked at Florence. "Uh, yeah, fine. You?" I asked because it seemed the polite thing to do.

He nodded. "Good. Yeah. Good. Listen, you girls are heading to the festival tomorrow night, yeah?"

"Of course."

"So, we'll see you there?"

I shrugged, playing coy. "You might. You might not." My eyes slid to Valen and I noticed he was watching me carefully.

I didn't want to use Apollo just to make Valen jealous, but it was tempting. I'd told Florence that, if it ever came to it, I would totally juggle them both. And I still thought that. But, there was flirting with Apollo to make Valen jealous, and there was flirting with Apollo because I wanted to and just happening to make Valen jealous. There were obviously some moral lines I'd cross, but intentionally using one guy just to rile up another wasn't one of them.

"I know we said it was friends' night this year," Apollo said. "But can I at least have *one* dance?"

I pretended to think about it as we walked into the chapel. Finally I nodded. "Okay. You can have *one* dance."

He grinned as he helped me into my spot on our pew. "Okay, then."

After Florence had elbowed me three times as my head dipped, mass was finally over. I kissed Apollo's cheek, and headed out to class with Florence. As I stood up, I somehow managed to flick my skirt up enough to reveal my garter, but not enough that my pants were on show for the whole school to see.

I snuck a look at Valen and knew, by the expression of fiery annoyance, that he'd seen.

When I paused to say goodbye to Florence outside my classroom, I felt hands at my waist, then a nose at my ear and Apollo's voice saying, "Have you changed something?"

Because of course he'd get there eventually. Maybe the garter had sent him over the edge? Based on the tone of his voice, I was rethinking this whole trying to seduce Valen. I'd forgotten that the last time I'd tried to do that, Apollo had definitely noticed.

For some reason, my heart skipped in my exaggerated chest, and I shook my head. "No. No, I don't think so."

One hand slid around to my stomach, pulling me closer to his body. Butterflies beat an unsteady rhythm on my ribcage and I suddenly felt hotter.

"Are you sure?" he asked. His voice was low, but I told my body to get a hold of itself.

Florence just smirked at me and slid off to class. I gave her the stink eye, promising to get her back later for abandoning me. Then, I turned to Apollo and gave him my biggest smile.

"I'm sure. Why?"

He shook his head and nuzzled my nose with his. "I don't know. You just look…"

I laughed. "Florence warned you about how you finish those sentences."

He got a cocky tilt to his lips and his eyes shone with cheeky mischief. It was…hot.

"You look insanely good today," he said. I'd never heard him have a deep, almost gravelly tone to his voice before. His hand slid to my waist and he caressed me gently. "And I mean, good enough to make a grown man lose his mind."

I wasn't going to use now to point out that he was not a grown man. Not really. Not with me anyway. It didn't feel like that kind of moment.

"Thank you," I said to him, honestly meaning it.

The aim might have been to seduce Valen, but I wasn't going say no to Apollo appreciating me.

He moved forward like he was about to kiss my lips, then

tipped his head to kiss my cheek. "I'll see you later."

I nodded. "Later."

He kept an extra tight hold of me when we were together for the rest of the day. Not so much in a possessive way, not like he was keeping me *away* from other people, or them from me. More like he just wanted to keep me close because he wanted me with him. The distinction might have been small, but it was enough to make me feel a little bubble of happy in my chest.

A bubble of happy that even Valen's insistent ignoring couldn't put a dent in.

It did, however, make me more adamant to make a lasting impression the next night.

The main night of the Death Harvest Festival was always celebrated large and loud in Bieityn. It wasn't as macabre as it sounded. Once upon a time, it had been two festivals: one celebrating the Harvest on November first; and a celebration of dead ancestors in mid-November. Over time, they'd been combined into one big festival that ran for a whole week in Bieityn.

The Saturday night, there was always a big bonfire and party. The music was always too loud for much else than dancing the night away. Until about nine, it was a family affair. But, once the kiddies had been ushered off to bed, that's when things got…primal. It wasn't a full-on orgy – people at least left for slightly more private areas to actually consummate their usually fleeting union – but it got pretty suggestive. For a town that had been under the influence of the Church for so long, they were still Pagans at heart.

"I think we need more smoke," Florence said as she finished my makeup.

She'd outdone even herself. Her red hair was hanging in loose waves and she wore a flower crown in black and silver. It had two big ram-like horns that curled over her ears. She wore a tight, peasant shirt under a well-fitting black corset dress.

She'd made me a similar crown to hers but, instead of ram-like horns, she'd given me antlers. My outfit was a very short red plaid skirt and a cropped black top with a low neckline, long sleeves and a hood. I wore thigh high black socks, showing the slightest skin between them and my skirt, and big, chunky black heels. The festival's pagan roots had turned somewhat Gothic over the years, and we'd used that to full effect.

We both wore black lipstick and had her perfected smoky eye going on. We'd spent all day painting our bodies with fake tattoos. Florence had found a perfect mix of marker and hairspray to keep them from smudging too much.

The Strawman was burning by the time we got there, and no kids were in sight. Already the dancing had become less disco and more tribal, as couples and groups twirled and spun around the Strawman in time with the music. It was what I could best describe as a trance-slash-techno kind of tribal beat.

Florence and I joined the crowds and completely lost track of time. At some point, God and his Angels found us. We pretended we weren't really dancing with them, even when Florence stuck her tongue down Marco's throat, making me and Apollo laugh. But this was the sort of time when they were good to hang out with as we all jumped and danced around the Strawman. At once point, I could almost have said I was dancing with Valen. His hand brushed my waist, and I could have sworn his nose went to my hair.

A little later, as I made my way through the crowd back to Florence, I ran full on into Valen. I didn't see him until my hands were on his chest and his were on my waist to steady me. For the first time that night, I took him in properly. He wore nothing but dark trousers, big black boots, and a big black jacket that fell to his knees. His cross was stark against his sweat-shined skin, and he wore smudged eyeliner, though not quite as heavy as me or Florence. Like most of the partygoers at that time of the night, his hair was somewhat limp and damp.

The whole atmosphere of the place was doing a number on my libido. My heart beat rhythmically along with the music and I felt amped up on nothing more than adrenalin and ambience. I was horny. I was horny and standing in front of a guy who got my motor running at the most chaste of times. There was no way he didn't see it on my face as I looked up at him.

Wordlessly, his hand skimmed lightly over the bare skin of my waist.

Our bodies swayed closer to each other.

My hand slid up his shoulder.

He licked his lips as he took me in.

"You might just be the death of me, Harlow Vanguard," he said, his voice little more than a choked rasp.

"Does the big, bad wolf like that?" I asked softly.

A different kind of darkness came over him. "It's the only way I want to go."

"Admit it," I begged, because it *was* more a beg than a plea. I didn't just want to prove him wrong, I needed him to be wrong.

"Admit what?" he asked, playing along.

"Admit you want me. Even if you can't have me."

"I won't do that, princess."

"Why? Because you don't answer to me?"

"I *don't* answer to you," was his answer.

"What is it you're scared of?" I asked him.

He frowned. "You think I'm scared?"

"Why else would you be doing this? You can't still say loyalty. Not now. Are you scared of hurting me? Of me hurting you? Of hurting Apollo?"

He pressed his mouth to my forehead with a strained groan, "Scared isn't the word I'd use," before letting me go and walking away.

I was getting to him. I knew I was. It would be somewhat immature and ridiculous to keep pushing him, but I did it anyway.

I spent all of Sunday with Florence, Exie and Triss. Between us, we tightened all my uniform, ordered some more bras online that would definitely show up under our white shirts, and ruined my school shoes so I'd have no choice but to wear my higher heels for the few days it would take to get another pair.

I walked around the school all the next week, flaunting all the goods I could with the self-confidence of a woman who was going to get what she wanted if it killed her. My skirt was shorter, my shirts were tighter, I wore my tie loose and my top buttons undone, and tall mary jane heels. Everyone noticed, but I didn't care. No one but the Sisters berated me, especially when I started a trend of wearing coloured bras under our white school shirts, and non-standard school shoes. With so many of us doing it, the most they could do was keep reminding people it wasn't quite seemly and wait for the fad to blow over.

By the end of the week, when my replacement school shoes had turned up, even the Sisters had given up sending any of us to change, so coloured bras and whatever black shoes we wanted it was.

Valen and I had barely exchanged a glance for the whole week. But Florence was my extra eyes, and she told me that, every second I wasn't looking at him, his expression was enough to make her blush. Apparently, he was staring at me so hotly I may as well have been walking around naked.

A (now) expected side effect was that Apollo had also taken notice.

His hands lingered on me longer. His touch was both softer and more insistent. Once or twice, goosebumps had flared and I'd found my heart fluttering like mad.

We already had a dinner coming up on Saturday with my parents at the Callahan Estate but, when Apollo suggested that he and I go into Bieityn on Friday for Club Night, I'd made myself so hot and bothered that I agreed on the spot.

I was still curling my hair on Friday evening when there was a knock on the door. I caught Florence's eye in the mirror and we exchanged our surprise.

"You expecting someone?" Florence asked.

I shook my head. "No."

"Huh," she said as she went to open the door.

"Your carriage... Oh, Flo," came Apollo's voice.

"*Flo-rence*," she sounded out to him like he was a moron.

I turned and saw he was brandishing a rose. He was brandishing a single red rose and was standing in our doorway.

"I thought I was meeting you at the garage?" I asked, putting the final touches to myself.

He rocked back on his heels and grinned. "I came to you."

Apollo was clearly very proud of himself.

I couldn't help looking at Florence.

There was something very weird about the whole thing. Florence and I had talked about this exact thing on my birthday. Talked about the fact that gods didn't go to princesses. But here he was. Maybe this wasn't a god. Maybe this was what a prince looked like.

I wasn't going to knock it. The quite proud 'are you proud of me, too?' expression on his face was sweet. It was endearing. It made me smile and look forward to the night out.

I took off my robe and threw it onto the bed as I shook out my curls. I heard Florence snort and looked at her, but she was watching Apollo. I turned to him and found him with his jaw practically on the floor. I had to say, it was the intended effect. I was just hoping that someone else would think the same.

I wore a backless pale rose gold sequin dress. It was the tightest piece of clothing I think I owned, so it was good that it barely skimmed my thighs because then I could still move in it. For all intents and purposes, it was a halter neck. The straps were made out of rose gold chain, which wound intricately around my neck a few times like a choker. There was also a strand that fell between my breasts, easily seen considering the neckline was only just above my belly button.

It was a piece of shit to get on, and there was a whole thing with tape that had required me jumping up and down for about ten minutes to make sure nothing was going to slip out at the wrong time.

My shoes were not-quite-too high, with buckles and straps, diamonds and small spikes. There were totally unnecessary, but they made my legs look like they went on for fucking miles.

I did feel almost naked, but I also felt amazing. Free and fabulous. And, if that didn't make me sexy, I didn't know what would.

"Eyes are up here, Casanova," I said to Apollo.

He spluttered and looked up at my eyes. "You look…"

I grinned at him and he smiled.

"Fuck me, Harlow. You trying to kill me?" he asked.

"Worried all your blood's gonna rush south so fast your heart won't have any left to pump?" Florence sassed.

Surprisingly, Apollo actually nodded. "Worried it's already happened, actually."

I snuck a look at Florence and we shared our surprise. But hers was also impressed; she might have hated Apollo, but she wasn't above admitting when he got something right.

"All right," she said. "Can you two get out, then? I've got my own date tonight and I'd rather you two didn't see him."

I smirked as I grabbed my coat and Apollo helped me into it. "Say hi to him for me. I'll see you later."

"Text when you're on your way back so I can kick him out!"

she called.

I waved as I took Apollo's hand and we headed to the garage.

"You driving tonight?" I asked him.

Apollo shook his head. "Nope. Tonight is all about you and me and zero responsibility. Valk's driving us."

As I'd expected. Hence the dress. Which Valen didn't see until we walked into the club when I pulled my coat off and casually threw it in his direction. He was forced to catch it so it didn't hit the floor along with his jaw.

I looked back at him and gave him a wink, feeling way more calm and confident than I ever remembered feeling. Me of a few months earlier wouldn't have been so brazen, wouldn't have called so much attention to myself. This was hardly sweet demure behaviour. And I fucking loved it.

Valen was a good little guard-slash-chauffeur. He spent the night at the bar, nursing a series of clear liquids I hoped were alcohol-free. But, given the scowl he wore while he watched Apollo and me, I wouldn't have been surprised if one or two weren't. He'd be driving us back and he took that seriously, so he would restrict his alcohol intake.

The same could not be said for Apollo or me.

We did shots. We cracked jokes. We laughed.

And we danced.

Oh, how we danced.

Apollo's arms were tight around me and mine around him. There was most certainly no room for the holy spirit between us. There wasn't a single millimetre between us. I could feel how hard Apollo was for me as we practically dry humped along with all the other bodies on the dancefloor.

There was a small, sub-conscious part of me that, knowing Valen was jealous, worried that was the only reason I was doing it. But, then I realised that I had spent very little time in Apollo's arms thinking about Valen at all.

As Apollo's hands slid over my body, all I thought about was him and us and that moment. As our bodies rubbed together, there was no concern about propriety or appearances, we were just us. With his forehead bowed to mine and that mischievous half-smirk on his gorgeous face, all I felt was him. I wondered what it would be like to kiss him now. I wanted to know what it would be like to kiss him now.

As though he could read my mind, Apollo's lips inched closer and my heart thudded in my chest. But it was a good thud. A warm thud. Anticipation, but not nervous. My first instinct wasn't to push him away. In some recessed, narrative corner of my brain, I figured that was a good thing.

But, just before his lips touched mine, he growled, pushed me out of the way, and walked out. I saw Valen by the bar watching us carefully. At the sight of Apollo leaving so purposefully, I saw him frown and quickly follow after his God. I had no choice but to follow as well, stopping for the shortest amount of time to get my coat from the check, but I didn't put it on.

By the time I got outside, Apollo was at the car and they were clearly arguing. Valen looked about ready to smack Apollo.

"What about her?" he snapped.

Apollo shrugged. "Fucking fine! You take her back, then. I'll get a car later."

And, with that, he shoved his hands in his pockets and stalked off.

"Apollo?" I called, starting after him

Valen stepped between us, his arm in front of me. It didn't touch me, but I felt the warmth of it against my bare arms.

"I wouldn't," he warned.

He sounded pissed. Furious. Seething, even. All contained behind that calm exterior, where the only hint was in how rigid he held his body and how rough his voice was.

God, but I loved when his voice sounded like that. It set my heart racing and clit tingling, and my breath threatening to stop. It didn't matter that I'd just almost kissed Apollo, my body reacted instinctively to Valen.

"I guess the night's over, then," I huffed.

"I'll take you back to school," Valen said.

"What about Apollo?"

Valen looked in the direction his friend and God had gone. He sucked his teeth before he answered, "Fucker can deal with his own shit tonight."

He went over to the car and opened the front door for me. His expression told me he wasn't going to put up with any disobedience on my part. I wanted to argue with him, to see how disobedient I could be before he saw fit to punish me. But I had a feeling I knew where Apollo was going and, knowing that I wasn't going to be allowed to seek the arms of another as well, I just wanted to go and curl up in bed while Florence commiserated about stupid boys with me.

So I got in the car, not missing Valen's surprise at my silent obedience. We were pulling into the boys' dorm garage when he finally broke that silence.

"You think you're proving anything in those outfits you've been parading around in?" he asked.

I glared at him. "I *allowed* you to bring me back to school without a fight, do not mistake that for any newfound subservience. I do not answer to you, Valk," I told him, throwing his favourite line back at him.

"You think you're achieving anything?"

"Since you've brought it up, yes."

He threw the car into park in its rightful place. "You *will* stop showing so much skin," he ordered.

A thrill ran through me. I liked it when he ordered me around. I liked the possessive streak shining bright, even if he was going to keep denying it. But that didn't mean I was going to submit.

"It's a free world," I told him, saccharine sweet. "I will do what – or who – I like."

Valen put a hand on the shoulder of my seat and leant towards me. "The only who you'll do is me," he snarled, full of that domineering passion.

Warmth flooded me and I felt my body leaning towards his, totally ready for him to use it however he wanted. I wanted him. I needed him.

But I couldn't have him.

As I started to get out of the car, I replied cavalierly, "Well, you don't want me, Valen. So, I guess I'll just have to find someone else to do the job."

I heard him growl and he was at my door before I'd finished

getting out of the car. He pressed me against the back door of the car, slamming my door closed as he did, and I could feel him hard against my hip.

He was breathing heavily, his eyes feverish like he was going mad. For once, he wasn't hiding behind a mask of annoyed indifference. Everything was on display. I saw it. I took one look in his eyes and I *felt* it.

My heart tripped and skipped. My stomach plummeted. My nipples tightened and my clit ached in response to the fierce need I saw in him.

Need. For me.

"You have to understand, princess," he said, his voice a strangled husk. "I need you to understand."

"Understand what, Valen?" I asked.

He dropped his forehead to mine with a heavy sigh. "Your life isn't yours? Well, my life's not mine, either. I was already pulled in two different directions... Now..." His rough chuckle was humourless.

"Now, what?" I breathed, afraid of the answer.

"Now, I need you to understand. One of us needs to walk away."

"Valen..."

He shook his head, still leaning on mine. One hand went to my waist and he gripped it tightly. The other hand reached up and cupped my cheek gently.

"One of us needs to walk away, Harlow..." he whispered.

Then, he pressed a deep kiss to my lips. It was slow and soft, but deliciously demanding. He took as much as he gave.

My heart jolted like it was restarting. But this wasn't a start. It was an end. I could feel it in the depths of my soul.

Valen finally pulled away from me like it took every ounce of his strength. He said nothing. As he walked out, he locked the car. I jumped as it beeped loudly behind me as though it was some twisted attempt at comedic relief against the sorrow I felt from Valen's goodbye.

Chapter Seventeen

The next morning, there was a knock on my door long before even Florence was ready to be awake.

"Ugh," she groaned as she burrowed into her pillows. "Shotgun not."

"Ugh," I agreed, hauling myself out of bed.

I opened the door, squinting blearily into the bright light of the hallway and took in the blurry sight of Apollo.

"What do you want?" I asked.

My morning voice was gruff and gravelly. On anyone else, it might have been sexy. The right anyone else. On me, it was definitely nothing to write home about.

"I wanted to apologise for last night," he said, no sign of morning voice. I didn't care if he didn't have one, or if it meant he either hadn't been to bed, or had been awake long enough to lose it.

"I'm really not in the mood for accepting apologies, Apollo. It's too damned early."

Apollo's smile was self-conscious. "Right. No. Should have thought of that."

I looked him over and realised he was in the same clothes as the night before. They were rumpled and his hair looked like he'd not had time to style it properly after sleeping on it. I felt my eyes narrow.

"Are you just getting back?"

He shrugged like it was nothing. Before he could say anything, I kept talking.

"I could have just met you there tonight," I told him.

He smiled. "No. I know. I actually thought about that, but Valen wasn't answering his phone, so I'm–"

"Not even here for me," I interrupted. "Great. Thanks, Apollo. Good to know where I stand in the great hierarchy of Apollo-fucking-Callahan's idiotic brain!" I snapped, just about done with his bullshit.

No. Not just about. Absolutely. I was done making excuses for him, done hoping there was a shred of the boy I loved still in there somewhere, done trying to save Frenella's son, and done thinking that we could ever have a real relationship.

After whatever had happened in the club – him still walking away and leaving me for some random Magdalen – and then the finality of Valen's kiss... My emotions were tangled and frayed and just so done.

I went to slam the door in Apollo's face, but his arm flew up to stop it.

There was a muffled clap from the direction of Florence's bed. "Woo, you tell him, girl," she mumbled.

But I wasn't that interested in Florence's reaction, because I was paying attention to Apollo's.

His eyes were wide and awe-filled. His mouth was only parted slightly, but it was his version of a jaw-drop, when there wasn't skin on display. He blinked twice in quick succession, then pulled himself together.

"No. Of course not," he said, losing all pretence of sweetly sexy man-child he pretended to be with me. "I'm not here just for Valk. I'm here for you, too. I needed to apologise. I *wanted* to apologise, Harlow."

I nodded. "Well, you have. So…"

He took my hand and held it to his chest. "I *am* sorry, Harlow. I shouldn't have left you last night. I was... I was all in my head, but that's no excuse for the way I treated you." He brought my hand up and kissed it softly. "I am sorry, Harlow."

Well.

As much as I wanted to be angry with him, as much as I wanted to slam the door on his pretty face and maybe smash it in a bit… I also...didn't.

In his eyes stood the boy I knew. The boy I loved. The boy I thought I was so close to losing. He held my hand to his chest. Not just his chest, his heart. Like he was reminding me I had a place there. Like he was telling me I belonged there. For the briefest of moments, I believed it. I knew it to be an irrefutable truth.

He was trying. He might not have been doing a great job, but he was trying. This was new territory for both of us, whatever territory had our hands on each other and our lips nearly meeting in ways they never had before. It was to be expected that we might not do it very well to begin with.

I nodded. "Okay, Apollo." I nodded again. "I forgive you."

He smiled. "Yeah?"

I gave him a small smile in return. "Yeah."

"Boo!" Florence mumbled, but I knew she'd forgive me faster than I'd forgiven him.

Apollo took a deep breath and laughed a breathy sigh of obvious relief. As his hand went to my cheek, he took a step forward and leant his forehead to mine.

"Thank you," he said. "Thank you, sweetheart."

"As lovely as this is," Florence said. "Can you do it anywhere but here?"

"Well," Apollo said suavely. "I suppose some of us *do* need their beauty sleep."

Florence's arm appeared out of her doona, and she pointed an angry finger at him. "You take that back or so help me, when I've had enough sleep, I'll remove you from your favourite appendage."

Apollo smiled. "Of course, I'm sorry. Rude of me to bring up something you can never hope to obtain."

Florence sat up and glared at him. It was impressive even for the fact that her hair was totally matted on one side, and she couldn't focus her eyes without her glasses.

"Well, at least I'm beautiful on the inside," she told him. She put her hand over her mouth. "Sorry, we're *not* mentioning things other people can never hope to obtain. My bad," she said sarcastically.

Apollo's eyes were full of mischief, but he smiled at her winningly. "I'll forgive you, Flo. Because I'm just that nice."

Her eyes narrowed. "*Flo-rence*."

I grabbed the front of Apollo's shirt and he turned his attention back to me.

"I'm going to get dressed, then you're going to get me breakfast," I told him.

He nodded. "Sounds like a plan."

I shoved him backwards, gave him a smile and closed the door in his face.

"Your *boyfriend* is a grade-A hole," Florence said grumpily as she flopped back into bed.

I nodded as I found some semi-clean clothes to change into. "Yeah. He is what he is, but he's all I've got."

"What about…?" she whispered.

My eyes slid to her as I kept getting ready. Her eyebrows were waggling half-heartedly in her sleepy state.

"Yeah," I huffed. "That's not…" I sighed. "I'm over it."

She snorted and I glared at her. "What?" she asked innocently.

"He's over it," I grumbled.

"That is just one hundred percent not true," she told me. "Although, we are back to normal Harlow, apparently."

I looked down at myself and found I'd put on my blue-grey jeans, and a pale pink, woollen, off the shoulder jumper. In my hands, I was holding my light brown, heeled boots. I sucked my teeth and I looked down at myself.

"Right," I said slowly. "Yeah. Let's… Let's put a pin in that for now, shall we? Especially for Saturday morning breakfast."

My fingers trailed to my lips as I remembered Valen's kiss from the night before. I was feeling far less in the mood to seduce anyone after the…finality of it all. I wasn't going to stop being what felt like a more real version of me, but I *was* going to hide behind the mask of Good Girl Harlow until I was back to full strength again.

"No," Florence said softly. "Fair enough."

Naturally, she just had to take one look at me realise something was up. I'd told her the night before that boys were stupid but that I didn't want to talk about it. We'd sat in the middle of her bed, my head in her lap and commiserated boys' stupidity. She knew I'd give her all the gory details when I was ready, and I wasn't quite ready.

I plastered on a smile as I pulled on my boots. "It's fine. I'm fine."

"No one asked, but great. Believable. Bring me back *un pain au chocolat*?"

I huffed a small smile. "Of course."

Apollo was loitering casually in the hallway when I opened our door. There weren't many people around at that time of the morning, but they all stopped and noticed him looking mighty dishevelled outside my door. I could only think what the school would be saying about that by the end of the day. He paid them no mind, though. He just took my hand and led me to the café. We were the only ones there for a bit, but slowly it filled around us.

It filled and emptied and filled again, and we moved on from breakfast to lunch.

It seemed that Apollo was in the midst of a very 'not caring about what anyone else thinks' day, because he wasn't keeping one eye on our surroundings for once. He barely answered when someone said hello to him. He didn't look at his phone once. His whole attention was on me, and I completely forgot myself in the sweet wake of it. We were laughing and joking, not caring if we were too loud or if anyone could hear the utter nonsense coming out of our mouths. We didn't stop even when one of us got up to order something more to eat or drink, carrying on our conversation over and through whoever was between us.

When I got a message on my phone and saw it was from my mum, I finally broke our little bubble and noticed the time.

"Shit, Apollo, it's almost three."

He looked at his watch. "Fuck. It is. What time did we say we'd be at my parents'?"

I breathed out as I thought about it. "Before mine. And mine have just landed at the airport."

"Fuck," he laughed. "All right. I desperately need a wash and a change. I'll text you when I'm ready and we'll meet you at the car?"

"I *think* I'm going to take longer than you to get ready."

He grinned. "Yeah, all right. Come and get me when you're ready, then?"

I nodded. "Better plan."

He leant over and kissed my cheek. "I'll see you soon!" he said as he hurried out of the door.

I checked we'd paid everything we'd owed, grabbed Florence's chocolate croissant, and hurried myself back to our dorm.

"I know!" I yelled as I threw the pastry at her and beelined for the bathroom.

"Where the fuck have you been?"

As I got undressed, I called, "With Apollo."

"All day?"

I nodded. "Yeah. We were just chatting and… He barely spoke to another person all day. He didn't look at his phone. He's…"

"If you say 'like a changed man', I'm gonna come in there and hurl on you."

"Fair," I admitted. "No. But something *has* changed, Floss. I don't what it is, but it's…"

"Good?" she guessed.

"Not bad," I corrected. "We'll see if it gets us through tonight."

"You do know what the school is saying after him turning up so early, don't you?" she asked.

"I can guess."

"If it was true, you'd have told me, wouldn't you?"

"Of course I would have. I tell you everything. He was out all night decidedly not because of me," I assured her.

"Okay, good. I mean, not good, but good to know you're not keeping secrets."

"I told you everything about Valen, would I hide Apollo from you? I'm *meant* to be with him."

"Yeah. Good point."

I was primped and primed in proper Princess Harlow clothes in a little under an hour.

Tea-length dress. Sensible pumps. Pearls. Soft curls. White headband. Clutch purse. Check.

"Sorted?" I asked Florence, doing a little spin.

She nodded. "Sorted. Perfect little princess."

"Great. Job done. I'll see you later."

She nodded. "Night."

I rushed to the boys' dorms, nodding to people as I passed. As I hit the third floor, a Magdalen was walking towards me. She made a big show of wiping the corner of her mouth as she gave me a knowing smirk. I guessed I was supposed to think she'd just been sucking Apollo's cock. Well, good for her.

I wasn't going to let that ruin the day I'd had with him. We had to take this thing with baby steps. If I was still trying to get Valen to admit he wanted to fuck me, then I presumably wanted him to follow through with it. I could hardly be pissy with Apollo for fucking around with Magdalens if I still wanted Valen.

I gave her my warmest smile and watched with pleasure as all her superior confidence was replaced with confusion. She gave me a nod, and we both went on our own merry ways.

I knocked on Apollo's door. "You decent?" I called.

"Come in and find out," he called back.

I pushed my way into his room.

Apollo was wearing trousers, but nothing else. He had a couple of shirts laid out on his bed like he was trying to decide between them.

Valen was slouching on one of the couches, his ankle crossed on his other knee and his elbow up on the arm rest. He was puffing away at a vape pen like the damned thing contained oxygen.

"That was fucking close," he said to no one in particular.

"You were quick," Apollo as though in answer.

I kept my smile firmly in place, pretending I didn't know what they were talking about it.

"Valk, go get the car ready," Apollo said as he picked a shirt and pulled it on. I noticed it was a soft blue, similar to my dress.

"Sure," Valen answered, getting up.

His eyes hadn't left me since I'd walked into the room. There was a hostility in him I hadn't felt in a few weeks. The air around him fair sizzled with some barely contained emotion.

"Cheers," Apollo said as he ducked into the bathroom.

When he was level with me, Valen paused and said quietly, "That's better."

"You think this is for you?" I asked him, raising my eyebrow.

"I think the good little princess knows what's good for her."

I huffed a laugh. "We both know I'm not a good little princess, Valen. I'm a fucking goddess, and you will worship me."

He looked me up and down. "Stick to what know, princess." He paused for a beat. "It suits you better."

"Does the big, bad wolf like the pretty little princess, Valk?" I teased.

The way his eyes flared burning heat told me yes. His words, however, weren't so forthcoming. "Do not push me, princess," he warned.

"Or, what?"

"Or, you won't like what I do to you," he growled, then was gone.

I just had enough time to get my breathing under control before Apollo was back and we were heading to the Estate to meet our parents.

In the car, Apollo and I were in the backseat. He had his arm around my shoulders and the other one ran up my leg. He looked into my eyes and his were feverish bright. He wore an utterly ecstatic grin. He dropped a kiss to my jaw, then play-nipped at my neck. I giggled at the tickle, and he pulled away.

Something was definitely different, but where it would go was another matter.

Valen took the curves like he was trying to beat some personal best down the mountain.

"Have you started drift racing?" Apollo chuckled to him.

"Like you fucking know what that is," Valen said roughly, but I heard the slight note of teasing humour in his voice.

Whether Valen was drift racing or not remained to be seen, but we arrived at the Callahan Estate in one piece each.

"I'll be in my room," Valen said as Apollo took my hand and dragged me out of the car.

We ran up the steps, laughing about how late we were and wondering whose dad would be angrier.

"Apollo. Harlow," Archer said as we bundled into the Parlour, both of us breathing heavily.

"Sorry, we're late," Apollo said with a smile for everyone. "We lost track of time."

Apollo and I split to say hello to our mums, who were tittering happily to each other about the young lovers losing track of the time. For once, the majority of their assumptions about the situation were true. It was a weirdly pleasing feeling.

"How's school?" my dad asked me as he hugged me.

I nodded. "Good. Fine."

He nodded as well. "Lovely."

As soon as the pleasantries were over, Apollo was back at my side. His hand was low on my back, but he was casual as you please.

As a family – as it were – we had a few drinks until the rest of the guests arrived. One could never have just a few people over. It was always about connections and business. Archer and Dad would use the time to show their guests their combined strength, then discuss their own business after the rest of us had retired or left.

Apollo not once left my side. Not even for a drink. He took me with him everywhere he went, every person he spoke to. It was lucky I hadn't needed to use the bathroom or we might have had a problem.

His nose nudged my ear. "Need another drink?" he asked.

I turned my face to his and our noses bumped. "I think I've had enough for a bit."

He had one hand around my waist. My hand was on his lapel. Our faces were very close together...

"Apollo, this must be the lovely Harlow?" a voice interrupted.

And so the schmoozing began again.

After the fourth interruption, Apollo's arm around my waist tightened and he leant his nose to my ear.

"Come," he whispered softly.

His hand trailed along my back before he slid it into mine and tugged gently.

Confused and intrigued, I didn't hesitate to follow him.

He weaved us through the party, expertly avoiding giving anything more than a few words to those he passed. He had a smile and a nod for everyone, as always. But the more people who tried to stop him, the firmer his hold on my hand became.

Once free of the room, he pulled me towards the stairs. I thought we'd go up them, but he sidestepped at the last minute, then he ducked into the door leading to the storeroom under them. It was nothing but shelves on three sides, holding linen for the dining room and downstairs bathrooms.

"What are we–?"

But my words were cut off as he closed the door and pushed me against it. One hand was on my hip, the other splayed by my head. His body was hard up against mine. In every sense of the word. I could feel him erect as he leant into me. His nose was in my neck, sending goose bumps skittering across my skin, a shiver running down my spine, and an irregular heat pooling between my thighs.

"Apollo?" I breathed, unsure what was happening. With him or me.

"Shh," he whispered.

He slid his hand purposefully up my body until it was loosely cupping my breast. His erection dug into me in a way that pleasantly shocked me, his hips pulsing gently against me in a way that made me want to rock right back.

"I thought we'd never get out of there," he said, more a purr than actual words.

I tingled at his proximity. I'd never done that before.

He kneaded my breast, his nose still trailing goose bumps over my skin. My body arched towards him instinctively. I couldn't have stopped it. I didn't want to anyway.

One hand kept kneading me as the other moved down to coax my leg around his hip. My knee hugged him tightly and a small gasp escaped me as I felt his dick rub against my clit. I felt him smile against my cheek.

"There's something different about you, Harlow," he said softly as we rocked together and his grip tightened on my breast. "I've noticed you."

Sudden panic welled at what exactly he'd noticed. If he had any suspicion about me and Valen, then… Well, what was this?

"My cock's noticed you," he continued, obviously not needing me to reply.

His hand left my breast, running smoothly down my stomach and between my legs. My nerves came alive at his touch, but he denied me what I really wanted as he peppered my neck with kisses. His fingers ran over me. Up and down. Up and down. But they stayed either side of my slit, never quite reaching where I was desperate for him to be.

I felt my hips buck towards him and he chuckled, the air blowing against my skin sending all new shivers over me.

"Do you want it?" he asked as I wriggled against his denial.

I bit my lip.

What the hell was wrong me?

First, I give in and fuck a guy I hated more than I knew it was possible to hate. Now, here I was with a different guy I hated in such a very different way.

"Tell me you want it, Harlow," he begged.

Oh. My. God.

Whether I was weak, a sleeper nymphomaniac, or maybe just

ridiculously lucky to have two devastatingly gorgeous men wanting to throw me against the nearest surface, I didn't really care at that point.

I wanted Apollo. I wanted him more than I hated him. More than I loved him. I wanted him to touch me, to ease this hollow, tingling ache between my legs.

I nodded, feeling breathless for no good reason. "I want it," came out a mere whisper, but he heard.

He pulled away just enough to look at me. As he looked into my eyes, I saw his were feverish, like he was a man possessed. They shone with deep hunger and desire. For me. He actually wanted me.

"Fuck," he breathed, his hand rubbing over me faster. He dropped his forehead to mine. "Say it again," he pleaded.

"I want it," I told him. I took his face in my hands and made him look at me again. "I want you."

It was almost like a shiver ran over him. Some kind of pleasant disbelief or excitement.

Then his hand was on my cheek and he was kissing me so hard he knocked the breath out of me. A rapid coil of something I didn't want to name spread in my stomach and surged upward, making my heart skip. He tasted like expensive Scotch and smoky cigars. My arms wrapped around his shoulders as my leg, still around his hip, pulled him closer.

"Jesus, Harlow," he panted against my lips as he fought my layers of skirts to find my centre once more.

While I was sure the skirts were annoying, I didn't think that was what the exhalation had been about.

His fingers slid over me, this time making no pit stops on the way to my clit.

As the first zing of pleasure ran through me, I nipped his lip and sucked a hard breath in. Maybe it was a mistake, or maybe it was the perfect reaction. Whatever it was, it seemed to make him ramp it up a notch.

Apollo pushed my panties to the side and slid a finger into me.

My hands fisted in his hair as my whole body clamped around him in the best possible way.

"Fuck, yes," he chuckled as his nose skimmed along my cheek and his finger pumped me slowly.

My back arched, my breasts pushing up and into him. He dipped his head and kissed the soft flesh above the cut of my dress' bodice. I lay my head back against the door and let him finger fuck me as his lips blazed flaming passion across my skin. I felt him slide a second finger into me, the middle two now by the feel of it, and he pumped me harder.

Pleasure twisted and curled, building deeper and stronger. As my breathing became more erratic and shallower, he didn't let up. He went harder. He went faster. My body writhed. His pinned me to the door, making me unable to get away from the onslaught of tingling, growing sensation he was hammering me with, but I didn't want him to stop either.

One hand snaked above my head like that was going to help me deal with the pressure building inside me. Apollo's reached up and pinned my wrist to the door. I looked at him and found him staring at me. My breathing was ragged. My legs were weakening. My voice was a whimper of entreaty.

"Don't stop," I begged him.

His eyes were liquid heat. He looked at me like he'd never seen me before. Like he couldn't believe he'd missed me until now.

He let go of my wrist and took hold of the thigh that was around his hip. The fingers in me railed me. No longer was he pumping them in and out. Not in swift, strong motions. It was more front to back. And it did the job. More than satisfactorily. The coil was tightening in me. I could feel myself on the precipice.

"Are you going to cum for me?" he purred in my ear.

He looked into my eyes and I nodded, biting my lip to stop myself from moaning his name. I wasn't sure how much longer I could keep it in.

"Say it," he commanded, his hand sliding up between us to close gently over my neck while the fingers in me were anything but gentle.

I whimpered as my body started involuntarily contracting around him. It was too much. Too sensitive. It wasn't enough. I wanted him deeper, harder, faster.

"Say it, Harlow."

I moaned, leaning my head back against the door again. My hands fisted in his hair and on his sleeve. All as though that could stop the eruption that was coming.

"I'm cumming," I told him, a desperate exhalation as he brought me right to the edge.

"Good girl."

His lips crashed to mine, his hand was firm but tender on my throat, and his pelvis wedged his hand between us. It was all I need to send me over the edge.

I pulled my lips from his as I cried out, "Oh, god!" and slapped a hand against the door behind me as my entire body curled around him, desperate to keep him where he was but loathe for any more stimulation.

He huffed an amused laugh as my whole body shook. He held me up, letting me collapse in his arms until I got my breath back.

"Apollo," I breathed, forcing my legs to take my weight, and letting the door do some of the heavy lifting.

He was looking me over with a soft smile on his face that reached his eyes.

"Fuck, Harlow…" he said, shaking his head.

Suddenly I felt self-conscious. "What?"

He shook his head again as his tongue darted out and caught his bottom lip, closely followed by his teeth. He just stood there, with a bemused but sinfully cocky half-smirk on his face.

"What, Apollo?" I asked.

He reached forward and brushed the backs of his fingers down my cheek softly. So, so softly. I never thought he'd have a touch that gentle, that tender.

I relaxed as I looked at him. "What?" I asked more gently.

"You're so fucking beautiful," he said, almost like he was in awe.

I swallowed. "Thanks?"

In one swift motion, he pressed me against the door again. But this time it was softer, laced with something very different to burning passion. His nose nudged mine. As I tilted my head, he snuck in for another kiss. Slower, more languid.

My hands gravitated towards his belt, but he drew away to look at me.

He shook his head and pulled his cock away from me. "Not now," he said.

I frowned.

"We need to get back," he said, pressing a lingering kiss to my lips, as though that explained it.

He looked me over, as though checking if I was appropriate for public display. The half-smirk that lit his lips was all arrogance and pride. As he reached for the door handle behind me, his lips lingered near my ear.

"You might want to detour past the bathroom," he whispered.

Then he was out the door and gone.

I took a moment to compose myself, smoothing my skirts back down over me like that would mask the fact that Apollo Callahan had just finger fucked me under his parents' staircase during one of their fanciest parties of the year disguised as a casual get together. I felt flushed. I felt confused. Mostly, I felt sated. Apollo had felt good. He'd tasted good. He'd made me feel good.

On my way back to the others, I passed Valen exiting the kitchen. I felt heat flood my cheeks and hoped my makeup was enough to cover the redness.

I knew I didn't owe him anything. He'd made it very clear where we stood. Even if he hadn't, he and Apollo got to fuck around, so why shouldn't I?

No, it wasn't anything I felt I owed Valen, but I did feel the first stirrings of uncertainty about what I wanted. Did I want to be the fuck around kind? Not just with Valen, but Apollo, too. And what exactly did fucking around with Apollo mean? Was our relationship suddenly real? Or were we just in another circle of our own special limbo?

All I knew for sure just then was that…

My God and my angel.

My prince and my big, bad wolf.

I wanted them both.

Chapter Eighteen

When I'd got back the night before, Florence had been asleep. She'd left a note on the end of my bed saying she was sorry she couldn't stay up any longer. So, I'd dropped into bed and stared at the ceiling for a few hours.

After sleeping fitfully for the rest of the night, I finally gave up trying to sleep at about seven and just sat on my bed and stared at Florence like I could wake her up with just the power of my mind.

Finally, she stretched and her eyes fluttered open. She blinked once. Twice.

"Ah!" She jumped up and grabbed her glasses. "You freak! Don't do that. It's creepy."

I opened my mouth, then closed it again.

As Florence's brain woke up, she started looking around.

"It's barely eight. On a Sunday. What are you doing up?" she asked.

"I suddenly decided to show my devotion to our Lord and go to Sunday mass."

"I'm not nearly awake enough for your sass, missy."

"I'm fucked."

"Dude, have you slept at all?"

I shrugged. "Don't know."

"What's up?" She was aiming for concerned support, but it was kind of ruined when she yawned.

"Uh...last night–"

"You gave in and fucked Valen. Big surprise." She waved her hand airily and rolled her eyes.

"Apollo dragged me into a storeroom and finger fucked me."

Florence's mouth dropped open. "Oh."

I nodded. "Oh."

"Okay..."

"Yeah."

"That is a surprise."

"Isn't it?"

"Did not see that coming." She amended, "I mean, he's clearly been dying to kiss you–"

"He did that as well," I told her quickly.

She blinked. "Okay. Not wasting any time there, then. I'm assuming you wanted it, otherwise you would have punched him in the nose."

"Little further south."

She snorted. "Good girl. Well?"

"Well, what?"

"Well, everything!" she cried. "How was it? Is it going to happen again? How do you feel about it?" She leant towards me. "Better yet, how does Valen feel about it?"

I blinked. "Valen?"

"Figures he'd be your takeaway." Florence nodded. "Yeah. Tall, brooding, dark, dangerous, totally fallen for what's between your legs. Valen Kincaid."

"All right!" I huffed, thankful the door was closed. "I know who he is – obviously. I meant what have his feelings got to do with it?"

Florence shrugged coyly. "I don't know. I'm asking you."

"Sometimes," I told her. "I hate you."

"No, you don't. You love me."

I frowned. "I think we both know those two things are *not* mutually exclusive."

"So Valen's feelings matter?"

I huffed and flopped back on my bed. "Only in so much as I want him to care. Is that bad?"

"I don't think so. Would you care if he was fucking around?"

"I think we both know he is."

"Okay, do you care?"

"I can't care, Floss. Same as I can't care when Apollo fucks around."

She nodded like she thought we were getting somewhere. "Okay. Pretend you can care. Do you?"

"Kind of..." I said slowly.

"Valen or Apollo."

"Valen. Both. Neither. I don't know!"

"Do you want to be told if and or when one – or both – of them have been fucking around?"

I shrugged. "I don't want it to be a secret, but I don't need details... Okay, no. I don't think I do."

"All right, so do you feel like Valen should know?"

"Maybe...?"

"Why?"

"I don't feel like I owe him anything, if that's what you're wondering."

"Wasn't. Interesting you thought I might be, though."

"It just..." I sighed. "I don't know what it means. With Apollo."

"Have you talked about it?"

"No."

"Do you want to talk about it?"

I wasn't against it happening again. I was pretty sure I wanted it to happen again, but I didn't want to talk about it. I didn't want to suddenly be in this monogamous relationship with new rules and expectations. I was ready for him to pleasure me, but I wasn't ready us to be more.

"No!"

Florence's eyes widened at the vehemence in my voice, but she just nodded. "Okay. Then don't. You don't owe either of those boys anything, babe. You clearly think you can't tell Apollo about Valen–"

"Because I can't!"

"And what's telling Valen about Apollo going to do except make him deny even harder that he wants you?"

"I don't know. What about honesty?"

"Do I need to point out how little sense that makes?"

She was right. It made no sense on any front. I *didn't* owe either boy anything. I couldn't – wouldn't – be honest with

Apollo, and being honest with Valen was only going to push him further away. I didn't want that.

I sighed. "No. Besides," I said as the thought hit me, "Apollo's probably bragged all about me with the Angels by now. Valen will know all about it."

"What do you think he's going to do?"

I dragged my hand over my face. "I don't know. He says things like 'the only guy you'll do is me', and then kisses me like it's goodbye. Does he think I'm just going to be a nun now? Of course not, because he knows I'll be with Apollo sooner or later, although it seems like maybe sooner now. Ugh, I don't know what he wants or what he'll do."

"Hang on," Florence said. "I've missed something very important here. Go back to the kiss. When did he say that?"

After the night before, it didn't matter if I was ready or not. I needed to talk to her about it.

I told her all about under the stairs. I told her about me and Apollo at the club on Friday night, about him storming out, about Valen and me in the garage. She didn't interrupt, only exclaimed in excitement now and then like a good listener was wont to do. When I'd finished she huffed out a breath.

"And then, Apollo dragged you into a storeroom and finger fucked you?" she clarified.

I nodded. "Yeah."

"Well."

"Yeah."

"I guess he could only deny himself for so long."

"What?"

Florence laughed. "You don't think he just woke up yesterday and decided that he wanted you, do you?"

I realised then that, no. He hadn't just woken up and decided he wanted me. "Fuck," I muttered. "That's why he walked out on Friday."

"Yep."

"He thought he shouldn't."

"Yep."

"Then he just couldn't help himself."

"Yep."

"Have you got anything more useful that 'yep' to add to the conversation?"

"Yep."

I laughed. "What is it then?"

"What is it about you that you've got two guys unable to control themselves around you."

"Must be my wicked womanly voodoo ways," I said with a smile.

"It's no small feat."

"What am I supposed to do?"

"Two guys, possibly simultaneously."

I snorted, appreciating her attempt to cheer me up.

"Seriously, babe. Do what you want. You want them both? Have them both. You don't have to have answers now."

I nodded. "Fair point."

"I mean, a vague idea of your principals and feelings would be good, but you know that already."

"I do."

"So, are we still trying to seduce Valen?"

I sighed. "How long do I try to seduce and man who says he doesn't want me?"

"Do you honestly believe he doesn't want you?"

"Maybe his restraint is better than mine?"

"So? Fuck his restraint. Fuck him."

"Preferably."

She snorted. "Exactly. Is it back to the pearls and pastels for Princess Harlow now, then?"

I shook my head. "Not always. That's not who I am, and I don't want to just hide away all the time. Not anymore. My future's no less mapped out, but if Apollo wants me – *me* – then maybe my future won't be quite as grey as I thought."

"So, in seducing Valen we accidentally seduced Apollo?"

"Seems that way."

"We're okay with that?"

I nodded. "I think we are."

"Okay, good. Good to know where we stand." She stretched. "But, if we're going to delve any further in this, then I'm going to need caffeine and pastries."

"Multiple?"

"Of course," she said like it was the most obvious thing in the world.

I nodded with a wry smirk. "Of course."

We got dressed and meandered down to the campus café. As we went, I got a message from Apollo

Apollo

Where are you?

                              Harlow

                    Why? Where are you?

Apollo

At your dorm.

                              Harlow

              We're on our way to the café.

Apollo

We'll catch up.

"Ugh," I sighed. "I think Apollo's going to join us."

Florence snorted. "So, he's fully whipped now?"

"What?"

"He wants to get you off *and* follow you around school?"

Now I snorted. "No."

"There she is!" I heard Apollo call behind us and we turned around.

Apollo was fair running towards me. Not quite, but enough that it was clear he was keen to get to me. Valen, Marco, Fender and Gage were all walking at a more stately pace behind him, like parents watching their offspring running amok at the park.

"Long time, no see," I said to him and he grinned at me.

Apollo's hands went to my waist, he picked me up and spun me around. "Hi."

The smile was deep in his eyes. I didn't think I'd seen him genuinely that happy in a very long time.

As my feet touched the ground again, he stepped closer to me and kissed me. Full on kissed. Right on the lips. In front of anyone who might be walking by. My heart stopped in my chest.

It wasn't that I didn't want him to kiss me, I just…also didn't want him to kiss me. I did and I didn't. How did that make sense?

He pulled away from me and ran his hand over my cheek. "How are you?"

"I'm fine. How are you?" I asked.

I liked this side of him, but it was very sudden.

I couldn't stop my eyes sliding to Valen over Apollo's shoulder. His face was a stern mask of detached indifference. Even his eyes were hard. No sign of any emotion in him at all. He might have been a robot or a statue for all the humanity I saw in him. He just casually puffed away on his vape pen, ignoring the elbow Marco stuck in his ribs. On the second elbow, he grabbed the front of Marco's shirt and pulled him around to face each other.

"You try that one more time, and I will end you," Valen growled.

Marco smirked at Valen as he held his hands up. "My bad. Twitch, you know."

"Take it somewhere else," Valen ordered.

"It's all right," Apollo told them both. "Valk's just itching for his fight."

"His fight?" I asked.

Apollo nodded. "Another idiot is challenging his supremacy."

"To be fair, he didn't challenge Valk," Marco said.

"No," Apollo agreed. "But Valk took the challenge."

Valen stretched his neck. "I'm going."

Apollo squeezed my arm. "We all better get going."

"Don't want to miss a blood bath," I said, acting chipper.

"You want to come?"

I shook my head. "Thanks, but no thanks. I owe Florence a pastry."

"Or, five," Florence added.

Apollo grinned. "Okay. I'll see you later." He pressed another kiss to my lips, then headed off with his Angels.

"Did you see that?" I whispered to Florence.

"The whole fucking school might as well have seen that," she muttered.

"Oh," I scoffed. "It's not *that* bad."

"Not *that* bad?" Florence asked. "Apollo Callahan has not once kissed a single person on the lips in the four and a half years he's been at Saint Benedicts. Not on their face lips, and not in public. And not counting that time with Marco."

"How do you know so much about anything?" I asked, annoyed at everything.

"I'm Florence Walton. I just know these things. It's my thing. I know things and I fuck."

I barked a laugh that surprised even me.

"You all right?" she asked.

I nodded. "Yeah. Fine. Just… Kinda overwhelmed."

"Valen legit could have punched Apollo just then."

"I wholeheartedly disagree."

"My magical cupid-senses tell you you're wrong."

I frowned at her. "I appreciate that, but I think, on this occasion, it's your magical cupid-senses who are wrong."

Florence shrugged. "I mean they're not, but I'll agree to disagree."

I looped my arm with hers and leant our heads together. "Agree to disagree."

At dinner that night, Apollo's hand was always on me. He kept kissing me. I got totally swept up in it. I didn't second guess anything, I didn't hesitate. I just went with the flow quite happily.

Florence later said that was because there was no Valen in the room to make me feel conflicted. Maybe she was right. Maybe I didn't want to think about it. Maybe I just enjoyed not feeling conflicted. Why should I feel conflicted? I doubted Apollo would feel conflicted about the next Magdalen he bedded. I knew for a fact that Valen wouldn't have been conflicted. So why should I?

I shouldn't.

I wasn't going to be sorry for wanting both of them. For enjoying what each of them gave me. Florence had been right, I didn't need answers now. No promises had been made, no conversations were needed. Not now. Not yet.

I was destined for Apollo, so whatever happened would unfold the way it would.

Valen and I knew, realistically, we couldn't keep doing what we were doing forever, so whatever happened with him would unfold – or not – as well.

For the time being, I just wanted to go keep going with the flow, take one day at a time, and see where life – or which boy – took me.

CHAPTER NINETEEN

Valen was still gone on Monday. His absence went from being meaningless and unsuspicious, to something that might have been cause for concern.

"Missus," Marco said to me with a deep nod as he walked past me.

I turned to watch him. "Uh, hi."

He gave me a cocky grin. "Caused quite the stir, you have."

My heart thudded in my chest. "I don't know what you're talking about."

His smirked suggested he certainly knew something. "Don't ye?"

I shook my head. "No."

"Funny, that. You've only got God all over you. Desperate for you. In five years, I've not seen him desperate, missus. Lucky the woman he lost his mind over was the one he's going to marry, isn't it?"

I swallowed hard. "What are you implying, Marco?"

He shrugged. "Nothing. Just, it would be a shame if someone wanted someone they shouldn't have, wouldn't it?"

I cleared my throat. "Would it?"

"It would."

"And you'd know, would you?"

"Maybe."

"And how would you know?" I asked indignantly.

"I'm not sure that's your business, missus."

"I think you've made it my business, Marco."

He took a step towards me. "Princesses and Gods aren't the only ones whose lives are planned for them, missus," he said. "Even the lowliest of Angels has powers higher than God that he must obey."

"And exactly what powers do you have to obey, Marco?"

He kicked his eyebrows. "It's not just me, missus. Or has Apollo's cock distracted you so much that you've not noticed his right hand is missing."

My heart skipped a painful beat. "I've noticed."

Marco nodded. "And have you noticed how it's affected our ruthless lord?"

I paused. "How has it affected him?"

Marco gave a shrug. "Can't rightly say. He doesn't confide in little old me. But he was up drinking all night with the worst case of the jitters I've seen on a man in a while."

"Is he okay?"

"He will be. Can't say the same for Valk."

Valen. Who'd killed people. Who'd probably done things I couldn't even begin to imagine. And if he hadn't done them, he knew someone who had. What could he possibly be doing that would worry any of them?

Because I saw all Marco's blustering for what it was. He was concerned. Say what you will about the nature of the Saints, but God and his Angels cared about each other.

When I saw Apollo at Lunch, my suspicions were confirmed.

Oh, he tried to hide it. Tried to hide his worry behind smiles and kisses, and jokes. But I saw through it. I saw the tightness in the corner of his eyes. I saw the way his jaw clenched. I felt the way his hand tremored in mine now and then. The way he reached for me like I was providing him comfort. The way his laughter was just a bit too loud, a bit too sudden, like he was compensating.

I did my best to be there for him. I left choir practice as quickly as possible and went straight to his room. He was talking to Fender, but seemed not to care when he saw me.

"I don't fucking care," Apollo was saying to Fender when I got there. "We said a full crate, so it better be a fucking full crate. For each piece missing, I'll take a finger. Tell the Polettis..." As he ran an obviously agitated hand through his hair, he turned and saw me. "Get out," he snapped at Fender, clearly not caring that much about whatever the Polettis needed to know.

Fender gave me a nod and hurried out. I saw on the Angel's face that he knew his God was in a mood. Apollo didn't often snap at his Angels. He was all charm and suave sophistication.

"You okay?" I asked him as he drew me into his arms.

"I am now," he said, leaning his forehead to mine. "I will be now."

He kissed me, strong and deep. One hand cupped my cheek, and the other went to my hip, gripping me tightly. Something welled from deep inside me. Something big and warm and powerful. It was sympathy. It was empathy. It was protective. It was defensive. It was ready to go to war for him.

It was love.

Because I did love Apollo. I loved him with every fibre of my being. Loving him was woven into the very fabric of who I was, who I'd always be. I needed him in my life. I needed to be with him.

Part of it was newly sexual, all of it was spiritual, but I didn't know that any of it was very romantic. Not yet. Potential. There was definitely potential for it to be romantic, but it would always be more than that. What I had with Apollo would always be familial. No matter where we went from here, he was my family. He was mine as I was his. Nothing could shatter that bond. And God knew that many Magdalens had tried.

I pushed Apollo down to sit on the couch and climbed into his lap. I didn't know what I was trying to achieve, what either of us might instigate, or where this might lead. I didn't have a plan. I just needed to be close to him. We'd never done feelings and emotions before, not like this, not for many years. And I doubted he'd talk about them even if I tried. So the only thing I knew how to do was kiss him and hope that it distracted him long enough to bring him some comfort.

Apollo kissed me with passion. His hands splayed on my back, holding me to him close. He wrapped his arms around me and brought me closer. My hands were in his hair and our bodies rocked together subconsciously.

I lost track of how long we just kissed.

His hand had ended up under my top and he kneaded me

gently. It sent a jolt of pleasure to my clit and I nipped his lip.

"Fuck," he groaned.

I felt him smile and he pulled his lips from mine and leant his forehead to mine again.

"You're nothing like I expected," he breathed.

"Is that good or bad?" I asked.

He kissed me quickly, but it didn't linger. "Good. So fucking good." His nose trailed over my cheek. "I need you, Harlow," he murmured. "I didn't know how much I needed you."

I hugged him close. "He'll be okay," I said firmly.

"He'll be okay." Apollo nodded and buried his face in my neck. "He'll be okay," he repeated, like it had become his personal mantra.

By the time Valen was back on Wednesday, he looked haunted. He was a pale, haggard shadow of the man I'd last seen four days earlier. There were circles under his eyes, and they weren't all bruising. Whether Apollo didn't care what Valen looked like, or it was just far better than Apollo had dared hope for, Valen's return put the spring back in Apollo's step.

It was back to holding my hand, surprise kisses, swinging me around in the hallway. I didn't see Apollo without a wide smile on his face all day.

"Tonight," he said to me, almost bouncing with too much energy. "You and me."

I looked at him. "Movie?"

He shrugged. "Don't care."

His happiness was infectious and I smiled. "Maybe. I need to hang out with Florence for a bit, but after dinner?"

Apollo nodded, then his eyes slid behind me. "Sounds perfect." He kissed me, then bounded off.

I turned to see him catching up with Valen, who was surrounded by a cloud of vape smoke like his own personal storm made manifest.

"Did you see Valen?" Florence asked me.

I nodded, my eyes still on him.

"Clearly someone has feelings about Apollo claiming you."

I shook my head. "It's just a coincidence," I told her.

"A coincidence that he left the day Apollo decided you were kissable in public?"

"Of course it is. Valen Kincaid doesn't just disappear because Apollo kissed me."

"No?"

"No," I scoffed.

But, the way Florence and I looked at each other, I knew neither of us fully believed that.

We watched the boys go and I felt like my heart went with them.

The man I loved.

The man I wanted.

The man with arms wide open.

The man who'd said goodbye.

I sighed, plastered on a smile and turned to Florence. She knew me well enough not to push, knew me well enough to not call me out on my mood. She just gave me a sympathetic smile, looped her arm with mine, and started ranting about Shakespeare on the way to class.

† † † †

As I was leaving the boys' dorm late that night, Valen was arriving from wherever it was he'd been. He barely looked at me. The sheer fury on his face was something I'd never seen before. He looked better than he had when he'd turned up at lunch, but not by much.

He wore dark trousers and a hoodie, the hood up over his hair and his hands shoved in his pockets. He looked like he hadn't shaved in days. If it was possible for Valen Kincaid to look small, he looked it now. Almost like he was hunching in on himself.

"I didn't expect to see you back in one piece," I said to him.

He stopped walking like he knew he had no other choice and sucked his teeth like he was praying for patience. "There's less of me than there was," he said, like it was a promise, like he thought that would please me.

I took a breath, torn between concern for him and annoyance at his attitude.

"Well, Apollo's definitely glad you're back," I said. I knew it wasn't like me to be civil with him, but I just needed to talk to him, to find out that he was really okay.

Valen scoffed humourlessly. "I doubt the fucker even noticed I was gone. His head's stuck in the fucking clouds. Rainbows in his eyes and stars up his fucking arse. Next he'll be singing and dancing in the fucking hallways." He didn't often have a thick accent, but it came out in full force now.

I frowned at him. "He's happy, and you're pissed about it?"

He turned to face me sharply. "I'm not *pissed* about it,

princess. I'm annoyed by it. He's annoying me. Fucking giggling and wanting me to have a good time."

"So now you just don't want anyone to be happy because it inconveniences you?"

"Of course," he answered sarcastically. "It's always all about me."

"He's your God, your closest friend, and you can't even let him be happy?"

He snarled. "This new sunny disposition he's frolicking about with, love? Let's not pretend we don't know why that is, shall we?"

I bristled. "Let's, Valen," I suggested. "Because I certainly don't know what you're implying."

He snarled at me again. When he didn't say anything more, I decided to push. My conversation with Florence was at the forefront of my mind.

"Weird timing," I commented. "You've never been called away during term before, have you?"

"What's that supposed to mean?" he snapped.

I shrugged. "Just that maybe someone left because they were jealous."

He growled again. "If I was jealous, would I have just spent the last few hours with my cock in a couple of Magdalens? Would I have spent the last three weeks fucking any idiot who'll spread her legs for me?"

I wasn't going to pretend that didn't hurt just a little because he was obviously suggesting I was one of those idiots. "I don't think the two are mutually exclusive, no."

"Apollo can have you. I don't fucking care."

"Well, he hasn't," I told him quickly, like it suddenly mattered that he knew.

"What?" For a moment, it looked like he did care.

"He hasn't… We haven't…"

Another humourless scoff. "Then, it's just a matter of time."

"And you don't care at all?"

He shrugged. "I couldn't care less."

"Seriously?" I asked. "You've got no feelings about me fucking Apollo?"

"Is apathy a feeling, love? Because I have loads of that."

"That feeling is mutual, Valen," I said with venom in my voice.

Anger flashed in his eyes. He'd been angry before, but this was something else. He hadn't liked that. He hadn't liked that at all.

"Apathy's a good colour on you, princess," he said. "Looks an awful lot like denial."

"God, I hate you," I snapped as I turned to leave.

He grabbed my arm, his other arm pulling me right against his body. "But you want me more."

"Do I?" I asked casually. "What makes you think that?"

"I know you. And I know how good we are together." He left the unspoken 'how good we could be together again' hanging, but I felt it.

"Here I thought one of us had to walk away?"

He growled. "And one of us will."

I frowned at him. "Right. And it will be me."

"Are you suddenly not interested, princess?"

"Whatever this was, Valen, it's over. It's done. It's never happening again."

"I've heard that before, love."

"Yeah? Well, I haven't forgotten how much I hate you now, so I can safely say I don't want you."

But we both knew that was a lie. The more I hated him, the more I wanted him. And he'd made me hate him something shocking.

There was a knowing mischief in his eyes, like he knew. He knew all he had to do was infuriate me and I wouldn't be able to deny him any longer. Well, he'd been denying me for nearly three weeks, I could surely hold out for the next few minutes until I found the effort to get out of there.

The corner of his lips kicked up into the most sinfully sexy half-smirk. "We both know that's bullshit." He leant down to my ear. "Just like you know I never stopped wanting you. Hate. Want. You and I, we can't do one without the other, princess."

I looked into his eyes and nodded. "Maybe not, but I *can* walk away from you."

"Just you wait," he told me. "It's only a matter of time before you're desperate for my cock again."

I gave him my own knowing smirk. "Who says I'm not already?" I shrugged coyly. "But I spent four years wanting you and not being able to have you, Valen. And I didn't have the luxury of idiots willing to spread their legs for me. All I had was eight inches of moulded silicon to bury inside me while I thought about your cock. For four fucking years. I survived those four years without anyone else touching me. I can survive again for as long as it takes. Can you say the same?"

Heat pooled in his eyes and his jaw twitched. That, he'd liked. I didn't care that I'd given so much away, it was worth it to see the desire and need in those stormy eyes. It was worth it to see it straining against his carefully crafted control like a beast dying to be unleashed.

Time to hammer the nail home.

"Only this time, I've got another who'll touch me." I widened my eyes cheekily at him. "Think how much longer I can survive with Apollo's touch to ease the ache between my legs that *you* cause in me." I leant up to his ear. "His fingers where yours could be. His cock where yours has been." I nipped his ear lobe playfully. "His name wrenched from my lips—"

Valen pushed me against the closest wall and kissed me hard. It was all desperation and passion and a fire that threatened to consume us. Anyone could come along and see us, but I didn't care. He was like water in the desert, like a big, soft bed at the end of a tiring week, like air after holding a breath for too long.

Lips and hands roamed freely, without purpose. Like all we needed or wanted was each other. We were in serious danger of just having each other there and then, consequences be damned. I wanted it – him – so badly. But not like this. Not now. He wanted to play games with me? Well, I could play games with him, too.

With all the strength I had, I pushed him away.

He stumbled backwards, breathing heavily, like he was at my utter mercy.

"Harlow," he begged.

I shook my head. "One of us has to walk away, Valen," I

reminded him.

"Neither of us want to."

No. Neither of us did want to, but he'd made it very clear there was a power struggle going on here and I was going to walk away with the upper hand this time.

"No. But one of us has to."

So, I did. I pushed past him and hurried back to the girls' dorms, fighting with myself the whole way there. All I wanted was to go back and have him drag me into the closest private corner and fuck me until I didn't want him anymore. I wasn't sure that was possible, to ever stop wanting him, so it was best to just not have him at all.

It made for a hellish next few days. The sexual tension between us could be cut with a proverbial knife, or a real one. Apollo didn't seem to notice and, if anyone else did, only Florence mentioned it. And she mentioned it a lot.

I told myself to just get over it – get over him – but I couldn't. Valen had become my own personal brand of heroine and I knew it was only a matter of time before I relapsed.

Chapter Twenty

What was I doing? Why was this my job?

I huffed as I hurried from the mail room to the boys' dorm the next Tuesday night.

It was raining, if only lightly, but there was a distant rumble of thunder, more like mere vibrations on the air. Whether the storm came this way or not, I didn't want to be playing errands for longer than necessary.

As I entered the boys' dorm, I looked around for anyone to help me. Marco saw me and jutted his chin toward me in what classified as a greeting to those Neanderthals.

"Can I help you, missus?" he asked.

I mentally rolled my eyes at him, but put in my saccharine smile. "I'm looking for Valen's room." I brandished the mysterious package. "Apollo wanted me to drop something off to him."

Marco nodded. "Quickest way... You know the cheeky service stairs?"

I shook my head.

Marco nodded as though he'd expected as much. "No. Right.

Third floor. Past God's room. Number nine." His thick Irish accent was the only pleasing thing about him.

I gave him a nod and scurried up the stairs.

"In and out," I muttered to myself as I headed for the third floor. "You'll just be in and out."

Which Valen most definitely wouldn't be.

I got to his room and knocked, but there was no answer. I knocked again. Still no answer. I looked at the package in my hand and swore under my breath. Apollo's instructions had been very clear: take the package from the delivery driver and take it straight to Valen, and it had to be put into Valen's hands.

I told myself the only reason I was going through with Apollo's cryptic and ridiculous orders was just on the off chance it was actually important. I knew they got up to shady shit. Exactly what wasn't my purview and they kept all that as separate from me as possible. So, whatever this was, if it had to be entrusted to me, it must have been important.

My obedience had absolutely nothing to do with me wanting to see Valen again after our last encounter.

As I looked around the corridor, I tried the handle to Valen's door. It was unlocked, so I opened it and peeked inside. So far as I could see, the room was empty. I opened the door further and took a step inside.

The Saints clearly got preferential treatment. I was a blinding beacon to that. I'd only had to share a room with one other person my whole Saint Benedicts career. Most of the girls shared in threes or fours until final year. Obviously, the old boys' club had special privileges one step further and it wasn't just Apollo who benefited.

There was only one bed in Valen's room. One giant bed with room for two people – or more. There was a huge window covered in thick velvet curtains. Two doors stood in the wall to my right which I suspected opened into his private bathroom and walk in robe.

The whole room was decked out in deep, red wood. Any coloured accents were black or grey. The bed spread. The couch. The TV unit and bedside tables. His desk and chair. Even a large wingback in the darkened corner. The fireplace to my left was cold and empty, even for this time of year, throwing no light on the lush rug in front of it.

The room was stark, offering no insights into the man who lived there. Nothing other than he was meticulous and tidy.

Still there was no sign of him. Wondering if I should just put the box on his desk and be done with it, I knew there was no way in hell I was leaving without seeing him. I looked around his room once more and decided the wingback in the corner looked the least likely defiled. I dropped into it and waited.

Sometime later, his door opened and I heard a distinctly feminine giggle. Valen walked in with a tottery, giggly Magdalen in the tiniest dress and tallest heels I'd ever seen. As she leant against his arm, I wasn't even sure she went to our school.

I got up as he reached for something on his desk, making the wingback scrape against the floor as I did.

Valen's eyes flew to me and I was almost scared of the look on his face. I stepped into the light and he visibly relaxed. He picked up what looked like his phone and pocketed it.

"Miss Vanguard," he said.

"Sorry I interrupted," I said coldly, not sure why I felt so sick all of a sudden.

"I'm taking her to Apollo," he said carefully, like it was a message. I just couldn't decipher it.

The idiot giggled. "I've got a meeting with God!"

I rolled my eyes. "You keep drinking in those heels and you sure will," I muttered.

It sounded an awful lot like Valen actually laughed. But it was only short-lived and poorly hidden behind a cough.

"Wait here and I'll be back," Valen said to me.

I hesitated. Technically my job wasn't done yet. That was the only reason I was staying.

I nodded like it was a hardship. "Fine."

I dropped back into the chair. Valen's hand went to the Magdalen's arm, and he paused before leading her out. I crossed my legs and jiggled the top one while I fiddled with the box in my hands and waited for Valen to return. He seemed to take an age.

Probably joined in, I thought.

"Why did you sit there?" he asked.

I jumped and found him leaning against the wall by the door, just watching me. Who knew how long he'd been there.

"What?" I asked.

He kicked his chin at me, pushed off the wall and headed over. His great long strides ate up the not insignificant room size and he was standing in front of me in moments. His crotch was level with my head, and I entertained the notion of releasing him from his jeans and seeing how he tasted. Only for a moment.

"Why did you sit there?" he asked again.

"On this chair?" I clarified and he nodded. "The one specifically designed for sitting?"

The corner of his lips turned up in a smirk. "That's not what it's for."

I leapt out of the chair with a yelp, running into his chest and nearly dropping the box. His hands caught and steadied me easily and he didn't move. The backs of my legs were so hard up against the seat of the wingback that I had no choice but to lean on him or fall back into the chair that wasn't as clean as I'd thought it was.

"I assumed it was the safest thing in here," I said, glaring up at him.

"Safest as in…?"

"As in the least defiled by your shenanigans."

He huffed a rough laugh as he looked me over hungrily. "Ah, you want the bed, princess."

Me, in his bed? I thought about it.

I pushed against him and shoved the box into his chest. "Apollo wanted me to bring you this. Although, I'm not sure why he couldn't do it since he wasn't busy…yet," I said pointedly.

"My fault. I was late picking her up."

"Lovely. Well, I've done my job. I'll be going."

He took the box from me but threw it away. It landed safely on the middle of his bed.

"Do you really want to go?" he purred, taking a step to force me back.

My legs buckled against the chair and his arm went around me to keep me standing.

My heart thudded in my chest and warmth pooled between my legs.

No. I didn't want to leave. I wanted him to throw me against the nearest wall and have his dirty way with me. Not that I was going to tell him that.

He dipped his nose to my hair and my traitorous body tilted my head to give him better access. A rumble of a laugh vibrated through him. As my hand slid over the bulge in his pants, his grabbed my arse. I rubbed over him again and he swore.

He swivelled us so my back was against the wall beside us, his forehead to mine as I stroked him through his pants. He breathed heavily and his hand roamed my body. He slid it over me firmly like he was committing it to memory, like his touch was worship in and of itself.

"Valen…" I started and my voice was a breathy plea.

He picked me up and pushed me up the wall so my breasts were in line with his face. One arm lay under me, helping to hold me up, while a hand kneaded me roughly and he sucked my other nipple through my shirt.

"You thought jeans were going to help you keep your legs crossed?" he asked.

I held his head to my body. "It was worth a try," I breathed.

I felt the vibrations of his laugh rumbling through his chest.

"Tell me you want it," he said.

"You tell me," I answered.

For all our playing at who was in charge, he always seemed much more in control of himself than me. I was sick of it. For once, I wanted to at least be as in control as him.

"I want you," he said, his teeth grazing my breast. He dropped me just so my head was in line with his. "I fucking need you, princess. Need to bury myself deep inside you and feel you quiver on my cock as you cum for me. Tell me you want it."

I was breathing heavily, and from no exertion on my part. I looked into storm grey eyes that were threatening to burn right into my soul. God, but I hated him. He was an arrogant, womanising, violent arsehole. But he played me like his own personal instrument, and I couldn't bring myself to deny him any longer.

"I want it," I told him.

"What do you want?" he demanded.

"I want you to fuck me," I said.

His breath caught and I noticed the heat rage in his eyes. He liked it. I'd excited him. It made me confident enough to keep going.

"I want you to play dirty."

I was worried he wouldn't understand me, but his next actions told me he knew exactly what I'd meant.

Valen dropped my feet to the ground, spun me around and pressed me into the wall from behind.

"Are you scared you'll like it?" I asked, harking back.

He chuckled, low and deep. "Scared isn't the word I'd use."

His had slid down between my legs and I parted them for him.

"Is this what you want, princess?" he asked. This time his voice was soft, tantalising.

I nodded as I pressed my arse back into him.

His fingers went to my waistband and he undid my jeans. His lips dropped to my neck and he kissed it as he pulled my jeans and panties down. He rubbed over my clit from behind as he kissed and nipped and sucked my neck.

I moaned and rocked back into him again. He splayed my arse cheeks with one hand and he undid his trousers with the other.

"Fuck," he breathed as his cock slid into me.

I breathed out heavily myself as he drove deep into me, both of us using the wall for support.

He started out slowly as his hands roamed around my body. Across my stomach. Kneading my breast. Over my back. Gripping my waist. Long, deep thrusts. Finally, his fingers dropped to my clit as his other hand lay gently over my exposed throat, pulling my body to his. My head fell back against his shoulder.

My breaths came faster and louder as the twisting coil of pleasure built up inside me.

"Valen..." I sighed.

"You gonna cum for me, princess?" he breathed in my ear.

I nodded against him as he thrust long and deep and hard. "Make me cum," I told him.

His finger circled my clit faster as he thrust faster. Unlike all our other trysts, I didn't worry about how much noise I made. I moaned his name and I bit my lip as the pleasure coiled and tightened, grew and spread.

My whole body tried curling in on itself as my orgasm washed over me, but Valen held me strongly against his body. His fingers and his thrusts slowing while I recovered.

"Is that all you've got?" I asked him as we rocked together.

"You wanna play rough, princess?" he growled appreciatively.

I nodded. "I wanna play rough."

He pulled out of me, grabbed my arm and threw me at the couch. He was behind me before I'd managed to stand up. His arm went across my shoulders, and he pulled my back to his front once more with his lips bent to my ear.

"Tell me if it's too rough," he said, almost as a challenge.

"You think I can't handle it?" I scoffed, not sure myself if I could.

I felt his laugh again. "I think it's more fun while you're enjoying it."

I understood what he meant now. I nodded. "I'll tell you."

"Good."

He lifted me up so my knees were on the couch and bent me towards the back as he plunged into me again. His thrusts were deep and unrelenting. He ploughed me hard and fast. When he slapped my arse, it surprised me so much I jerked up and looked back at him.

His eyebrow quirked in amusement. "You didn't like that?"

My eyes narrowed. "I don't know that I did."

He nodded. "Duly noted."

His arm wrapped around my body and pulled me to his front again. He squeezed my breast hard as he drove into me again and again.

"How's that?" he asked.

I nodded.

"You like that?"

"I like that."

"Good to know."

My legs started trembling as my orgasm built and I quivered in his arms.

"You do like that," he purred, proud approval dripping from his voice.

It was all I could do not to just go limp in his arms.

"Valen," I moaned. "I'm…"

"Gonna cum for me?"

"Fall," I managed to say.

His other arm wrapped around me tightly. "I've got you," he whispered in my ear.

His grip on my breast was so tight, but the pain twisted and turned until there was nothing but pleasure. He hammered into me without mercy or any sign of slowing. He kept right on going until my body convulsed with the force of my orgasm. And even that didn't stop him. He just held me tight and kept hammering me.

I came twice. Three times.

He bent me back over to lean on the back of the couch and his hand went to my clit. He rubbed it furiously. His pace matching his thrusts.

Four times. Five.

I honestly didn't know how much more my body could handle.

Finally, he turned me around to face him and sat on the couch. He helped me stand as he pulled my jeans down further and pulled me into his lap. My feet were bound by my jeans, but my knees fell to either side of his legs as he pulled me down on his cock. And still he rammed me.

"I think you've got one more in you," he said.

I managed a weak smile. "Are you sure?"

His lips went to my neck and yeah…I had one more in me.

My whole body shook with the force of it, and I clenched tightly around him as I moaned his name.

"Fuck," he moaned as he took one massive thrust into me and paused.

I felt him pulsing in me. Steady throbs that made me want more. So, I took it. Took more. I rocked against him. I rolled my hips, rubbing him up inside me. I saw the look in his eyes. Approval. Pride. Enjoyment. He put his hands on my waist, pressing me further down onto him, pushing himself deeper as I rode him.

"Yes, love," he said, a crooked smile at his lips. "Fuck, yes."

I went faster and I saw the point he lost control. It was like a switch flipped in his eyes. He grabbed me to him and drove deeper and deeper into me until he came hard.

As we got our breaths back, we clung to each other as though we'd slip into the abyss if we let go. Both breathing hard, hearts pounding from exertion. Our heads on each other's shoulder.

He ran his hand over my side, and I shied away from the tickle with a breathy laugh.

"You're ticklish?" he asked, brushing his nose along my neck.

"If I cum hard enough, yeah," I answered lazily, enjoying the feel of his closeness. Not that I'd tell him that.

"What was that? Like five times?"

I nodded against him. "Mmm. Seven?" Then I laughed at how ridiculous that sounded.

He ran his hand over me again. It was still ticklish, but less. I still twitched.

"You liked it," he said, sounding surprised.

"Was that not the idea?" I asked.

He huffed a rough chuckle as he wrapped his arms around my waist and buried his nose in my shoulder. "I just didn't expect the good little princess to like it dirty."

"What *did* you expect, Valen? I'd be all vanilla and only let you do me missionary?"

"Mm, no," he said, and I felt him smile against my neck. "Not really. I don't know."

"Did you think about it? About me?"

"More than I should." His hands went to my waist, and he sat up to look in my eyes. "I thought about the day we met. I thought about our first class together three years ago. Being stuck in the same room as you where all I could think about was how much I wanted to bend you over Mr Galikani's desk and make you mine."

I broke out in a smile which would not suppress a laugh.

"What?" he asked, searching my eyes.

"I thought about that, too."

At the look of awed disbelief on his face, I buried my face in his shoulder again to hide my smile.

"Fucking hell," he muttered, brushing my hair back to kiss my neck.

I tilted my head to give him better access.

"You still think this won't happen again?" he asked.

"You do?"

"The only hope we have is for you to fuck me out of your

system."

"Oh, you'd like that. Wouldn't you?"

His lips grazed over my throat, trailed across my cheek and brushed a whispered kiss over my lips. "So would you."

My clit very much agreed with him. Had it been in charge, I would have definitely tried fucking him out of my system, whatever exactly that entailed. But my larger head was in charge.

"It's irrelevant and not at all necessary because I don't need to fuck you out of my system."

"Say it again," he purred against my throat, making my nipples pull taught.

"Say what?" I asked.

"Like you mean it this time." I heard the humour in his voice.

I pushed him away from me in annoyance.

"You are so arrogant," I spat. "You honestly think people have nothing better to do than lie in their beds, wishing you were pounding them?"

The fact I had done so once – or twice – had no bearing on my point.

"You say you're done, and yet here we are. Your face still flushed that pleasant shade of pink from what I did to you."

I stumbled in an effort to stand up. He was there, like protecting me was instinct. I let him only until I got my jeans buttoned back up. By the time I was done, he was tucked back into his trousers.

"You just don't take no for an answer do you."

"You didn't say no."

I couldn't refute that. "Well, I'm saying no now."

His fingers tickled the waistband of my jeans and my body went to him willingly. "We're going to have to work on our safe words, princess. I don't want any mixed messages."

I batted his hand away from me and he chuckled, sending tingles through my stomach.

"Your lips say no, but your hips say yes," he purred.

It was true, but still.

"Ugh!" I grunted. "You're insufferable!"

"You're the one who wants me," he said.

"Last I checked," I answered flippantly, "the feeling was mutual." I glared at him. "I hate you."

"Last I checked," he said cheekily, "the feeling was mutual."

"And they say you're a master of seduction," I scoffed sarcastically.

He closed in on me, standing a hair's breadth away from me, and staring down at me, his eyes dark and narrowed. "I don't have to like you to fuck you. To want to feel your body tremble with every orgasm I give you. To want to pound you until I can't hold on anymore. Again. And again. I can hate you and still leave you craving more."

"Can you?" I asked sceptically.

"Yes."

"And what makes you so sure about that?"

He span me to pull my back to his front and his hand was at my throat. His other hand pressed my hips back into him. He was already hard again. "Because I can't stand you and this is what you do to me."

I didn't need to check to know the feeling was mutual.

I struggled out of his arms and started for the door, but he grabbed my arm. I ripped it out of his hand so forcefully that I almost fell over. Instinct took over and I reached for it again. As he always was, he was there to steady me.

"Don't touch me," I said harshly.

His hand came off me like I'd burned him with more than words. "You can't just…" He swore.

"What?" I scoffed. "Walk away? Clearly, Valen, I can."

His mouth twisted angrily. "Walk out the front door," he snarled.

I blinked. "What?"

"I told Apollo you left an hour ago. You can't go out the front door."

"Oh," I said sarcastically. "You don't think he's actually finished with her yet, do you?"

He huffed a laugh. "He'd like to think he can last as long as me."

I rolled my eyes. "It's not a pissing contest," I said as I started for the door again.

"No. It's a literal fucking contest," he growled and that stopped me.

"Excuse me?"

"One day, he'll be forced to have you," he said as he walked towards me. "On that day, the only cock I want you thinking of is mine."

A thrill of excitement ran through me. "I'm sure I'll forget you by next week." Lies.

He shook his head. "I've tried being patient with you,

princess."

I put a hand on his chest. "You don't give the orders here, Valen," I warned him. "I do. And I say I'm leaving now. You can't stop me."

"Fine," he said, though it was obviously anything but. "At least leave with a little discretion."

"What? With a bag over my face?"

He growled. "Never," he said forcefully. "Never talk about yourself like that."

I shrugged. "What am I supposed to do?"

"Service stairs," he said, like that was an answer.

"Cheeky little service stairs?" I asked, remembering Marco's words.

Valen's eyebrow rose. "You know where they are?"

"No, Valen," I huffed. "I don't. I haven't had any cause to be sneaking out of the boys' dorms before."

Another angry twist marred his lips for a moment. "The only room you'll be sneaking out of is mine," he said, another warning.

"Where are they?" I asked, both thrilled by and sick of the possessive streak.

"I'll show you."

He pushed past me and went for his door. He held his arm over me as he looked out into the corridor, then nodded and held the door open for me.

"A girl might mistake you for a gentleman," I teased.

"A girl isn't that stupid," he said absently as he kept scanning the corridor as though he thought someone was going to see us.

He led me the opposite way from the main stairs, closer to his room.

"Here," he said, stopping at a door. "This'll take you to the quad in front of your dorm."

"That's where they go," I mused. Florence and I had always wondered where that door went but, the only time we'd been brave enough to investigate, it was locked.

I nodded and started for it, but he put an arm in front of me. I looked up at him and the moment was charged with something I didn't want to name. For a moment, I thought he was going to kiss me. Then he shook his head, dropped his arm and kicked his head towards the door.

"Go."

I went, not wanting to stay in that moment that so easily could have become something else.

The ache had been sated. For now.

But I knew there was a much deeper need in me to feel him again.

He'd said I needed to fuck him out of my system? Well, I didn't know exactly how to do that, but I was going to find a way to try.

Chapter Twenty-One

"Yeah," Florence said with a cheeky grin the next night. "But it's a party. On a Wednesday. In the common room."

I was trying to do my homework and not think about what Valen had last done to me.

I smiled. "And I said you could go if you want."

"I won't get in without you!"

"Tell them I sent you," I laughed. "Go on. Marco's probably waiting on you."

"Marco's probably got his tongue down some Magdalen's throat. Wait." She grimaced. "Ew, does that make me a Magdalen?"

"No!" I shook my head. "No. You're like me."

She snorted. "I'm *never* going to be a goddess. Much less *the* Goddess of Saint Benedicts. That's all your fate, babe. I will leave that to you."

I laughed. "Not what I meant. No. You're not a Magdalen. You'll never be a Magdalen. You could fuck Apollo himself and still not be a Magdalen. I won't allow it."

She gave me a side eye. "I've thought about it, you know."

"Have you?" I smirked.

She nodded. "Yeah. I didn't hate it."

"I'll bet you didn't!"

She scrunched her face up and nodded. "You don't mind?"

"Mind?" I chortled. "Floss, you get to do whatever you want in the privacy of your own brain. Besides, I can hardly complain. I think I'm still sore, and Valen was…only just last night."

She chuckled. "Yeah. Just the sound of that gave me a touch of green envy."

If a guy was ever going to challenge you to fuck him out of your system, that had definitely been the kind of sex to do it after.

I still thought about it. Vividly. I was replaying it in my head so many times, I felt like a broken record up there.

It wasn't just that the sex had been good – better than good. It was how it had felt. How we'd felt. The air of passion and possession and obsession that had swirled around us, encompassed us. Something had shifted, albeit very slightly, and I doubted it would ever be the same again.

I sighed. "It was amazing."

"It sounded it. And you're still adamant it's not happening again?"

"He said the only chance we have is if I fuck him out of my system–"

"Which you don't want to do," she reminded me, but it felt more like a question.

I nodded. "If I do that, then I have to actually acknowledge that it means...something."

She looked at me like I was an idiot. "And what's wrong with that?"

"Floss, I can't have any kind of *something* with Valen Kincaid. It doesn't matter if it's good sex–"

"Great sex," she corrected.

"Tremendous sex," I agreed. "And it doesn't matter if it's just sex or more or whatever. I can't have anything that means something with him. Fucking him out of my system acknowledges that it's something."

"I think we're past that point, babe."

"Yes." I nodded. "You and I know that, but Valen doesn't know that."

She laughed. "I think he knows."

"Okay. He knows. I know. He knows I know he knows. I know he..." I shook my head. "You know what I mean, but we haven't talked about it. We haven't put it into words. We haven't *made* it something."

"Haven't you?"

Had we? We'd talked about how much we hated each other. How well we did hate and want. It wasn't the kind of something one often intentionally aspires to, but it *was* still something.

"Not... Not really." I sighed. "Maybe."

"You can admit you just don't want it to end..." she said slowly, hesitatingly, like she wasn't sure if giving me permission was what I wanted or needed.

I looked at her as I took that in. "Oh, God. I don't, do I? I don't want it to end."

She shook her head. "And that's okay."

"No, it's not. I'm supposed to marry Apollo."

"As long as Apollo's fucking around, you should be, too."

It wasn't just that. That was a good point and I agreed, but... Forgetting the fact I was meant to end up with Apollo and therefore any fucking around with anyone would have to end eventually, Valen was...well, Valen. I couldn't afford to get attached to anyone, and I certainly didn't want to already be attached to Valen-fucking-Kincaid. Problem was...

I nodded. "Yes, but if I don't want it to end with Valen, then it's beyond just fucking around. It's most definitely already something. I haven't just forgotten I hate him..."

"You like him."

I frowned. "I wouldn't go that far."

"I would."

"Florence!"

"Okay. Fine. Let's just say, you don't hate him."

"Ugh. That sounds worse!"

Florence laughed. "Okay. So let's go to the party and we'll put Valen behind you."

"Yeah," I scoffed, vividly remembering the previous night, where that's exactly where he'd been. "If only."

She snorted. "That's the spirit!"

I threw my pen down and stood up. "Fine. Let's go to the party."

Sometimes, I felt like Florence just wanted an excuse to dress up. That she'd have been just as happy dolling ourselves up and then just sitting around watching rom-coms. And, why wouldn't she? She was gorgeous first thing in the morning on the first day of her period. Of course she was. A self-confident, vibrant personality like hers was going to make her sexy. It didn't matter she wielded her sensual curves and perfect bone structure to full effect, she was also a gorgeous human on the inside.

We paused at the door to the common room, hand in hand. The party was in full swing. At least, what counted for full swing for one of these get togethers. There were Saintlings on each door to keep out the rabble and the riffraff – both staff and student. This was an exclusive gathering, reserved only for final year Saints. And Florence.

One of the Saintlings at the door looked Florence over and I knew what he was thinking. I shook my head at him.

"She's with me," I told him.

He visibly gulped. "I...I should check with Gage..."

I shook my head again. "You want me to tell your God that *you* denied his princess' wish?"

Another visible gulp, and his little Saintling friend whispered, "Dude! That's Harlow Vanguard!"

They did look young. Probably Year Sevens. It wasn't their fault they didn't know who I was yet. I knew from my own introduction to Saint-dom that there was no orientation. You learned on the job or you got booted.

The first Saintling looked me over. "Isn't she one of the Magdalens?"

Florence's hand shot out and slapped him. Then it flew to her mouth in surprise. Then she frowned and doubled down.

"Fuck you," Florence chastised him. "This is your goddess and you will bow down to her!"

"Oi, oi, missus," Marco said as he saw us. "Trouble with your ticket?"

"These little Shitlings you arseholes like to boss around thought Harlow was a Magdalen," Florence told him.

Marco's gaze narrowed on them.

"It was him," the second told Marco. "I knew who she was."

Marco gave a pale imitation of the growl Valen was so well known for, and slapped the first kid upside the head so hard he took an involuntary knee. "You will respect Miss Vanguard. You will do as Miss Vanguard says. Do ye hear me?"

They both nodded.

Marco smiled at me. "Right, then. Now that's settled. Thank ye for walking Miss Vanguard, Florence. But I can take it from here."

Florence took a step towards him, but I held a hand out to stop her.

"Florence is my guest, Marco. Consider her my plus one."

Marco opened his mouth to argue, but I continued.

"Or will you disobey Miss Vanguard?" I sassed.

The corner of his lips tipped up and I guess I could see what Florence saw in him. Like the good little dramatic Angel he was, he took a very voluntary knee in front of me.

"Your wish is my command, missus," he said as he lay his fist over his heart.

I gave him a little pat on the head and a wink as I stepped passed him. He returned the wink.

"Cheeky," I warned him.

"Right back at ye, missus," he said, but I heard the note of respect in his voice.

"Remind me why he calls you 'missus' again?" Florence said.

"Because I'm going to be Apollo's missus eventually," I said absently as I looked around. "He figures he may as well get a head start."

"And what happens with them when we graduate?"

"What do you mean?"

"Who are you looking for?" she countered, then continued. "I mean with the other Angels. I get Valen has some kind of bond with Apollo, but what about the others? Do they get to put 'Saint Benedicts' God's Angel' on their resume or something?"

I shrugged. "They come along for the ride as well."

"Really?"

I nodded. "I think so. Dad's security and closest people were his Angels, so," I shrugged again, "I guess they'll go wherever we end up living."

"You came!" I heard Apollo say and turned just in time for him to throw his arms around me and kiss me hard.

"Hi," I laughed as he pulled away.

"Hi," he said, then turned his smile to Florence. "Flo. Who do I have to beat to keep out the plebs, these days, huh?"

I knew Apollo beat up the Saintlings with very little cause, but his grin was clearly infectious. I could see Florence trying not to smirk in return.

"Don't worry," she answered, "I did it for you."

I nodded to him. "She did. She smacked one of your Saintlings."

"They thought Harlow was a Magdalen!" Florence said in defence.

Apollo looked at her. "I'll allow it. Maybe God needs five Angels?"

Florence scoffed. "First female Angel?"

For a moment, I thought she was considering it. I could just imagine Florence Walton kicking arse and taking names. She'd definitely give Valen and Marco a run for their money. She'd never best them in a physical fight, but she could destroy them mentally and verbally.

After a heartbeat, she rolled her eyes and continued, "Yeah, no. I'll pass on that one."

Apollo shrugged. "Suit yourself. Job's yours if you want it."

Something made me look to the door while they continued arguing about Florence's potential first female angel status.

Valen stalked into the room and my whole body tingled. He had a bruise blossoming on his cheekbone that hadn't been there when I'd left his room the night before. My hand twitched by my side like it wanted to run my fingers over his face, hold it gently, and seriously consider his words from the previous night.

His grey eyes scanned the room, barely even pausing as they passed over me. Like I wasn't even there. He exuded indifference as he flicked his hair out of his face and sucked on his vape pen. He looked bored. He looked like he had better things – or maybe people – to do.

I wondered why he'd even bothered turning up. Then he headed straight for one of the Magdalens and it all made sense. I wanted to say he wasn't ensuring I saw him making moves on her, but I couldn't stop thinking he wanted me to think I meant nothing to him.

Even his indifference, especially his indifference, got to me. It made my blood zing, my whole body flush, warmth pool between my legs, and my heart skip in my chest. He was utter deliciousness is a tall, dark and dangerous package.

Did I want to fuck him out of my system?

Well, I'd just recently realised that I didn't want it to end. I didn't want to give him up. He was addictive. He was fire and passion and being in the moment. He made me feel alive. He made me forget the bars on my cage. I didn't feel like a bystander in my own life anymore. I wasn't waiting for life to start. I was living.

But...should I fuck him out of my system?

Probably.

As I'd told Florence, I didn't want to admit to him that between us was enough of something that I needed to take drastic measures to overcome it. And that's exactly how fucking him out of my system would feel; drastic measures.

Then there was whatever was blossoming between me and Apollo. At some point I'd owe it to him to give Valen up. Like I expected – rather, would demand – there was a point where he'd owe it to me to give up his Magdalens. But I had no idea when that would be. I had no way to know what his cut off was. When we finally had sex? When we got engaged? Married?

Without knowing, there was no reason to give Valen up for Apollo. Not yet.

But maybe I had to give Valen up for me.

Maybe it was time to cut the cord. I was already in dangerously deep. The fact I desperately wanted him to look at me while he was whispering something no doubt deliciously dirty in Mina's ear was enough to tell me I was in too deep. I was very close to letting emotions get the better of me. Emotions that weren't just hate and annoyance. Emotions like jealousy.

And if I was even considering feeling jealous, then I needed to get out.

I needed to fuck him out of my system. Because God knew – or, hopefully didn't – I wasn't getting over him cold turkey.

An embarrassingly high pitched squeal left me as arms went around me and Apollo nuzzled my neck. By the time my eyes found Valen again, he was glaring at me. His hand was on the wall next to Mina's head, his face was right next hers, but his eyes were burning blazing contempt in my direction. Mina whispered something in his ear and the corner of his lip turned up. It wasn't so much a challenge as a promise.

A promise I fully wanted to know more about, but Apollo started kissing my neck and Valen was temporarily forgotten.

"I didn't think you were coming tonight," Apollo whispered in my ear.

Goose bumps chased across my skin and I felt my nipples pull taught. I span in his arms and he wrapped them closer around me.

"I wasn't going to," I replied.

His nose trailed across my neck, my jaw, my cheek. "What made you change your mind?"

"Florence wanted to come."

I felt him chuckle against my cheek. "I'm finding less and less to dislike about her lately."

"Here I thought you'd be jealous I didn't change my mind for you."

290

"Oh, I am," he said, and I heard the humour in his voice. "But you're here, and now I'm going to make you glad you came."

"How do you plan on doing that?" I asked.

He kissed me. Hard. His hand going to the back of my neck. I wrapped my arms around his shoulders and, just as I thought it was heated enough for a public place, he picked me up and sat me on the back of the couch beside us. He stepped in close between my legs and kissed me like I was life itself.

I forgot about everything and anything except Apollo Callahan and his lips on mine, his hands on my body, sliding up under my top, his pelvis rocking against mine...

A commotion to our right pulled Apollo's attention.

Valen was being physically restrained. It took Marco, Fender and Gage to hold him back from whichever unfortunate he'd turned his eye to at that moment.

"Fucking hell," Apollo muttered. "That's the third fucker tonight…" He looked at me, an apology in his eyes. The apology was not about his language. "I'd better go and sort him."

I nodded, thinking that was probably in everyone's best interests. "Okay. No worries."

Valen whirled on Marco and took a swing at him.

"Fucking get off me!" Valen roared.

I slid carefully off the back of the couch, my eyes glued to Valen.

Apollo skidded to a stop in front of Valen, his hands up like he was dealing with a skittish or scared animal. "Valk, come on, man."

Valen turned an eye on him and I saw his lip was now split.

He spat to the side and wiped his hand over his mouth. "Don't fucking tell me to 'come on'. You just go back to your princess. Don't want the wee lass getting frightened by the big, bad wolf."

A shiver ran over me.

"Scared isn't the word I'd use," I said, loud enough for them all to hear.

Apollo turned a proud smile on me. If only those words meant what he thought they did. What they all thought they did. All but Valen. Valen would know what they meant.

Not that I paid Apollo that much attention.

Because Valen looked at me, too.

I crooked my eyebrow at him, a challenge. Did he dare say anything in front of his God? Did he dare try to insult me further?

Although, Florence was probably the only person beside me and Valen who knew the insult wasn't actually to my character, but by pretending it was all about me.

Valen didn't need me as an excuse to 'behave'. He didn't need me as an excuse to misbehave. But he was apparently not above using me as one anyway.

We stared at each other and a battle of wills played out. To anyone else, it was Apollo's goddess facing off against the wolf, taming him to her coming rule. We knew better. Oh, I was taming him to my rule all right, but not as Apollo's. I was doing it as my own self.

Finally he snarled, grabbed Mina and strode from the room.

There was a great raucous applause for my perceived win. I smiled and gave a little bow but, when my eyes met Florence's, she saw my real feelings.

I hadn't really won.

Valen was quite happy to let them all think I had, but we both knew I hadn't tamed God's most sinful angel. He had the last laugh. He got to bury himself in some Magdalen when we both knew Apollo would probably do the same later.

I doubted Valen knew my true feelings about Apollo's 'infidelities', but I was sure he was smart enough to guess that I'd feel something about them both fucking Magdalens instead of me. Even if it was the tiniest of somethings, it still stung. It stung all the more knowing Valen was making it sting on purpose.

I took the first opportunity to leave Florence and the others partying, hurrying back to the girls' dorm through the cold. But, under the wisteria, Valen stepped out of the shadows and I pulled up short.

"Figures you'd slip away," he said. "Going to cry in your pillows?"

I bristled. "Where's Mina? Couldn't get it up, so she went to find someone who can?"

"I got what I wanted out of her. She's probably taking those sloppy seconds straight to your boyfriend."

"Ugh, you're insufferable."

I made to keep walking but he stepped in front me.

"Yet, you know I'm right," he said smoothly.

"Apollo's business is Apollo's business."

"And he'll make it my business when I get a text to get rid of her."

I wasn't going to pretend that Apollo would go to his bed alone that night. Even if I'd stayed, it wouldn't be me he took back to his room to fuck, use up, and discard. Putting it like that, I guess I was lucky.

I didn't need to admit that to Valen, though. He didn't need to know the intricacies of my 'relationship' with Apollo. If Apollo hadn't seen fit to tell him, I wasn't going to. Besides, this wasn't about Apollo and me. It was about Valen and me.

I stepped closer to him and his head dropped towards mine. We didn't touch, but we didn't need to for heat to engulf me. He was so tantalisingly near, the ghostly feeling of his skin touching mine a delightfully torturous tension sizzling between us.

"I don't need to explain my relationship to you," I told him. "Apollo and I have never promised each other anything. I didn't ask for, expect, nor do I want his fidelity–"

"No, if you had that, how could you justify fucking me?" he snarled.

Instead of pushing him away, I leant into him. "But I'm not fucking you," I reminded him softly.

"You want to fuck me."

"You want to fuck me," I countered.

He rested his forehead to mine as his hand went to my hip, and may as well have burned a hole in me and my clothes.

"Of course I do," he said, his voice gravelly and deep. Had I not know Valen so well, I'd have said it was choked.

"Well, tough fucking luck, Valen," I said, but I nuzzled against his face.

"Tell me you want me," he begged.

"I want you," I told him, and it was barely a whisper.

He leant his lips towards mine and I let him kiss me.

It was soft and gentle and made my heart do things it was not supposed to do. As our bodies closed the gap between us, it wasn't just my clit that tingled for him, that warmed for him. So did my chest. My stomach fluttered like I was nervous about something. I just didn't know what.

Finally, I pulled away and put a finger over his lips.

"I crave you, but it's not happening again," I told him cheekily.

Every fibre of my being wanted to push him against the closest wall and make a liar out of me. My hand dropped from his lips and to his chest like I would do just that. Thankfully, I managed to control my smaller head.

"You think you're in charge?" he asked.

I nodded. "I know I'm in charge. You've admitted you still want me, Valen, and I'm not hiding I want you, but I can want you and still deny you."

He growled. "We'll see how long that lasts."

I nodded again as I stepped away from him. "We will," I promised him.

Before I waked away, I caught the look on his face. He'd understood the promise of my words. I wouldn't – couldn't – deny him forever. But it was going to be interesting to see how long I could go before admitting to both of us I needed to give him up and fuck him out of my system.

Chapter Twenty-Two

Florence and I were lying on my bed on Thursday afternoon, staring at the ceiling.

"How's Marco?" I asked.

"He's Marco," she said.

I nodded. I knew what she meant. Marco was Marco. They'd been hooking up, but that didn't mean that there was anything more between them.

"Do you think he knows about you and Valen?" she asked.

I looked at her in panic. "Why? Has he said something?"

She shrugged. "No. I'm just wondering. He seems…" She paused. "What's the word? Way too observant for his own good."

She said it like she was taking the piss as much as making a genuine observation, but the humour in it didn't put a dent in my mood at the idea Marco might know.

I sighed and looked back up at the ceiling. "I doubt Valen's the kiss and tell type, but I don't know if Marco's worked it out on his own."

We lay in companionable silence for a bit longer.

"Do you think he'd tell Apollo if he did?" I asked finally.

"I dunno. Marco and I don't exactly...talk," she said suggestively.

I laughed. "Fair."

"I've seen him talk to you a bit. He seems to have taken to you."

I laughed again. "He, for one, appreciates his future goddess."

"As opposed to Valen."

I nodded. "As opposed to Valen."

"What are you going to do about him?"

I sighed. "I think I'm going to have to fuck him out of my system."

Florence rolled to her side to face me. "Seriously?"

I nodded. "I don't want it to be over, but I also don't want to want him anymore. It's...tiring."

"So it has nothing to do with God pulling his finger out?"

I scoffed. "He might have pulled his finger out, but he's still got something else in the Magdalen of the day."

"So? If Apollo gets to fuck around, why can't you?"

Because that was not the objection here, as much as I knew it looked like it.

"No," I agreed. "I know. I just don't... I want to go back to hating Valen and move on with my life before it becomes more complicated than it needs to be."

"Are you falling for him?" she gasped.

I smiled at her outburst, then went back to serious. It was perhaps well past time for an admission to myself as much as her. "I don't know. Sometimes, I worry I could. Sometimes, I honestly forget that I hate him. Then I remember, and I wonder if I really do anymore."

Florence was quite simply the best friend in the world. Instead of berating me for stupid choices as though I even *had* a choice, she was just supportive. Instead of asking what I could possibly see in an arsehole like Valen Kincaid, she was just there for me. Instead of reminding me how much we hated him, she just tried to be helpful.

"Okay. So, Operation Khaleesi is back on?"

I knew she was semi-joking, but I'd heard of worse plans. "You know what?" I asked.

"What?"

"I think it might be."

"Great. How can I help?"

"Remind me how to seduce a guy."

"I don't think you have any problems in that department. Not with Valen."

I laughed. "It would seem not. Only problem is, I told him I was going to hold out as long as possible."

"That sounds delightful," she sassed. "And other than the horrendous vaginal equivalent of blue balls you'll get, how is that a problem?"

I snorted very attractively. "Because...I'm afraid if I don't do it soon, I'll never do it."

Florence nodded. "Riiight..." she said slowly. "So basically, you either fuck him out of your system like right this second, or you'll just keep fucking him whenever you want for as long as you want?"

A splutter of a laugh escaped me. "No. I'm not saying that."

Although, that is how it felt.

"Good, because I'd seriously advise you to go for the latter. That's a much cheerier path to take."

Same, Floss. "I was thinking it could wait until tomorrow."

"Oh, at least," Florence said semi-sarcastically, but in a supportive way.

"I am looking to you for guidance, Floss. Ideas. I need you to help me formulate a plan."

"Are you suggesting we kidnap a Kincaid?" she gasped and I batted her with a pillow.

"No!"

"Good. Because, babe, I've got connections. But even my connections pay Kincaids for kidnappings."

A shudder ran through me as I said, "I'm sure Kane would pay *us* to kidnap his brother."

Florence audibly shivered as well. "Ugh, even for a Kincaid, that man gives me the creeps. I would rather find myself in a deadend alley with Neo AND Cillian, and that other... What's her name...?"

"Her?" I asked.

She nodded and clicked her fingers. "The girl... Valerie? Victoria? It was V-something."

"Who was?"

Florence smirked at me. "Are you jealous of a woman who shares Valen's last name?"

For someone who wasn't, my heart fluttered weirdly. "No," I scoffed.

"Well, good. Because even though I'm ninety percent certain

that incest isn't a Kincaid thing, the mum took her home to the motherland."

"Valen has a sister?"

"Valen undoubtedly has an army of discarded female siblings, but the Kincaids have no use for them. At least their mothers seem to appreciate them."

"The Kincaids don't think much of women?" I mean, I'd guessed. It had been implied. But a confirmation never hurt anyone.

"They do not," Florence laughed. "I heard Cillian's mother only survived because she killed his dad and took his place as head of the Family until Cillian came of age."

"How do you know these things?" I asked her.

She shrugged. "Dad entertained a contract with the Volkovs for a bit, but he went with the O'Malleys instead."

There was a lot to unpack in that sentence. Namely, who were the Volkovs?

But, "You've been fucking the help," is what I led with.

She laughed. "Marco hasn't really been involved with the family biz yet. Is that because he's promised to Apollo?"

I thought about it. "I don't know. Sure doesn't stop Cillian expecting Valen to jump at his every command."

"You almost sound like you care," she teased.

I nudged her. "I do care," I admitted, as scary as that was. "That's why I have to fuck him out of my system."

"Before you care too much?"

"Before it's too late to stop caring." I ignored the small voice in the back of my head that asked, *But is it already too late?*

"Ouch. Yeah, okay," she agreed. "And were you serious about tomorrow night, or...?"

I shrugged. "It's as good a time as any. Is there anything on that I can, like, hide behind?"

"Hide behind?"

"Like hang outs that'll keep Apollo busy, but not Valen."

Florence breathed out heavily as she thought. "Uh... Not that I know of. But you'd know more about Saint plans than me."

I nodded as I grabbed blindly by my head for my phone. I finally found it and texted Exie and Triss to ask them if they knew about Saint plans for the next night. While I waited to hear back from them, Florence and I kept staring at the ceiling.

"I suppose I could be persuaded to keep an eye on Apollo tomorrow night, if need be," she sighed dramatically.

I laughed. "I appreciate the lengths you'll go for our friendship, Floss, but I wouldn't make you do that."

She chuckled in relief. "Thank fuck. I mean, if you asked, I'd do it in a heartbeat. But I won't be offering again any time soon."

I gave her a grin. "No. I get it. All good."

"Do you have a plan?" she asked.

"Not really. The best I can come up with is to wear some sexy lingerie under my coat and hope he's in his room."

"I mean, it's as good a plan as any."

"You think?"

"I know."

"How do you know?"

She grinned. "I tried it on Marco."

"Oh, good. So I'm just copying you now." I wasn't angry at

her, but I was annoyed with myself for my lack of originality.

She snorted. "Me and a million people through the course of history. There's a reason it's done. Because it fucking works."

My phone buzzed and I looked at it.

"Parties?" Florence asked.

I shook my head as I opened it.

Exie

The boys have some kind of macho wank-fest planned. I hear it's well private and very intimate. None of the girls are supposed to know, but I overheard a Magdalen saying something about it.

"Well, we know what kind of orgy– sorry, party they're having then," Florence muttered, reading over my shoulder.

"Yes, but that's perfect."

Florence chewed her fingernail. "Okay, but what if Valen goes to the party as well?"

"Then the whole thing will be an embarrassing non-event."

"Okaaay," she said slowly. "And if you therefore can't fuck him out of your system? What are you going to do then?"

"Try again on Saturday night?" I suggested.

"You are determined to do this?"

"You don't think I should?"

Florence cackled. "Fuck no," she chortled, tears threatening. "I definitely think you should. I'm just checking you think you should."

"Should I not think I should?"

"Oh my God," she laughed. "Stop over thinking. I shouldn't have said anything. Let's do it."

My answer was distracted by another message coming through.

Exie

By the way...is it true that Apollo secretly

proposed already?

Florence and I shared a look.

"What's that supposed to mean?" I asked her.

She shrugged. "I don't know. Ask Exie."

Harlow

What do you mean?

Exie

Well, everyone's noticed something's

changed. Bets among the girls is that

that he popped the question. The boys

think he knocked you up.

"He what?" I spluttered. "He hasn't even touched me. Barely," I amended.

"I knew the rumour mill was fanciful, but that's…" Florence breathed. "I mean, neither of those things are ideal… Are they?"

I felt like chucking my phone into the nearest wall. "Why not? What other use do I have in life than to either be someone's wife or someone else's mother. Preferably both and preferably before I grow too many brains to fight back."

"Too many brains?" Florence asked gently.

"Everyone knows that once a woman hits her mid-twenties, she becomes an argumentative shrew."

"Have you been binging Regencies again?" she asked kindly.

I huffed. "I honestly wonder sometimes if anything's actually changed for women."

"I hear tell that outside the ridiculousness of far too much money, and in normal human society, girls get to choose who they marry, and even *if* they marry. They're also allowed to go to uni and get jobs and have pursuits that are not limited to throwing successful parties, keeping up with the latest fashions, and pumping out male heirs."

"Fiction, surely."

She gave me a smile and I found a small one to give back.

"Who knows," I said. "Maybe Apollo's going to sweep me off my feet?"

Florence nodded. "A few months ago, I'd have said there wasn't a chance in Hell. But now, even I can see the possibility."

I snorted as I started typing out a reply to Exie. "Coming from you, that means a lot."

Harlow

Neither. There are no rings, secret or otherwise, and defs no babies.

I sighed. "Well, if I've got any hope of Apollo sweeping me off my feet, then I need to eliminate every potential competitor. And if I'm fucking Valen out of my system tomorrow night, then you get to help me choose what I'm going to wear."

"Oh, sexy fashion parade?" Florence asked excitedly.

I laughed. "Sure. Sexy fashion parade."

Chapter Twenty-Three

"I cannot believe I'm doing this," I muttered as I finished applying my makeup in the mirror. "I must be insane." I gave my hair one more fluff, like that was going to do anything to calm the nerves racing around my body.

"Insanity would be passing up what is being freely offered," Florence said from our room.

"I don't know about that," I said as I walked back out of the bathroom.

Florence's jaw dropped. "Fuuuck," she breathed.

I did a dorky little turn. "All right?" I asked.

She nodded eagerly, then shrugged coyly. "If you like that sort of thing." Then she smirked at me knowingly. "He's gonna love it."

"I don't even know why I let you talk me into buying it."

She indicated me. "For this exact reason."

"This reason wasn't a reason when I bought it," I reminded her.

"But it is now," she reminded me.

I rolled my eyes. "Well, at least it's getting some use."

She laughed. "Go and seduce your man."

"He's not my man," I told her. "I hate him."

As my best friend, she didn't even bother contradicting me. "But you love his cock."

I couldn't disagree with her. "Love his cock."

I pulled on my overcoat and tied it up tight.

"I won't wait up," she said with a wink.

"Shut up," I said before sliding out our door.

As I made my way from the girls' dorm to the boys', I felt like a terrible parody of a secret agent. I saw a few people out and about but, if any of them thought it odd that I was heading to the boys' dorm at almost ten on a Friday night, then they said nothing.

"He's probably not even there," I said to myself as I hurried up the cheeky service stairs.

There was no one about on their floor, but I couldn't guarantee it would stay that way. I beelined for his door and tried the handle. It was unlocked. I pushed open his door and my heart beat slightly more steadily that my stealth run wasn't in vain.

He was lying on his big, soft bed in nothing but long pyjama pants. He had a book, of all things, and seemed lost in his own little world. As I closed the door behind me, he finally seemed to hear me. He pushed himself up onto his left elbow and looked me over.

It felt like the first time I had to really take my time as I looked him over. It wasn't like I hadn't had plenty of opportunities to see him just as naked before. I'd seen his scars, his muscles, and his tattoos. I'd seen them often enough that a cursory glance – all that was appropriate, of course – had, over time, let me commit his torso to memory. At least, I'd thought I had.

In reality, with real time to actually drink him all in, it was so much better than my fantasies. The way his pecs shifted as he sat up straighter and put the book on the nightstand beside him, never taking his eyes off me. The way his stomach muscles tensed as though with very little effort as he moved. The way his chest rose and fell with each slow and steady breath, bringing my attention naturally to the glint of the cross he always wore.

I felt myself lick my lip as I realised that all this – provided my seduction went well – was all mine for the night. He had been all mine before. But this was different. Tonight wasn't just some quick, unplanned hook up where anyone might catch us. We had all the time in the world. I hoped.

Valen's eyes wouldn't leave mine. The space between us was charged with something. I could have walked in there in a cardboard box, and I think the sexual tension would have been enough to melt me. As it was, I had no doubt that Valen was wondering what was going on under my coat.

Time to oblige him.

I slowly pulled on the tie of my overcoat and dragged it open. By the time the overcoat was sliding down my arms to pool on the floor, he was sitting up, his eyes pinned on the very little I now wore.

I sauntered towards him, letting him have full view of the lingerie I'd chosen for him.

I'd leant into the innocent vibe with a peek-a-boo bra and panty set, finished with a pair of tall white mary janes. The lingerie had floral panels, but was mainly white lace. The major bits were all covered, but the cut-out sections – at my hips and lower breast – gave it that added sense of anticipation. At least, that had been the plan.

By the look on his face, the plan had worked.

"Harlow…" he whispered as I reached the foot of his bed.

I lay a finger on my lips as I climbed on to the bed to straddle him. His hands went to my waist, but they were soft, almost reverent.

I undulated my hips, rubbing my slit over him. Running my hands up into his hair, I pressed my breasts against his bare chest. I felt him harden under me in a matter of seconds. My clit tingled as we rocked together slowly, and I moaned in his ear.

"What are you doing here, princess?" he asked as his hands trailed over my naked back.

"Fucking you out of my system," I told him.

I lay my hand over his throat. As I eased him down onto the bed, my body followed, my nose almost brushing his the whole way. His eyes watched me with a hint of amusement.

"What's so funny?" I asked, trying not to let in the fear that he thought this whole thing was funny, that he was laughing at my attempt at seduction.

He shook his head as he grabbed my arse with both hands and sat us back up again. "The fact that you think you're in charge," he answered.

"Oh, you think you are?" I scoffed.

He flipped me over, leant his arm on my chest, and lay between my legs. "You came to me. I'm in charge."

I could have fought it. I could have told him I was in charge or

I was walking. But the gruffness in his voice, the erection pressing into my hip, and the look of intense dark heat in his eyes had me wanting him in control.

For good measure, I strained against his arm as I reached my face towards his. "Then take charge," I said carefully.

As he stood up, he pulled me with him, spinning so that his back was to the bed and my front was to him. I looked at him expectantly and he smirked at me. It sent a shiver through me. An all too pleasant, needy shiver. Whatever he was about to do to me – to make me do – I wanted it.

"On your knees," he commanded.

I held my ground. "Or what?"

"On your knees," he said, his voice even and calm.

"I won't bow to you," I said.

He ran a hand agonisingly softly up my side as he leant down to my ear. Goose bumps broke out across my skin and my nipples felt tighter.

"No one said anything about bowing," he whispered. "A challenge."

I pulled back to look at him. "A challenge?"

His fingers trailed between my legs and rubbed me lightly. "A challenge. You want to be in charge?" he asked and I nodded slowly. "Make me come undone for you and you can be in charge."

"You don't think I can."

His grin was all cocky arrogance. "No one can."

I'd take that bet. "Fine."

I got down on my knees and pulled him out of his tracksuit

bottoms. I ran my hand along his shaft slowly, looking up at him through my eyelashes. He definitely liked the view. As I took him in my mouth, his hand alighted on the back of my head. He didn't push, he didn't even try to guide, he just rested it there as I ran my lips over him. I placed my hand on his shaft to work him with my mouth.

He breathed deeply and I heard him groan once or twice.

I went faster, then slower, dragging my lips over his head on the way out. Faster again. I felt his hips start to sway in time to my rhythm. I snuck a look up at him and found his face turned to the ceiling, a look of pure satisfaction on his face. I upped the pace, letting him fuck my face as my hand took the rest of him.

"Fuck," he grunted, and I felt him shudder.

He liked it.

The next thing I knew, he was sitting on the edge of the bed with me in his lap and he was pressing into me. He slid in quickly and easily until I'd taken him all and was sitting on his lap.

"Fuck me," he instructed, his eyes hard as they looked into mine.

So I did. His hands ran over my body like he couldn't get enough of me as he let me do all the work. I didn't hide my pleasure as I rode him. I didn't hold back a single moan or whimper and breathy encouragement. The closer I got to release, the jerkier my movements got, the more vocal I was.

Valen groaned appreciatively, wrapped his arms around my body and nestled his face in my shoulder. As I came, he held me tight and I felt him thrusting gently, drawing my orgasm out as his tip rubbed inside me.

"I win," he said, his voice gravelly.

"Round one, maybe," I told him, my head bowed as I got my breath back.

"Just how many rounds did you think there'd be?" he asked, tilting my face to his.

"How many have you got?" I challenged.

"I've got more than you can take."

"Is that so?"

He nodded. "It is. I'm going to fuck you all night, princess. I'm going to make you cum for me until your body can't take it anymore. Understood?"

I knew what the word was now. I knew what this was. Consent. Valen Kincaid might have been a lot of things, but he didn't just say the things he did – or want me to say the things I did – because he liked to talk dirty. I didn't doubt he did like it. A lot. But it served a higher purpose. It made sure there weren't any misunderstandings or crossed lines.

I smiled as I nodded and bit my lip. "Understood."

"Are you really here?" he asked.

I wrapped my arms around his neck. "I'm really here. And, tonight, I'm all yours."

"All mine?" He got a quirky tilt to his lips. "Is that a promise?"

I nudged his nose with mine. "Until I walk back out those doors, I'm yours," I told him. "I'm yours, and you're mine."

"If you think walking out those doors is going to stop you being mine..." he said slowly.

"One night is all we have, Valen."

He nodded. "One night's all I need," he said as he kissed me.

"One night and you'll be over me?" I asked as my heart hitched.

"One night and you'll never forget me," he clarified, giving me a smile to melt everything in me.

"You only needed a pool table."

"We've got more than a pool table now, princess," he said as he dropped kisses over my jaw and down my neck, and undid my bra. "And I am going to rock your world." He helped me out of my bra, and threw it I didn't care where, but his eyes never left mine.

He stood up, with my legs still around his waist. He smiled widely, and it reached his eyes. He turned and threw me down onto the bed. His eyes took me in hungrily as he dropped his trousers. His eyes still didn't leave me as he took my shoes off. He kissed my ankle and he stared at me.

"You pick this out just for me?" he asked.

I felt my cheeks heat. "Florence made me buy it. Do you like it?"

"Like it? Princess, I love it. Every single inch of you is dangerously lickable. And I plan on tasting it all."

He reached down to peel my pants off me, then pushed my legs to either side of his body as he settled between them.

The sinful smirk on his face would have made me dripping for him, had I not already been. Then he dropped his head between my legs and sucked my clit. Hard.

"Fuck!" I breathed in.

I felt rather than heard him laugh.

"You're enjoying this," I accused.

He lifted his head to look at me. "Of course I'm enjoying this. I have Harlow-fucking-Vanguard, princess of Saint Benedicts, a fucking goddess, in my bed. Willing. Wanting. On offer. What isn't to enjoy?"

Something hit me. "We're in your bed..." I said slowly.

He trailed kisses up my stomach as he pinched my nipple hard. My back arched off his bed as I sighed in pleasure.

"We are in my bed. Would you rather be somewhere else?"

I shook my head. "God, no. I just remembered you saying this was the least defiled place in your room."

I felt him nod as he kept creeping up my body. "You're the only one I'll fuck in my bed, love."

"Is that a promise?" I teased.

"It's a fact. Can facts be promises?"

"I don't know," I answered as his face drew level with mine. "How many?" I asked suddenly.

"How many what?" he asked as his lips dropped to my neck.

"How many Magdalens did it take for you to pretend you didn't want me?" It was an embarrassing whisper, but I needed to know.

I felt him tense. "You don't want to know that number, princess."

"What if I do?"

"Trust me, you don't."

"I do, Valen."

"Please, don't ask me, Harlow."

"Why not?"

"Because, if you ask again, I'll tell you and neither of us wants that."

"I want that. How many have there been since the Halloween party?"

He groaned in reluctance as he coaxed my leg around his hip. His cock pulsed at my opening. Once. Twice. Then he plunged deep inside me. It wasn't until he was buried deep in me that he spoke.

"None."

"What?"

"I haven't fucked anyone else since the holidays." He thrust hard. "Is that what you what to hear?"

"Only if it's true."

"Well, you're in luck, love. Because it's true."

He clearly wasn't taking any more questions because he crushed his lips to mine as he pounded me relentlessly. It was like he had to draw a stark contrast between his words and his actions. Not that I was complaining. He didn't stop kissing me as he made me cum once, twice, three times, and, on the fourth, he finished with me.

He groaned my name, more like a prayer than a curse, and held me tight as we both got our breath back. Finally, he pulled out from me slowly as he trailed kisses down my body. He paused at my nipple and bit it playfully. My back arched from the bed as my hand gripped his hair, and I felt him smile.

"The things I could do to you…" he purred.

"I thought you *were* doing them to me," I sassed.

He grazed his teeth over my breast lightly. "I'm not going to get to show off all my tricks in one night, love."

"Those tricks you've spent years practising on all those Magdalens?" I asked, telling myself I wasn't jealous.

He shook his head as he kissed over my stomach. "No," he mumbled into my skin, his hands hot on me. One on my hip, and one under me like he was holding me close. "No. Some of them I saved."

"For the right girl?" I asked sarcastically.

"For you."

I could have sworn he'd nodded when I asked, 'for the right girl?'. I propped myself up on my elbows and he looked up at me in question as his fingers traced over me lazily.

"For me?" I clarified.

One eyebrow rose like he was daring me to ask him to be sorry. "I might never have thought I'd taste you, princess, but it didn't stop me thinking about it." His hands went to my hips, and he pulled me down the bed to slide into me, hard again already. He punctuated every sentence with a languid thrust. "It didn't stop me imagining what I'd do to you. What you'd do to me. But even I didn't imagine you'd taste so sweet and yet fuck so dirty."

I felt my cheeks flush. "I'm sure you've had dirtier."

And I was sure. I had no lofty ideas about my sexual prowess. I wasn't winning Kink of the Year or anything, but I felt like I wasn't going to win Vanilla of the Year either.

A mischievous smile crossed Valen's face as he looked down at me. "I've had dirtier, but I'll never have better."

Then, much like before, that was clearly all he was saying on the topic as he crushed his mouth to mine and fucked me hard but also somehow gentle.

His lips never left my body and I was completely at his mercy. The use to which he put that was to wring as many orgasms out of me as possible before he couldn't hold on any longer.

"You still claiming you don't come undone for me?" I asked, nipping his lip playfully.

Humoured heat danced in his eyes. "How many times have you cum for me now?"

I smirked. "It's a lot easier for women to have multiple orgasms. I thought it was just good practice to give her as many as possible."

"I thought I was your first?"

I nodded. "You were."

"So where are you getting ideas about good practice?" His voice was teasing, but I heard the possessive streak shining through.

I bit my lip. "Books. TV. Movies… Porn."

"Porn?"

"What?" I asked. "Is the good little princess not *allowed* to watch porn?"

He looked me over. "If you were my princess, I'd hope you were."

It took us both a moment to realise what he'd said. Then he blinked, pressed a kiss to my temple, and swung out of bed.

He went to a mini-fridge and threw me a bottle of water. "Drink it."

"What's this for?" I asked him.

He grinned. "Can't have you dehydrating on me."

I caught sight of the book on the bedside table. The one he'd been reading when I walked in. I recognised it.

"That's my book!" I said as he climbed back into bed beside me.

His lips dropped to my shoulder. "So?"

"You're reading my book, Valen."

"Am I, princess?"

"Yes. That's the book I was reading when we first..."

"Say it," he begged.

"The night we first..."

"Say it."

"Gave into whatever this is."

His lips were trailing lazily over my skin, and I felt the smile. It wasn't what he'd wanted me to say, but he'd take it. "And what do you think this is, love?"

"I think this is wasting what little time we have together, Valen."

I felt him smile against me, then he nipped me playfully, his teeth grazing the flesh of my neck and sending goose bumps chasing each other down my arms.

"If you say so, love."

He took the water bottle from me, threw it at the end of the bed, and dragged me down into the pillows with him. I laughed and I could feel the answering smile on his face as he buried it in my shoulder and his cock deep in me once more.

Chapter Twenty-Four

I felt a coolness on my stomach where I'd been sure it had been warm moments before. I blinked and realised I'd fallen asleep.

As I sat up, I looked around the room. For a moment, I forgot where I was and why I was naked. Then it all came flooding back as I felt the tenderness between my legs. I had a feeling I'd be sore for a while. But it was a good kind of sore. A satisfied kind of sore.

I was alone. There was no sign of Valen in the dark room, but the door to the bathroom was ajar. No light spilled around the curtains, so it must have still been the middle of the night.

I dropped back against the pillows and was overwhelmed by his scent drifting around me, encasing me. I closed my eyes and let myself smile. I didn't know if I drifted between sleep, or just relaxed there for a few moments, but I felt the bed shift and opened my eyes to find Valen getting back into bed.

"I didn't mean to wake you," he said as he rolled onto his side, facing me, and leant his head on his hand.

"Just give me a minute and I'll go," I told him, doubting very much that he was the snuggling kind.

"You got somewhere to be?" he asked. For a second, I thought he sounded jealous.

I shook my head, revelling in the softness of his bed. "Nowhere but my own, far less comfy bed."

"Did you finally get enough to get me out of your system?" he asked.

I rolled my head towards him. Only being drunk on the pleasure he'd wrung from me and the remnants of sleep could make me so honest. "No, but I'm sure you've had enough of me."

I started to sit up, but he stopped me.

"Stay," he begged. "Just a little longer."

"Are there students about to see me leave?" I teased.

"Yes, but that's not why."

"What then?" I laughed. "Do I have something you want?" I joked.

"Everything," he said, drawing me back onto the bed.

Valen rolled over me, nestling back between my legs. He dropped kisses along my breasts, my neck, my jaw. He seemed in no hurry. Neither to go another round – despite the erection hard against my thigh – or to get me out of his bed.

As he lifted his head in line with mine, his hand ran up my body, over the contours of my stomach and my breast. He looked deep into my eyes.

And then he kissed me.

He'd kissed me a lot that night. A. Lot.

Every single one had been toe-curling and stomach-churning and clit-tingling deliciousness.

This…

This was heart-warming and wrapping my arms around him and wishing I never had to let go. So, for now at least, I wasn't going to.

In moments, he was inside me again and fucking me hard. But there was something different about the rough this time. It wasn't just rough, or even just passionate, but it was special. It wasn't just about sexual tension and hating someone more than you thought possible. It was about realising that there was indeed a very fine line between love and hate.

I came hard and fast, and he flipped me over to press me into his mattress as he kept pounding me. The way his hands gripped my body felt like he couldn't get me close enough. His arms wrapped around me, and he pulled my back up to his chest, kissing my neck as he drove into me. He fisted my hair and tugged lightly, forcing my lips to meet his. His other arm lay between my breasts with his hand over my throat.

The action had long since stopped being threatening. In fact, I wasn't sure I'd ever felt threatened by it. There was something about Valen that, no matter how dangerous I knew him to be, I could never believe he'd ever hurt me. At least not, as he said, unless I asked.

Valen had me the proverbial six ways from Sunday. Behind. On top. Cowgirl, and reverse. Lying side by side, where he had the perfect angle to finger my clit. Standing.

When we eventually paused for a break, I was too scared to see what the time was because it might tell me I had to leave.

I took a swig of water and stretched my neck.

Then, suddenly Valen had put something around it. Something

light and warm. I looked down and saw a cross sitting slightly lower on my naked chest than the one I always wore. My fingers touched it gently as I felt Valen doing it up at the nape of my neck.

"What's this?" I asked him.

He kissed the side of my neck. "That would be my cross."

"Why is it your cross?"

"Because my mother gave it to me for my confirmation."

I couldn't stop touching it, my eyes glued to it with an emotion I didn't think I could name had I wanted to. "No. Why is it your cross around my neck?"

"Because," he said as he trailed lazy kisses over my neck, "he might own you, but your body is mine. This might be goodbye, but I'll know you were mine first."

First.

Because Apollo would claim me one day. Whether soon or not. The day was coming.

"And I suppose you expect me to wear it all the time?"

I felt him nod. "You will not like what I do to you if you take it off."

The gentleness of his touch belied his words, but I knew not to push Valen Kincaid too far.

"I can't wear two crosses, Valen. Someone will notice."

He raised his head and I felt his fingers at the clasps of the necklaces. He undid mine and lifted it off me. I swivelled and held my hand out to take it from him, but he shook his head.

"You're not throwing that out," I told him.

He shook his head again. "No."

I watched, slightly mesmerised as he undid the cuff on his left wrist, wrapped my chain around it, did it back up, and slipped the cuff back over the top.

"Now, we'll both have a secret," he said.

I looked down at his cross nestled, alone now, on my chest. "I thought we already did."

His finger went to my chin and tipped my face to look at him. "Ah, but this ends when you walk out of my room. Fucked out of your system. After that, no more secret."

I didn't like the way he said that. I didn't like the sound of that. His voice was hard, his eyes were inscrutable. I neither understood nor wanted to understand the message in them.

"Well, I'm still here, so I guess the job's not quite done," I told him.

He almost looked thankful. I nearly believed he didn't want me to leave either. "Do you want another secret?" he asked.

I bit my lip, wondering what on Earth he could mean. Nothing that my heart should flutter over, I was sure, but it did that anyway. I nodded as I steadied my breath. "Sure."

He slid off the bed and settled between my legs. His hand lay over my breast and squeezed it hard as his other ran up my leg. I looked down at him, not sure where this was going or how this counted as a secret.

Valen pressed a soft kiss between my breasts, just below his cross. As his lips headed south, he coaxed me to lie down on the bed. He sucked my clit gently before slowly dragging his tongue over me.

"I've been undone for you since the day I met you," he said quietly, reverently, his lips fluttering against my clit as my heart stuttered in my chest.

I tried to sit up, but his hand held me against the bed firmly. "Valen–"

He shook his head. "Just let me have now, love," he whispered.

I laced my fingers with the hand on my chest as best I could, and he seemed to take that for the agreement I'd intended it to be. He rearranged our hands so his was on top of mine, but our fingers were still laced. It was one of the most intimate actions I'd ever experienced. Which I realised wasn't difficult considering my history of intimate experiences.

Valen buried his face between my legs and didn't let up until I'd cum for him three times. It felt different. It wasn't hard and fast. He got nothing out of it. It was all for me. From him, for me.

I tried to tell myself to breathe his name slightly less…whatever it was, because it felt like something that had the potential to be incredibly powerful. The whole moment filled me with light and warmth and the firm belief that I was wanted. Me. Not the princess. Not the future goddess. Just me.

Emotions were running high when he finally dragged his face up to mine, and I saw I wasn't the only one. I scooted back on the bed, my finger under his chin for him to follow me. And follow me he did. For a split second, I felt like Valen Kincaid would follow me to the ends of the universe.

"Valen…" I whispered.

"Harlow…" he seemed to agree.

I pulled him down to the bed with me as I kissed him. He tasted like me, but there were worse things he could taste like, I was sure.

We rolled so he was nestled between my legs again and he slid in easily.

We moved together slowly, him pressing deep inside me in long, steady thrusts. We hugged each other close. My heart soared in my chest, but I ignored it.

"Fuck, you're so… Ugh," he whispered in my ear. "I've had addictions, love…"

"Are you saying you're addicted to me, Valen?" I breathed as we rocked together.

"If they kill me tomorrow, I'll die a happy man."

"Why? Because you had me first?"

He nuzzled his face against mine. "Because I had you at all. Because…" He started increasing his pace, fucking me deeper, "there was a time I called you mine."

A breathy moan escaped me. "I want to say I'll always be yours," also escaped me and we both froze to look at each other.

My heart pounded in my chest and the unreadable expression on his face made me panicky. I didn't know what he was thinking. It wasn't the first time I'd given too much away, but this was different. This served no purpose. I didn't win anything by telling him that. I only lost. Potentially everything.

Finally, he cupped my cheek and ran his hand up my body as he pumped me again. The look in his eyes, for a moment, was discernible. And, thankfully, it wasn't all bad.

He dropped his lips to my ear and whispered, "No one will ever get as close to my heart as you have."

I noticed his word choice. He didn't say his heart was mine. He didn't say I was in his heart. But I'd come close, and that was going to have to be enough for me. He might not have been with anyone else since Halloween, but I'd be the naïve fool he used to believe I was if I thought he'd never fuck around again. Before tonight, he hadn't owed me anything, but after tonight, he definitely wouldn't owe me anything. He wouldn't owe me anything and this would be over. For good.

I wanted to tell him he'd always be in mine, but would it mean as much to him as it did to me? Would he prefer not to know? And was it true? For a night that was supposed to be just all out carnal physical pleasure, there'd been a lot of emotion involved. What was a bit more?

"You will always have a piece of mine," I told him.

"Fuck, love…" he breathed. "Just…" He pulled back to look at me. "Fuck it," he said and he kissed me.

This. This was it. This was no holds barred. For perhaps the first time in his life, Valen Kincaid held nothing back. He wore no mask. There was everything in that kiss. Everything I knew we'd never speak about, never even acknowledge. But I knew. I knew we both felt the same: maybe in another life.

It wasn't just heat and lust and passion that swirled around us as he thrust harder and deeper and faster. Emotion and feeling and the tiniest spark of the potential for love tied us together. Hands roamed freely. This wasn't fucking for pleasure's sake. This was connection, pure and simple.

Breathy nothings passed between us, meaning little outside the little bubble of moment in which we'd found ourselves. The coil in me tightened and wavered on the precipice for so long, it felt like one long, drawn out orgasm. But as Valen's hand tightened on my hip and my leg shifted, and he slid deeper, I couldn't hold back my moans.

As my orgasm enveloped me, I felt him throb inside me and he exhaled sharply as he came hard. After a few languid thrusts, Valen slid out of me, rolled over and pulled my back to his front. Valen Kincaid was actually spooning. He was also dropping little lazy kisses all over me.

Had I not been utterly spent and exhausted – both physically, but now emotionally as well – I might have found that funnier. As it was, I just enjoyed the feeling of behind tucked warm and safe in his arms, committing it to memory as though I knew there were dark days to come for which I'd need comfort.

As much as I wanted to stay there forever, I could feel myself falling asleep and knew that it was time this came to an end.

"I really should go before someone sees me," I told him with a laugh as he peppered my neck with kisses. The neck that now housed Valen Kincaid's cross.

"I suppose you should."

I sat up, holding the blankets to my body as I looked around for my lingerie. He grabbed the blankets and pulled them down, exposing my breasts. He leant down and sucked on one of them. A jolt of need shot straight down.

"Where's my bra?" I asked, trying to distract him before I jumped him again.

"In a safe place," he said.

I grabbed his hair and pulled his head to make him look at me. "Excuse me?"

The cheeky and pleased grin he gave me was, frankly, almost sweet. "You didn't think I'd let you go with them, did you?"

"What am I supposed to wear back to my room?" I asked.

He shrugged. "That coat suited you on your way here, it'll suit you on the way back."

I looked at him incredulously and he just shrugged. Was he not Valen Kincaid, I might have considered it adorable.

"At this rate," I told him as I turned to climb out of bed. "You'll own more of my underwear than me."

He scooted over behind me and pressed a lingering kiss to my neck. "Maybe that's the plan."

I made a mental note that next time I'd just not bother wearing any underwear. Then I realised that there wouldn't be a next time because this was us fucking each other out of our systems. I cleared my throat and stood up, dragging his sheet with me as I went to pick up my overcoat.

"Have you got a problem with being seen naked?" he asked me.

I turned to find him standing on the other side of the bed in all his naked glory. He stretched his hands behind his head as I looked him over.

"It's never been done before," I told him.

"Drop the sheet," he commanded and I very nearly dropped it right there.

"You've seen it before."

He shook his head. "Not like this. All at once. Unhampered. On display."

I trembled at the force of his words. Slowly, I prised my fingers from the sheet and let it fall to my feet.

A softness came over his face then as he walked towards me.

His hands went to my waist as he looked me over. My hand reached up and I cupped his cheek.

I felt it. This was the end. When I walked out his door, the bubble burst and whatever this was would be over. I was okay with that. It felt right. I honestly believed that I could walk away and I'd be over whatever insane attraction I had to him. It didn't mean there wasn't a part of me that would mourn the end, it would just be a very, very small part. The same one that used to wonder what my life could have been like if my future wasn't all planned out.

I gave him a nod, pulled on my overcoat, picked up my shoes and went to his door. I couldn't help myself having one last look at him. The him that had been all mine, even for a moment. And what a him it was.

I slipped out his door and into my own bedroom without seeing another soul. The rest of the school was still soundly asleep at just before six on a Saturday morning.

After changing in the bathroom, I climbed into my own bed and saw that Florence was still fast asleep and breathing deeply.

For a while, I stared at the ceiling, loathe to sleep only to wake and find it had all been a dream. But I was exhausted – Valen had exhausted me – and I could only fight sleep for so long.

As usual, Valen invaded my dreams, but it was a different Valen. A softer, more gentle Valen. One who made my heart flutter and warm.

When I woke that afternoon, it was after one and Florence was gone. There was no sign on our message board or my phone that she knew what time I'd come to bed. All she said was

Hope you had fun 😀 talk when you're awake.

I texted her to let her know I was awake and, boy, did I have some stories to tell.

Chapter Twenty-Five

I walked into the world on Monday morning like I was starting again. It wasn't without some trepidation. It wasn't without a sprinkling of regret. It wasn't without some tenderness between my legs.

It wasn't without a few clouds, but they were silver-lined.

My morning was bittersweet.

I felt some sadness at the potential I was leaving behind. But I knew, as much as I might have futilely dreamt otherwise, that potential would – could – never be more. It seemed as though I'd still want Valen until my dying day, but I'd be stupid to think I could have him. It would be stupid, and I didn't want that kind of marriage. Not when it looked like Apollo and I had the potential to have a decent union.

And that potential was one I could foster. It would take time and effort, but so did all relationships. It wasn't a pipe dream that had the power to leave me broken and despondent when it all came to its inevitable end.

Florence, as always, was by my side. She would be by my side for everything and anything. She, of course, had been given as detailed a play-by-play as I'd been able to give her, and she was convinced I'd made the wrong choice in giving Valen up. It hadn't been what I wanted to hear, but she'd apologised and promised to be on Team Apollo.

"Mrs Callahan, for the endgame!" she'd said, as absolutely positively as she could, and I knew she meant every word of it, even if she didn't want to.

She held my hand as we walked out of the girl's dorm towards Mass on Monday morning. I paused for a moment and let the sun shine down bright on my face. There was always tomorrow. And today was just yesterday's tomorrow. I could do this. I could get over Valen. I could go on with my life – and my duty – and be happy.

And I did. For most of the day, life was almost like it was back to normal. Valen was his usual wary self around me, but the contempt didn't quite reach his eyes anymore. For all intents and purposes, nothing had changed between us. We'd never touched, let alone spoken for more than was absolutely required between two people who were bound to Apollo Callahan for life.

So far, so good.

But on the way to lunch, I bumped into Valen without anyone else to buffer us.

"Miss Vanguard," he said, his voice all smooth and suave with not an outward hint of impropriety about it.

But in his eyes, as though an answer to mine, was our secret. It was a tiny point of warmth – of light in the darkness of his soul – and it was me. It was an unspoken promise between us. We were done. Even if we both had to pretend we didn't want more, we were done. There was a civility, a mutual understanding, that made it feel like it was going to be okay.

There was the briefest of sizzles between us, as though it was a mere echo of what we once felt. A pleasant reminder of something once shared. I felt – no, I knew – that it was a tiny thing, just waiting for the spark that could reignite it back to full flame, but I'd said my goodbyes and I had to be happy with them.

Valen lifted his left hand and, as his thumb brushed the corner of his mouth seemingly innocuously, there was a flash of silver under his cuff. My cross. As promised, he wore my cross.

I nodded to him as I reached up to my neck, and I saw he understood; I was wearing his, too. "Valen."

As my fingers grasped Valen's cross under my shirt, I saw Apollo up ahead at the door to the dining hall. I gave him a warm smile. I'd always have a part of Valen, as he'd always have a part of me. But it was for the best that I put him behind me now and walk towards my future.

The big, bad wolf would always be a comforting shadow in my life, but my prince was waiting for his princess.

PRINCES & WOLVES

Harlow, Valen and Apollo's story will continue in *Princes & Wolves*. Available in eBook and print. Check out the webstore for ALL print cover versions.

A falling prince. A ruined wolf. And the goddess between them. In the epic finale to the duet, who will Harlow choose?

If you liked *Gods & Angels*, share the love and let me know! While the duet currently sits as a standalone, I've got ideas for a whole series of follow-ups, including a sequel to turn Harlow's story into a trilogy, Valen's and Apollo's POVs, a HEA for Florence, 'next gen' plotlines, as well as a sequel to the alternate endings.

Print Books

Print versions of the Sinners of Saint Benedicts duet will be available from Elizabeth Stevens' webstore. They come in three versions:

1) the original duet version with all endings

2) the Harlow trilogy version, which will be what the Main Timeline (books 3+) follows on from.

3) the Why Choose trilogy version, which will tie-in with a sequel for the three of them.

tHE LORDS OF PHOENIX HALL

If you liked *Gods & Angels*, you might also enjoy E.J.'s next release, *the Lords of Phoenix Hall*. A New Adult superhero bully academy romance, it's described as 'Sky High' meets 'the Boys'.

At Phoenix Hall, even the heroes are villains.
In my world, there are three kinds of people.
Heroes. Villains. Plebs.

Heroes save the world.
Villains try to take over the world.
Plebs just try to get through Chemistry without losing their eyebrows.

I'm Ruby Raddish, pleb. The lowest of the low. The utterly powerless child of two of our most famous heroes. Or I was. Until I accidentally blow up Lord Hero himself after one too many bad jokes at my expense. Now the target on my back has just tripled.
No matter which way I turn, I can't win.

My new powers unearth old secrets and soon it's not just my life in danger.
Lord Hero wants my head between his legs.
Lord Villain wants his between mine.
I just want to graduate and disappear into the normalcy of a human life.

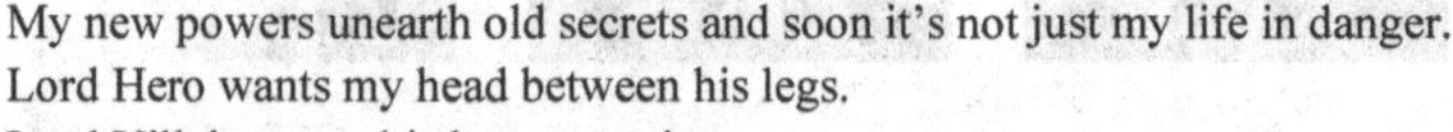

Goos & Angels

Thank you so much for reading this story! Word of mouth is super valuable to authors. So, if you have a few moments to rate/review Harlow's story – or, even just pass it on to a friend – I would be really appreciative.

Have you looked for my books in store, or at your local or school library and can't find them? Just let your friendly staff member or librarian know that they can order copies directly from LightningSource/Ingram.

If you want to keep up to date with my new releases, rambles and writing progress, sign up to my newsletter at https://landing.mailerlite.com/webforms/landing/y1n6q2.

You can find the playlist for *the Sinners of Saint Benedicts* on Spotify: I also have a generic writing playlist you can check out 😊

Follow me:

THANKS

I had so much fun writing this book! Thank you, dear spark, for finally coming back to me and giving me these characters.

Thanks, too, go to Charny for letting me talk at her ALL the time about Valen and Apollo, and Marco.

To my lovely beta readers, both my Beta Team and the new ones I found for this new branch of sub-genre. Thank you for reading so many drafts and letting me chat about the plot and where it was going, especially when I realised it was not a standalone, but a duet with the potential for MANY sequels.

A massive thank you to my husband, as always, for keeping the household running, even though you do actually have a day job to deal with now.

My Books

E.J.'s list is just getting started. While you wait for the next release, you can find where to buy all my books in print and eBook at the website; www.elizabethstevens.com.au/.

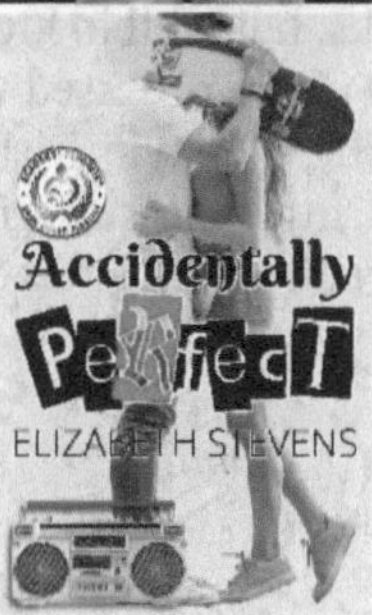

About the Author

E.J. Knox is the Darker/Bully Romance penname of Elizabeth Stevens. E.J. is the name to read if you want darker/bully romance in the Mature YA/NA crossover space. Think high school, college, and academy. E.J. brings my usual wit, banter, and repartee in good old enemies-to-lovers showdowns between alpha males and the sassy heroines strong enough to knock them down a peg or two. There'll be fake-dating, love triangles, kidnapping and danger, second chances, and more.

Writer. Reader. Perpetual student. Nerd.

Born in New Zealand to a Brit and an Australian, I am a writer with a passion for all things storytelling. I love reading, writing, TV and movies, gaming, and spending time with family and friends. I am an avid fan of British comedy, superheroes, and SuperWhoLock. I have too many favourite books, but I fell in love with reading after Isobelle Carmody's *Obernewtyn*. I am obsessed with all things mythological – my current focus being old-style Irish faeries. I live in Adelaide (South Australia) with my long-suffering husband, delirious dog, mad cat, two chickens, and a lazy turtle.

<u>Contact me:</u>
Email: ejknox@elizabethstevens.com.au
Website: www.elizabethstevens.com.au/ej-knox
Twitter: www.twitter.com/writer_iz
Instagram: www.instagram.com/writeriz
Facebook: https://www.facebook.com/elizabethstevens88/